MW01027085

Shards of Desire

DRAGONS OF SIN

R.L. CAULDER

Copyright © 2024 by R.L. Caulder

R.L. Caulder reserves all rights to and/or involving this work as the author. This is a work of fiction. All characters, places, incidents, and dialogues are products of the author's imagination or used fictitiously. Any resemblance to actual people either living or dead, or events is purely coincidental unless the author has express permission from a living person to use their namesake. No part of this book may be reproduced in any form or by any means whether electronic or mechanical, including information storage and retrieval systems, now known or hereinafter invented, without written permissions from the author, except for brief quotations in a book review.

Cover by: Merry-Book-Round

 Created with Vellum

For my daughter,

The world can be a cruel and unforgiving place, but I never want you to bend to the rules and limitations society will try to place on you.

Be your own person.

Believe in yourself and your dreams.

In the moments that you can't, I will believe in you enough for the both of us, always.

Love, Mom

EDATH

ANDRATHYA

ISOMITHYA

SANCTUM

ERUTHYA

SALARYA

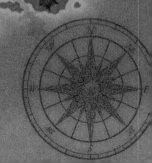

Kingdoms of Edath

Northern Kingdom
> Name: Andrathya
> Element: Water
> Dragon classification: Undine

Southern Kingdom
> Name: Salarya
> Element: Fire
> Dragon classification: Ember

Western Kingdom
> Name: Isomithya
> Element: Air
> Dragon classification: Zephyr

Eastern Kingdom

Name: Eruthya

Element: Earth

Dragon classification: Lithi

Glossary

Edath (Ee-dath)
    Andrathya (Ann-drath-EE-ah)
    Undine (Uhn-deen)
    Salarya (Sah-lare-EE-ah)
    Ember (Ehm-bur)
    Isomithya (Iso-myth-EE-ah)
    Zephyr Dragons (Zeh-fr)
    Eruthya (Eh-ruth-EE-ah)
    Lithi Dragons (Lith-ee)
    Drackya (Drack-EE-ah)
    Siyana (See-ahn-AH)
    Takkar (TAH-car)
    Kaida (Kay-duh)

Chapter One

SIYANA

In all my twenty-five years of drawing breath in this world, my father had never requested my presence at a council meeting. The letter I'd received from him in the early evening hours yesterday broke that streak, and it didn't sit right within my heart or mind.

Today I was expected to join him.

I had always known that I was a pawn for the kingdom as heir, and that one day I would be played. But how and why?

My mind circled back to the same thought all night. *Did this have anything to do with the increased dragon sightings and the women who had gone missing from our kingdom? And if so, how did I factor into it?*

The cool steel of my opponent's blade tore into the fabric of my tunic as my mind drifted, pondering the reasons I might be summoned. The weapon nicked the soft skin of my upper arm deeply enough that I knew, if the searing pain and warmth of blood trickling down my arm were any indication, it was going to leave a scar. My teeth ground together as I let out a hiss in both appreciation and pain from the wound.

I spared a brief second to let my eyes fall to the crimson stain that slowly seeped through the sleeve before letting a wolfish grin take over my lips. I wondered, not for the first time, from where the darkness inside of me blossomed–the deep recess of my soul that purred in the midst of a fight. I relished in it and welcomed the wave of coldness that settled into my bones as I looked up into my opponent's eyes.

Would I be as brave as I was in my current battle if I was staring up into the slitted eyes of a dragon instead? My heart yearned to know what it would be like to stand at the foot of the beasts of ice and water we used to be allies with.

Despite my well-founded fear of their sheer size and magical affinities, I still wanted to stand in the presence of one to test my mettle. I'd even settle for an undine drackya–a beast that could shift between both human and dragon forms–despite their dragons being smaller than that of their full-blooded undine counterparts.

A wistful sigh escaped my slightly parted lips. It was a shame I'd never be allowed the opportunity to join our soldiers on the battlefield and feel the adrenaline coursing through me as the dragons soared above.

I'd already accepted I'd never see the other elemental dragons of fire, earth, and air since they were sequestered to their chosen terrains that established the four kingdoms of Edath.

"Come on, Siyana, focus," Brenson goaded as he bounced on the balls of his feet, waiting for my rebuttal attack. "We wouldn't want to mark up the precious princess of Andrathya, now would we? We can't have all the men with frail egos seeing your wound and realizing a dainty woman has been allowed to train with a sword for years and could actually put them on their asses in seconds."

A deep pit in my chest kindled with fire at his words. That was exactly what I wanted deep down.

My eyes rolled of their own accord as I parried his next slash toward my midsection, not allowing me time to be the aggressor. "Yes, what a horrible thought, that their wives and daughters could be as competent and fearsome, if not more! We can't have that."

Condescension and sarcasm were so thick on my tongue, I found it hard to get the words out. What a shame that this was our reality. But at this moment, I didn't don my tiara, only my sword. I could allow myself to just *be*.

The clash of metal against metal sent tingling shockwaves through my upper arms until they found a home within my chest, right next to my heart. My chest expanded as I took in a deep, satisfying breath. This was where I belonged–where I flourished. My upper lip curled back in a snarl of excitement as I gave myself fully over to this fight, body and mind.

With each day that passed, I found it increasingly exhausting to live this double life. I grew tired of biting my tongue and mincing my words. Forced to be a perfect princess to the public, while hiding that my heart beat to the drum of a warrior's song. Forever torn between who I knew I could be and who I *had* to be. Lost somewhere in the middle without a path out.

Dropping the tip of my sword to face the ground, I jumped back a few paces to give myself a moment to reassess the fight in case he charged me.

A lop-sided smirk tilted one corner of Brenson's full lips before he took the break to run a hand through his short mess of blond curls that laid across his forehead, damp from exertion. "Don't tell me you're tired and giving up already, Sia?"

Cocking my head at him, I arched a brow. "Don't tell me you're scared enough of this battle to resort to using one's looks for hopes of an advantage, Brenson?" Letting out a tsk of disappointment, I smirked back. "Especially when we both know that will never work on me."

My father had once questioned if there was a romance between us and we'd struggled to not openly laugh in his face. I'd once seen Brenson use a poisonous noctura leaf to wipe after he'd relieved himself in the woods while we were playing tag, and after he flashed me while running to the stream to stop the burning sensation, I knew there was no coming back from that. We were completely and firmly in the friend zone.

This time I gave him no time to respond, rushing in

with my blade following behind me. As he lifted his blade to block, expecting an attack from the front at my current trajectory, my foot planted into the ground and I spun over my shoulder, swinging my sword around with me as I barrel-rolled through the air. Our eyes locked as I pulled my blade just short of cutting deeply into his neck as soon as my feet hit the ground. The smallest trickle of blood ran down from his rapidly beating jugular as his eyes widened.

"Maybe I need to lay off the ale the night before our sessions," he breathed out, shaking his head in seeming disbelief. "You're getting damn quick on your feet."

Our breaths mixed in puffs of steam floating through the cool, early morning air. We needed to end this soon, if the tendrils of light beginning to crest over the mountains in the distance were any indication. My eyes swung around the secluded training yard that was tucked behind the armory in the northern corner of the ward. It felt like a second home at this point. We'd practiced here undiscovered for years, since it was blocked partially by the stone wall of the storehouse.

"Admit defeat," I demanded as my eyes narrowed, knowing this battle was not over until one of us did so. We'd graduated to the *anything-goes-until-the-other-admits-defeat* part of training long ago. After all, it wasn't as if real opponents would play by a code of conduct.

The cool metal hilt between my palms heated the longer I held it, showing our fusion. The blade was a part of me, and I, its master, and I'd be damned if I was ever forced to give it up. Even my own father, the king of Andrathya, hadn't been able to stop me from sneaking in sessions as a teenager despite his grumblings. I'd had nothing on the line then. What was he going to do, take away my crown if I took up the blade? He'd be doing me a favor.

Brenson's crystal blue eyes ran along my face and body in a slow, practical way, trying to look for an opening out of our current positions.

A dark laugh bubbled in my chest. Leaning in close, despite him towering a few inches above me, I fluttered my lashes while looking up from beneath them. "If you don't, shouldn't you be afraid of the boys under your command coming out soon and seeing your ass on the ground, with the edge of my blade to your throat? I'm guessing that wouldn't be good for morale within the ranks. End this."

The crown princess fighting a commander of our army—and winning? Unheard of.

We'd grown complacent in the preceding centuries of peace with the dragons who resided within our kingdom's territory. There was no cause to have a well-trained army at our disposal, be it men or women, but ever since a curse had supposedly plagued the drackya in our lands twenty-seven years ago, the way of life our kingdom had known crumbled to the ground.

We weren't able to withstand the year-round frigid temperatures of the most northern reaches of Andrathya.

The majority of our food supply came from the oceans bordering the dragon's tip of the mountain range. With being cut off from that, besides the few rivers that ran from the ocean and into our land at the southern tip, we'd been forced to overhunt the forest. Soon, rations would need to be established to prevent in-fighting amongst our citizens.

I wished that was our only problem...

In recent years, there had been an increasing public outcry for us to deploy our army to find all of our missing citizens who had been taken by the beasts, driving my father into the position of a possible mutiny if he didn't soon acquiesce.

Although I wasn't sure how he expected to win a war against the dragons, if that was the route we were heading in, considering none of our men had ever seen war and our numbers were nowhere near enough for that scale of an attack. They'd wipe us out with ease. We were mere humans against dragons, after all. Even if the undine dragons left the war to the drackya to handle, we couldn't win.

Dirt and small stones scratched underneath Brenson's boot as he tried to shift his weight, and I pressed my sword in harder. "Don't try it," I hissed out in warning.

His feet stilled and he shrugged, a small, deceptive smile gracing his face. "I think you have me for the day."

Still, he didn't say the exact words needed to call the duel to an end. Did he think he could trick me with a mere switch of words?

I shook my head and let out an exaggerated yawn that likely appeared fake for the dramatics of the moment but was mostly real. I was running myself ragged having spent every hour in our royal library since receiving that letter. That voice within me spurred me to search for any information I could find that had to do with our northern enemies. I wanted to be able to participate in discussions, and offer my own thoughts, but quickly realized I'd never looked too deeply into the history of our lives before the curse.

I was well-versed on the ley lines that provided the magical affinities of dragons and drackya, while also maintaining the climates needed to support their specific element. But if it were about the bonds and relations between humans and the beasts, my knowledge was severely lacking.

It wasn't like I had anyone around to ask about it, considering those who were old enough to remember those times, that still lived within our lands, were very hush about the subject. It was as if they feared the curse could transfer to them if they even spoke about it. It was said that the drackya were cursed while in their human forms, to not be able to fully shift back, leaving glimpses of their inner beasts on display. How that could be transferred to us, considering we didn't have the ability to shift, was beyond me, but I digressed. Fear was a palpable force.

"Oh yeah?" I retorted, refusing to move a muscle. If he wanted to fake being conversational, I could play that game. "I was up all night in the library trying to prepare for a council meeting I've been summoned to today. How does it feel to know that I'm still kicking your ass after getting no sleep?"

His jaw dropped, and I wasn't sure if it was from the admission of being included in a council meeting, or that I was truly running on no sleep and still handling our fight with ease.

I thought back to my night as he pondered my words.

What I learned about the drackya from my tutor growing up was that they were the voice for the full-blooded dragons, who vehemently refused to mindspeak with humans, unless said human was a rare rider.

It was openly discussed in our history books that the drackya were the male offspring of the elemental gods, and witches were the female offspring. What wasn't discussed in the books were the whispered bonds that humans and drackya supposedly shared before the curse.

I'd not been born until that symbiotic relationship between the undine drackya and the humans of our kingdom ceased to exist, so having a soulmate that was half dragon at heart sounded like the thing of tales. It was almost as unbelievable to me as the thought of a curse being placed in our lifetime. Witches were rumored to have been eradicated centuries ago when the dragons and drackya teamed up, coveting the magic of the ley lines.

Brenson let out a throaty growl seconds before he used his height to his advantage, boldly shoving his shoulder up into the blade as his head pulled away from the deadly-sharp blade.

"About time you make a move. I was growing bored," I murmured, flashing a toothy grin as I gave in to the heady rush of dopamine that flooded my system at his refusal to concede.

He did exactly what I expected, and I side-stepped quickly, noticing all his weight shifting into his left foot that had crept back, showcasing his intent to surge forward and knock me back onto my ass with brute strength alone. Brenson was the only person I'd ever fought, but from observing our guards for countless hours, it seemed the majority of men relied far too much on their weight, rather than their nimbleness.

Pulling the pommel of my sword up behind his head as he staggered by me, I wasted no time in bringing it down hard into the back of his skull. He crumpled to the ground, like I imagined the stone walls of our castle would if the weight of a dragon was to bear down upon them. There was no recourse as he lifted his hand to the area I'd struck.

"When did you become so fast?" he groaned with his face still firmly planted against the dirty ground. "This is getting embarrassing. Truly, I need to be sober for these fights now."

I bent down to pat his leather-padded shoulder. "Whatever excuse makes you feel better about yourself, Commander. Take pride in knowing it was at least you that's trained me all these years."

He'd proven to be the only swordsman in this damned kingdom that cared about my desire to learn the blade and stick up for me.

Before he could respond, a roar echoed from the edge of our territory, sending a shiver of excitement and dread down my spine as my eyes snapped in that direction. A dark shadow flew high through the morning mist that still coated the mountains. The dragon was far enough out that I couldn't make out its color or true size to know its abilities, but it didn't matter, as long as it wasn't silver. Only the royal line of drackya shifters were silver, the full-blooded undine dragons remaining shades of blue, so if we saw a silver beast, I feared their own army would be only moments behind them, following their king into battle.

I held my breath as I waited to see what direction it flew in, but quickly released it as the dragon faded into the higher clouds. Likely scouting. They were becoming emboldened by the month, coming closer and closer without retribution from us, *yet*. I hoped today's meeting would give me insight on what my father planned to do about it. For far too long women had lived in fear of a taloned foot plucking them into the air as we went about our day to day lives. If they didn't want to wage a war for that sake alone, they needed to do it before we began to starve to death.

My head jerked toward the sounds of scurrying of feet, light enough in their steps that I knew it wasn't one of Brenson's men on patrol. None of them were that graceful. Only the tail end of a gray dress caught my eye before it disappeared, the person ducking into one of the small doors near the foot of the storehouse that I knew opened into a small servant's corridor leading in the direction of the kitchen.

Shit. We'd been seen.

Chapter Two

SIYANA

I TOSSED my sword onto the rack of practice weapons and a breath later had my cloak securely fastened around my shoulders and the hood drawn over my head.

"I'll see you tomorrow morning, Brenson," I called out in a rush as he began to push to his feet, "I have a matter to tend to that can't wait before my council meeting."

I had to imagine his skull was still ringing from a mixture of that blow and the ale from last night. Telling him our session might have been witnessed by someone, despite him taking the early morning rotation where he would be responsible for monitoring the northern rampart wall that overlooked the armory, would not go over well. Best I handled this with a deft hand than to have a roaring commander alerting even more people to an issue.

He lifted a hand to wave me off. "Yeah, yeah. Tomorrow I'll get redemption for this, so be prepared."

His half-hearted warning made the corners of my lips pull up into a gentle smile. There were definitely days when he left me sore and bruised, but it had been a good bit of time since then. I wasn't sure if I was improving that much or if, for some reason, he had begun taking it easy on me.

I took off in the direction of the stranger, hoping I was fast enough to catch up with them. If they were in a dress, it was likely they wouldn't be running anywhere— that was highly frowned upon for the workers within the castle and would draw too much attention. It was still early enough that only the staff would be awake, though, and that might embolden the person.

I was more grateful than ever for my leathers at this moment, feeling my legs extend to their full stride without a dress holding me back. The brisk morning air whipped at my face as I pumped my arms to propel me faster. I had to catch whoever this was.

Anxiety swiftly pooled within my stomach and chest at the thought of our session being made known to the public. Had we gotten too lax in our routine, since it had been years and no one had discovered us?

My father only allowed Brenson and me to have these sessions under the strict rule that we were not to be observed, to prevent any rumors about my love of the blade from starting. Brenson had vouched that it would be his head on the line if we were ever discovered. As one of the youngest to rise to station of commander, he held a lot of respect, and in particular with my father, but this was a misstep that would not be tolerated.

I wiped at the bead of sweat trickling down my temple, the heat in my body rising with my anxiety and racing heart. I was willing to risk going against my father when it was just the chance of myself being reprimanded as a teen, but now that Brenson's station and honor were on the line, things were drastically different.

Turning a corner that led to a wider corridor toward the kitchens and great hall, I increased my pace until I reached the end. It forked in two directions. My braid whipped me in the jaw as my head swiveled both ways and indecision plagued my gut. My fingers curled until my nails dug into my palms, the painful bite grounding me in the moment. *Which direction, Sia?* I couldn't allow everything Brenson had worked so hard for to be thrown out because of me.

The tell-tale sound of a wooden door creaking open had my feet carrying me down the left corridor instantly. I ran toward the end of the hall before sliding around the corner, the flat bottoms of my boots not catching well against the smooth floor. The breath was knocked from my lungs as my shoulder collided with the wall for a brief moment, but my eyes locked onto the woman going into a room at the end of this hallway, and I grinned.

Found you.

I collected myself, steadying my breath as I walked toward the door. Now that I'd discovered her, what was I even going to say? My hand fell on the door handle but stilled before I could pull it open.

Would she want to be paid for her silence?

My brow furrowed at the scenarios rolling through my mind before a sigh puffed over my lips and my shoulders fell. Whatever she wanted for her silence, I'd have to give it to her. There were only two people I considered true friends, and Brenson was one of them. I'd not allow his life to crumble due to his support of my secret training.

I'd negotiate my way out of this. I was a lady raised in the political sphere, after all.

With a deep inhale, I pushed the door open and came face to face with a wide-eyed young woman I didn't recognize. She must have been new, as I made it a point to befriend all of our staff. All that was in her small room was a small bed, a table with a steel pitcher and matching cup for water, and a small chest of belongings at the foot of it.

Her gray eyes darted behind me toward the door, as if she was contemplating escape. *Absolutely not.* Instinct came over me, and in mere moments, I had the dagger that was hidden in my boot pulled out and at her throat, trapping pieces of her straw-colored hair against her fair skin as I did.

I snarled as I closed the distance between our faces,

"Tell me exactly what you saw back there before I cut into your vein and leave you to bleed out."

Well, there went my attempts at a polite negotiation. I tried.

The girl's large eyes widened in terror, her breath coming in short, panicked gasps. Her voice shook as she stuttered, "I-I didn't see anything, Your Highness! I swear it!"

So, she knew exactly who I was, despite me not being in my typical royal attire. That would most certainly be a problem.

I pressed the blade harder against her skin before snapping at her, "Don't lie to me!" Her bottom lip quivered as I ground my teeth together and forced myself to take a deep breath. "I will ask once more...What did you see?"

Tears welled in her eyes as she trembled. "Please, Princess Siyana, I meant no harm. I was just delivering linens and I got lost. I heard the clash of swords as I tried to find my way. I...I was curious. I only watched for a moment, I promise!"

If the hay I smelled on her was any indicator, she'd also taken a trip to the stables this morning, which was nowhere near the training yard. That was a considerable distance to cross, and there were no linens to be delivered there.

My eyes narrowed. "Why do you smell like you've lain with the horses, if you've been delivering linens as you said?"

Her mouth popped open with a sharp inhale. Pink warmed the apples of her cheeks as she stammered, "I...I shouldn't speak of such things with you, Your Highness, it isn't acceptable."

Color my curiosity doubly-piqued.

I studied her oval face, searching for any sign of deception that I might have missed. Finding none, I slowly lowered the dagger to my side, though I kept it clutched tightly in my hand. "What's your name?"

"Mira, Your Highness," she whispered as I took a step back to allow for the slightest amount of room between us. Her hand came up reflexively to smooth over the skin my blade had just been held to. There was no wound— I'd been careful—but it was natural to want to ensure your throat was indeed intact.

I gave her a moment to assure herself of that fact before I felt her focus entirely back on me. Slipping my dagger back into my boot, I crossed my arms in front of my chest.

"Well, Mira, as you just saw, I'm quite the fan of things that aren't acceptable." The barest of smiles turned her lips up at my words. "Humor me."

Her anxiety was palpable from the rigid set to her shoulders and the way her tongue kept darting out to wet her lips.

"I wasn't lying with the horses, Your Highness," she answered, lowering her voice and dropping her eyes to the ground, "just the stableman."

My eyes widened and I couldn't stop the laughter from pouring out of me.

"Good for you," I answered, composing myself. "Just a word of caution: Sebastian is known to not have the best loyalty when it comes to his partners."

It was her turn to laugh, and I found a smile returning to my lips as she did. It was a sweet laugh that instantly put me at ease.

"I appreciate your honesty, Princess Siyana, but you don't have to worry about that," she admitted with a wink. "I don't have all my eggs in one basket, either."

My smile turned into a full-fledged grin. I officially liked her.

Her words seemed genuine, and if she was indeed new like I thought, the story of getting lost was entirely plausible—it wasn't a small castle, after all. She was either a terrific performer, or I was a gullible oaf.

Despite my heart telling me she was being honest with me, there was still a matter to settle. One that I couldn't let go so easily.

I stepped back to lean against the wall. "So, Mira, what do you intend to do with the knowledge that I was sparring? It isn't common knowledge, and it needs to stay that way."

Mira's eyes widened as she smoothed her hands down the front of her dress, a flicker of something I couldn't quite place dancing across her face. Why did she suddenly seem nervous?

"Do with it? Nothing, Your Highness. I..." Her eyes

rose to meet mine, her shoulders rolling back as she admitted, "I admire you. The way you moved with that sword, it was like watching poetry in motion. I couldn't look away until the dragon's roar shocked me out of it."

I blinked, taken aback by her unexpected response. There was an earnestness in her gaze that gave me pause.

"You admire it?" I asked, incredulity coloring my tone.

Mira nodded earnestly, her earlier fear of me seemingly forgotten. "Yes, Princess. I've never seen anything like it. The strength, the grace..." She let out a soft sigh, "It was beautiful."

A warmth blossomed in my chest at her words, a feeling I wasn't accustomed to when it came to my secret passion. I had to temper down my inclination to want to preen like a peacock at her praise.

I felt my guard lowering despite just having met her. There was something in Mira's eyes—a spark of genuine admiration and longing–that resonated deep within me. I recognized that look. I'd seen it in my own reflection countless times when I thought of watching the new recruits train as a young girl.

"Tell me, Mira," I said softly pushing off the wall, "have you ever held a sword?"

A wistful smile played on her lips. "Only in my dreams, Your Highness." She hesitated, then the words tumbled out in a rush. "Ever since I was a little girl, I'd practice with sticks in secret, imagining I was wielding a real sword."

Her confession stirred something within me, a kindred spirit recognizing another. This was a woman who'd join me in burning down the patriarchy, if there was ever a time for it.

I felt a smile tugging at my lips, unbidden. This girl's passion mirrored my own so closely it was almost uncanny. For a moment, I saw myself in her—that burning desire to break free from the constraints society placed upon us, to prove we were more than delicate flowers to be admired from afar.

"Mira," I said, my voice barely above a whisper in case someone walked by, "what if I told you that your dreams don't have to remain just that? Dreams, I mean."

Her eyes widened, a mix of hope and disbelief shining in their depths. "Your Highness?"

"I could teach you. In secret, of course." My brows pinched together as I started to work out the details in my head. "It won't be easy–you'll have bruises, blisters, and aches in places you didn't know existed. But if you're willing to put in the work, I can show you how to wield a blade."

Mira's face lit up with an inner fire that I recognized all too well. But as quickly as it appeared, doubt clouded her features.

"But Your Highness, I'm just a servant. Surely I'm not worthy of such an honor. And what if we're caught? I couldn't bear it if I caused you trouble."

Her worry for me only proved I was right to like her. Here I was, offering her exactly what she wanted, yet her mind jumped straight to ensuring I wouldn't get in trouble for it.

I waved her off, turning for the door. "Don't call yourself just a servant, Mira. You're a human, just like me. I don't care much for titles."

Pausing as my hand fell to the handle, I turned to look back at her. "Ask for Tillie. She's my cousin, but also technically my lady-in-waiting. I'm supposed to have at least two, but until now, I'd never found someone else I wanted to fill that spot. If you're sure this is what you want, I'll inform the castle steward of your position change this morning, and that will give us the time together to train. Tillie will ensure you know your new route, so you don't get lost again."

My voice was light and full of mirth, poking fun at our unusual cause for meeting this morning. I expected to see glee on her face, so when tears brimmed in her eyes before a few escaped, trailing down to her jaw, I blinked rapidly at her.

"Mira?" I questioned, concerned I'd offended her somehow.

"That is the kindest thing anyone has offered me, Your Highness," she admitted, lifting a hand to brush away the stray tears. "I don't know how to repay you for this."

My chest tightened with her display of emotion. Swords and crass words were my comfort zone, not this.

"Think nothing of it," I reassured her, wondering if it would be rude of me to ask her to stop crying. I quickly came to the conclusion that it likely would be and swallowed the words. "You can repay me by continuing to be curious and open to what the world has to offer us. There isn't enough of that around here. It's refreshing and gives me hope."

"Mira!" a voice yelled from the hall suddenly, though it was still far enough away that I had time to hide behind the door if needed.

It wouldn't be unusual to see me down here with the staff, but the way I was currently dressed would be cause for far too many questions. Questions that would make their way back to my father.

Mira seemed to understand that and pushed me to the side before yanking the door open and sticking her head out. "Yes, Margaret?"

The head of the kitchen was a kind woman, but she scared me a little bit. You could regularly hear her barking orders at her staff from the level above. Through stone. I shuddered at the thought.

No one could say she didn't take her job seriously, and my stomach rather appreciated it. Her food was a thing to be marveled over.

"I know you aren't on my staff, but there's an important meeting this morning, and the King has sent word that he wants us to prepare a large breakfast for his guest. Why he'd require so much food for one guest is beyond me, but that's the king for ya," she breathed out, voice clearly tinged with judgment.

She wasn't wrong. My father often seemed to either

forget, or blatantly ignore, we were heading for hard times. You'd never gather that, from the routine feasts he called for.

"I didn't know of it until now," Margaret admitted on a weary breath, "and I just got word from the castle guard that Leah was taken by a dragon this morning while foraging for herbs, leaving me short of a hand. Do you have any skill in the kitchen?"

My mind whirled. Leah was taken? Was it the dragon I spotted during sparring?

How could Margaret be so nonchalant about one of our own being snatched by a dragon? Yes, it was becoming more common by the week, but this was still a human being taken. Someone with a life, a family, and their own dreams. Had we really grown so complacent to the thought of being weak in comparison to the dragons that we simply no longer cared?

Fire built within my belly. They had to be stopped, and now more than ever I hoped this meeting was about doing exactly that. Nothing else mattered.

"I may not be trained, but I have enthusiasm and a listening ear, if you'll instruct me," Mira answered, making Maragret let out a huff.

"That'll do. Please clean off quickly from your morning activities so that we keep the kitchen and food a clean environment."

I thought back to Maragret's other words, that a guest was arriving. I'd assumed that it would just be the usual council when my father had told me I'd been requested to attend the meeting. If that was the case, Margaret wouldn't refer to any one of the councilmembers as a guest.

Who was visiting our castle, and why hadn't my father told me earlier? Though I wasn't welcomed into meetings, I was usually privy to the knowledge of any visits and told to brush up on the territory and the guests before they arrived. During the meals we had together, I was expected to make conversation with guests and make them feel at ease.

The door shut quietly as Maragret walked away, leaving Mira and me in private once more. I began pacing the small room, back and forth as I tried to piece together what was going on.

It would be one thing if my father just happened to neglect telling me about the visitor, but the fact that he hadn't alerted the staff to be prepared for a guest until this morning...It was unheard of. He'd never risk Andrathya looking ill-prepared.

My gut churned. My unease over this meeting was rising rapidly. If he'd hidden it from everyone, that only meant one thing: whoever was coming would cause a large stir in our kingdom. Rumors would likely swirl if people were given prior knowledge of these visitors' arrival.

I'd almost rather risk the wrath of the dragon from this morning coming to our castle instead of walking into that meeting later.

The sound of the door shutting snapped me out of my thoughts.

"Are you okay, Your Highness?" Mira questioned, reaching out a hand to my shoulder, startling me from my thoughts and determination to wear a path in the floor with my pacing.

I forced a smile to my lips and grabbed her hand, squeezing it lightly to show my appreciation for her concern.

"Please, call me Sia in private, but, yes, I'll be fine, thank you," I answered, stepping around her toward the door. "I must leave and prepare for that meeting. When you're done helping Margaret, go to the steward and he will escort you to your new quarters that are near my own in the west wing."

She nodded, worry still ever present in her eyes. "Are you sure you're okay? I watched you look every bit the seasoned swordsman this morning as you defeated a man twice your size, yet this meeting seems to have filled you with dread."

My chest rose with a deep breath as I tried to paint my face with my proper princess facade. Her worry spoke to the good-nature of her heart, but it wasn't something I needed to burden her with. "All will be well. I'll see you later."

I didn't waste another second, knowing I was already pushing it with the time that was needed to bathe and ready myself for this meeting. Tillie was going to have her hands full helping me, and I prepared myself for a good chiding from her.

Ensuring my face was covered with my hood, I escaped to the back stairs that spiraled up to the west wing. Upon reaching my door and hearing Tillie letting out a string of curses about my absence, I settled the palm of my hand on my stomach and took deep, calming breaths.

Despite what I told Mira, I had a sickening feeling that this meeting was going to change everything.

Chapter Three

SIYANA

"Will you just keep your head straight for one more second!" the fiery redhead I claimed as my best friend growled, stabbing me in the skull with a hairpin in the process.

"Ow, Tillie!" I exclaimed, sending her a withering look in the mirror in front of us. "Why do you have to be so cruel to my hair?"

As the second person I considered a friend and confidant, she'd always been privy to the knowledge of my training with Brenson, encouraging me on the days I had wanted to give up in the beginning. So I knew her mood wasn't due to my morning training session.

Her hazel eyes rolled in response to my pouting as she stabbed me with another pin, cinching a long strand into place atop my head. "Oh shut it, Sia. You didn't flinch when I cleaned off and bandaged your wound from this morning, yet a hair pin will be your demise?"

I grumbled about that being entirely different and she talked right over me.

"It's your fault that we didn't have time to wash and dry your hair properly. I'm having to work magic on your messy waves this morning! I mean, seriously, what did you expect when you spent your time with Mira this morning?"

There it was.

I tried to bite my lip to keep my shit-eating grin to myself but failed when she narrowed her eyes at me in the reflection. It was just too much fun to rile her.

"Do you have something you'd like to say to me, Sia?" she asked in a saccharine sweet voice, holding a pin in the air.

I mimed closing my mouth and throwing out the key, shaking my head.

Stab.

I winced. Well if she wasn't going to drop it, neither was I.

"I just find it funny," I mused, reaching for my cup of tea resting on the vanity. "I've never seen this jealous side of you."

She leaned down to inspect her work in the mirror, picking at a few strands to give them more volume. "I told you, I'm not jealous, I just don't know how someone managed to convince you to become your lady-in-waiting in record time, when your entire life you've denied the other candidates presented to you."

I blew on the piping-hot liquid, it steaming as I raised

the cup to my lips. My eyebrows rose just before I whisper-sang, "Jealousssssss."

I'd already made it abundantly clear that Mira hadn't asked for the job, therefore she didn't convince me of anything. I'd freely offered the position. Harping on that fact was only going to start our argument back up, though, so I didn't bother correcting her. In the end, all she was concerned about was my safety and being used by someone, so I couldn't begrudge her that. I would have done the exact same as her if the situation were somehow reversed.

I let out a huff. I actually would have been an absolute menace in comparison.

Although Tillie was stuck with me by blood as my cousin, I'd claimed her soul in this life and the next. I could never replace her, but it was amusing to see her hackles rising when I filled her in on Mira and the young woman's new appointment.

"Don't you have a meeting to get to?" she countered with a raise of her eyebrow as she stood to her full height, popping a hand on her hip.

My mood dipped instantly. I'd mulled it over every which way while in the tub and had come to the conclusion that the meeting had to be in regards to the talk of war with the undine. There was nothing else of importance that would garner such discretion. Had my father found allies from the other kingdoms? It seemed unlikely, so I pushed away the hope that threatened to blossom in my chest.

"I don't like being kept in the dark and walking into something I'm not prepared for," I murmured, putting my tea down as I rose to get dressed. "Am I overthinking this?"

As she grabbed the soft blue gown laid out for me, I slipped off my robe. Her head shook as she approached and I raised my arms to assist.

"It's unsettling," she agreed, tossing the dress over my head. "If it is concerning a war, it could just be to protect whoever is offering us assistance as an ally?"

My lips thinned as I pondered her words, letting her fasten the dress in place in silence. It was a possibility, but there was peace on the continent with all the other kingdoms right now. Though skirmishes with their own dragons were always handled without assistance from others, none had faced what we had for the past twenty-seven years. A complete dissolution of an alliance between human and undine, due to the drackya.

The last I'd heard of there being an issue in another kingdom was last month, in regards to the Salarya territory to the south of us. An issue with the line of succession with their ember dragons was causing some civil unrest. The human council was being called upon to help them settle the matter, which was unheard of here, where the humans and dragons had their own governing rulers, with no crossover.

From what I gathered in our texts and my political studies, each of the kingdoms in Edath had an entirely different relationship with their dragons. In Salarya, the humans and dragons supposedly coexisted—and also referred to the embers as dragons, no matter if they were drackya or full-blooded dragons.

I suppose that's exactly why I was so curious about our continent as a whole. Each kingdom and their dragons had such unique ways of life together, and being forever sequestered to Andrathya as the precious princess, I knew I'd never have the chance to satisfy that thirst for exploration.

A knock came at my door a few minutes later as Tillie and I exchanged a hug.

"Are you ready, Princess?" a guard called, reminding me just how bizarre the situation today was. I'd never needed a guarded escort within our own castle walls.

Who was here that I needed protection from? Distrust for the situation was understandable, but why did mine feel so deep-seated?

Tillie squeezed my shoulders as she took a step back and gave me a once over. "Whatever is waiting for you in that room, they have no clue what's coming for them. Remember exactly who you are, Sia."

Her words chased away the tingling bundles of anxiety in my stomach. I nodded at her and raised my chin, letting my shoulders fall back.

Slipping my dagger into the sheath wrapped around my thigh before I headed to the door, a blanket of comfort washed over me as the familiar coolness of the hilt pressed into my skin.

I dared someone to threaten me or my kingdom.

The walk down to the council room was quick, not allowing me the time to second guess the confidence I wore like a suit of armor. As the guards stationed at the door gave me a nod of greeting and opened the doors, I blew out a breath.

"Announcing Princess Siyana of Andrathya," the guard on my left called out to the room, "heir to the throne."

The council room was filled with the scent of freshly polished mahogany, the lingering smell of incense and candles, and the subtle hint of expensive cologne and leather from the men's attire.

Countless men gathered around the long table, standing to their feet with my arrival, but one pair of eyes drew me in amongst the sea of the rest.

Eyes like navy blue flames, radiating with a dangerous magic that ensnared my very being. But it wasn't just the shimmering color that held me captive—it was the left pupil, slitted like a serpent's and the skin encircled by shimmering, silver dragon scales that trailed from his temple to the inside of his nose. Strands of his wavy white hair were tucked behind his ear in a lazy attempt, considering they were too short to stay in place as his head tilted. A slender scar ran from the top of his face and over his eyelid, ending at the top of his cheekbone. I noted more silver scales running the length of his neck and peeking out on his collarbone.

There was no hiding exactly what he was. A royal drackya, with his curse on display.

It was all true. The curse was true.

His lips curved into a smirk as my gaze traveled down, igniting a fierce anger within me at his dismissive response to my open scrutiny. My nostrils flared with irritation as I tore my eyes away from him and sought out my father at the head of the table, though not before taking in every detail of the infuriatingly handsome man. His sharp jawline and towering stature were no surprise, considering he could transform into a massive dragon at will—yet it still left me breathless and on edge.

Considering his looks, I placed him to not be much older than myself. He was likely their prince, if I had to guess.

I must not have been hiding my agitation well, for when my eyes locked onto my father's brown ones, they all but screamed '*behave.*'

It took every ounce of strength and patience that I could conjure to not tell him to shove it where the sun doesn't shine.

How dare he blindside me like this?

There was an open seat on his right that I presumed was for me as I made my way over. He pulled it out for me to sit, grazing my cheek with his lips in a quick greeting before whispering into my ear, "I have indulged your desire to wield a blade and never forced you into a marriage proposal, but today I will be asking you to do your duty for this kingdom, Siyana. Do not let us down."

I could have sworn the drackya prince let loose a

breath of ice with the way my blood instantly chilled from my father's words.

Giving me no time to react, he squeezed my shoulder, turning me toward the rest of the room that waited for me to sit. Giving the room a small curtsey, I inclined my head. "Please be seated," I called out, ensuring my voice was strong and loud, before taking my own seat.

Pain lanced through the inside of my cheeks as I bit down on the tender flesh to keep myself from demanding answers here and now. I barely recognized the warning in my father's tone. Despite not being as progressive as I wanted him to be, he'd shown me small bouts of kindness growing up. I believed he loved me in the way he could, as someone struggling to be both a ruler and father in one. Apparently, he'd just been waiting to hold those things over my head until it suited him.

The betrayal from that realization cut deeply, and I wished my mother was in attendance so that I could see if it extended to her as well. She wasn't one to dabble in politics willingly and often told me she didn't understand my desire to be involved. We might have looked identical with our tanned skin, dark waves that fell to our hips, and general stature, but we couldn't have differed more in our minds and hearts.

I felt a gaze burning into the side of my face, from my father's left, as everyone took their seats, but I refused to meet *his* eyes. I had assumed this meeting would likely entail discussing the situation with the dragons, but I'd never dreamed they would ever actually be at this meeting.

It all made sense now, why my father had kept the meeting entirely private. Our people would be furious to know we welcomed the dragons into our walls willingly.

I focused on the weight of my dagger against my leg to ground me and stop my hands from trembling with rage as I folded them in my lap.

"Thank you all for coming today on such short notice," my father began, staying on his feet as he addressed the room with his booming voice. "The past twenty-seven years have been hard for both of our peoples, and it is time that we put our struggles behind us, in order to forge a path to peace and prosperity for the whole of Andrathya."

Hard on our people? That's what we were going to call the abduction and likely murder of our citizens at the hands of the undine drackya? An interesting choice of words that I wouldn't have personally used, but here we were.

I kept my face blank as I digested his statement, not wanting to give anything away with our enemy at his side. Perhaps my father was setting a trap for them, luring them into a false sense of security with the promise of a treaty, to keep them unaware before we attacked them.

"King Takkar, please," my father said, urging the undine drackya I assumed to be their prince to stand and take over the conversation.

King.

My spine stiffened at the distinction. He seemed far too young to be the king. What I read of their current political structure was apparently outdated, because he looked nothing like the king I'd read about, who I now realized must have been his father.

Still, I refused to look at him as his chair screeched against the floor before he stood. He'd done nothing to earn that respect from me.

My father elbowed me lightly as he sat down, jostling me slightly, forcing me to incline my head just enough to appear like I might be giving the dragon any of my attention.

"I look forward to ending the senseless struggles of both of our peoples through this marriage."

His words sent my heart into overdrive, and I felt as if I was going to collapse at the sudden rush of blood to my head.

I couldn't have heard him right, being distracted by the deep timber of his voice.

His calculated gaze shifted to settle on my face before he smiled and announced, "I know I can speak for Princess Siyana, and myself, when I say that we will work dilligently toward a new path forward."

How dare he.

The tips of my fingers dug into my thighs, through the fabric of my dress. "The curse will be our number one priority, and we will not stop until we find a way to lift it and restore the life the generations before us speak of with fondness."

My blood boiled beneath the surface, and I couldn't stop myself from surging to my feet and staring him down as my hands flattened against the table.

I didn't recognize the cold, venomous tone of my voice as I looked him in the eyes and seethed, "You most definitely cannot speak for me."

"Siyana, sit down this instance!" my father roared as he attempted to pull me down by the sleeve of my dress.

The fabric ripped at the force in which I tugged my arm out of his grasp. My burning gaze swiveled to focus on the man who was shipping me off to our enemies, without even having the decency to discuss it with me beforehand.

Never before had I realized just how little my voice, wants, and needs mattered to my father. The bar had been low in my mind, but to be happily handed over to the beasts that have historically terrorized us, for the off chance that it may eventually bring peace?

My head shook of its own accord as a dark laugh bubbled out of me. "Is this an order from my king, or my father?"

His lips thinned, and for the briefest of moments, I thought I saw a flicker of shame or remorse in his gaze, but then it was gone. "Both."

The room was completely silent as I turned to look at the beast my body had been promised to. I found him studying me with open curiosity as I asked, "And what if I refuse?"

A chuff came from him, sounding almost as if his

beast was trying to laugh from within. His broad shoulders shrugged, his voice tinged with amusement as he answered, "You can't. The marriage certificate was already signed by myself and your father, prior to your arrival."

It was like a bag of stones had been tossed into my gut.

The fight bled out of me and my eyes fell to the table as I struggled to wrap my mind around his words. Marriage certificate. Signed.

My eyes drifted back up toward the monster my fate was now tied to, and the predatory grin that I found on his face had my blood icing over.

"Hello, wife."

Chapter Four

SIYANA

Wife.

My body trembled with rage as I stood in the center of the room, surrounded by the men who had just used me as a pawn in their schemes. Their voices faded into white noise as my own thoughts consumed me, searching for a way out of this desperate situation. But there was none—my fate had been decided without any consideration for me as a person.

There was a minuscule part of my brain that was trying to rationalize that there may yet be some good to come of a treaty between our people, but I wasn't ready to accept that my life had been the cost of achieving that.

There had to be another way.

As the room cleared, leaving only myself and the two kings, I abandoned all pretense of propriety or decorum. With fire in my eyes and trembling hands that were balled into fists, I unleashed a torrent of rage and defiance at the two figures who held my fate in their hands.

"I hope one day you both are brought to your knees and made to feel as powerless as I do now, and I pray the elementals allow me to have a hand in that moment."

The weight of their power and control crushed down on me, but I refused to break beneath it.

My father opened his mouth to rebut, but the drackya king lifted his hand, those haunting eyes still trained on my face as he cut him off before he could get words out. "Not now, my wife is speaking."

The burning rage within me was momentarily tempered by his words, not in appreciation, but confusion. The most insane part of this moment was that my father actually closed his mouth in response.

My anger came rushing back like the waves crashing against the northern bluffs, chipping away at the essence of the sediment. Much like it, I found pieces of myself deteriorating. The gentle and kind portions of my heart were nowhere to be found.

"I don't need you to defend me," I spat, hating the way I couldn't even fume without intervention from a man. My fists clenched and unclenched, over and over again at my sides.

Was nothing my own anymore?

His chest rumbled with laughter before he turned for the door, dismissing me. He didn't even bother to look back at me before answering. "I just wanted you to have your chance to get all that brewing hatred out before we journey to my home. Consider this your warning that I won't put up with it when you inevitably direct it at me, so, this is in your best interest."

My brow rose at his words.

Oh, he thought I was a timid woman who was going to just get over this and be a good little wife? The elementals were smiling upon me now, ensuring my betrothed had no clue the woman he'd tied his fate to.

Air puffed out of my nose as a deep chuckle worked itself through my chest. His feet stilled as I retorted in the most sarcastic tone I could muster, "I hate to break it to you, *husband*, but you just signed up for a lifetime of 'putting up with it,' so go ahead and prepare yourself now. My nonexistent marriage vows include making your life as miserable as I can."

Abruptly, he spun on his heel and leveled a piercing gaze at me, filled with a coldness and malice that I had only heard of in the whispers surrounding the drackya king. It seemed that coldness had been inherited by his father. His eyes seemed to bore into my very soul, sending shivers down my spine as I stood frozen in his presence. The rumors about what I realized was *his* cruelty suddenly felt all too real at that moment.

"Well, it's lucky enough for me that I can just lock you in a room and never have to deal with that, now isn't it?" he retorted, raising a single dark eyebrow that contrasted the snowy white strands dangling over it, as if daring me to defy him. I almost rose to his bait, but it was becoming clear that he wanted to rile me, to bask in my utter despair of my situation he'd helped concoct. Upon seeing I wasn't going to respond, he shrugged, "The marriage certificate was all I needed. Those flowery words for your council mean nothing to me. You will do as I say and behave yourself while in my castle, or you can remain imprisoned in a room for all I care."

This was my future.

He was my future.

"That is not what we agreed upon!" my father roared, stepping in front of me, attempting to obscure me from view, but not doing too great of a job considering he was the same height as me and just about as slender.

My head reared back at his outburst. Did it suddenly matter now how I was treated? Interesting.

I wasn't sure who I was more pissed at: my new husband, who was showing how little I mattered to him already, or the man who put me in this position to begin with. My lip curled in disgust. They could both burn in the eternal pits of the fire elemental's domain for all I cared.

My betrothed pulled a scroll from the inner pocket of his dark coat and made a dramatic show of opening the cream-colored parchment and narrowing his eyes on the words as he scanned it.

I couldn't help but wonder if his vision was sound or not, having a dragon eye and human eye warring with each other, not to mention the scar running down the right side. Everything we knew about dragons as a species spoke of their superior genetics. Sound, sight, strength, agility. I tucked that thought away, knowing I needed to find a weak spot—if ever the chance was presented to me to make use of it.

After a few beats, he surmised, "Yeah, I'm not seeing in here where it says how I have to treat her once she's in my possession. If that actually mattered to you, you would have ensured it was a part of our contractual agreement."

As he rolled it up and put the scroll of doom back where he'd retrieved it, my father spluttered. I stepped from behind him, finding his face blotted with red stains, as he spoke, "Well, I...I shouldn't have to specify basic decency in a contract of wedlock! Have you no honor?"

His words were rich with irony, and for the first time, it was clear my husband and I agreed on something, our laughs echoing through the air in unison. It was slightly unnerving and I settled myself instantly, glowering at the beast.

My father spun to look at me, bewilderment clear in his wide-eyed expression. "Siyana, I swear to you," he pleaded, reaching for my hands, "I had many talks with King Takkar about what this arranged marriage would look like for you, as well as his feelings about it. I never would have agreed to this if I knew of his true nature."

A pang echoed through my heart and I pulled my hands back just before he could enclose his around them. Everything in me wanted to believe him. It was easier to stomach than thinking that he was throwing me to the beast to be slaughtered without thought. But as we gazed into each other's eyes, I spoke the truth of the matter.

Sorrow filled my voice as I asked, "It doesn't matter now, does it?"

His mouth opened as he struggled to find the words he wanted, but I shook my head and made it simple for him.

"There are no words to make this okay. Don't waste our time continuing to search for them. I need to pack my things and say my goodbyes to those I love."

I felt the hollowness of my words and hoped the subtle distinction that he wasn't a part of that group was loud and clear.

A loud sigh came from King Takkar as he opened the heavy doors. "You will have everything you need provided to you at my castle, and we don't have the time for you to say goodbye to whomever. It will take us all day and into the night to make the trip on horseback."

Horseback? He was a king and could shift into a dragon, yet we would be riding horses?

Once again, I sensed something was off, and I nestled that information away. I assumed we'd either fly back or have a carriage and escort befitting his rank.

It was on the tip of my tongue to tell him the least he owed me was my goodbyes, but a scuffle from the corridor took my attention.

"Sia!" a familiar voice yelled.

My eyes widened and my heart skipped a beat. *Tillie.*

"Sia!" she screamed once more as guards informed her she wasn't allowed into the room.

Despite being my lady-in-waiting by choice, she was still a member of the royal family. The guards never defied her. Clearly my father had warned them to not let her in.

The terror in her voice had my throat tightening and my feet moving swiftly toward her. A large arm jutted out as I made to pass through the doorway, my eyes clashing with my dearest friend for the briefest of seconds before the guards hauled her down the hall, kicking and thrashing within their grasps.

"Tillie!" I cried out, pushing against the arm that blocked me.

"We are leaving, now," the dragon stated dryly as his hand traveled down to grip my wrist tightly, drawing my eyes up to his cold, uncaring gaze. "I don't have time for your sorrowful weeping and empty promises to stay in touch."

I glanced back to my father, seeing if he would try to rectify the wrongs one last time, but I was met with a blank stare from a man I was beginning to realize I never truly knew the heart of.

"Unhand me right now!" Tillie screamed as a guard let out a curse, and I felt my fire return with her fight as I whipped my head back to my enemy.

I bore my teeth at him, feeling the familiar energy I had when sparring with Brenson wash over me. "I will gouge your eyes out with my nails if you block me from going to her one more time!"

He lowered his face until our noses were a mere inch apart, his presence overwhelming me, yet sparking my indignation even more with his attempt to intimidate me.

"I think I'd like to see you try that," he whispered darkly as his serpentine pupil widened, like a predator enthralled with the thrill of a hunt.

Chills covered my arms. "Let go of me now, or else," I stated calmly, preparing myself to make use of the dagger hiding under my dress.

"That's enough out of you!" a guard yelled just before a grunt of pain came from Tillie.

I didn't think, moving on pure instinct as I used my free hand to draw my dagger out, cutting my dress in my rush. I glared up at the hulking shifter, holding the tip of my steel to his abdomen. Our breaths mixed as we held each other's gaze, a battle of wills taking place.

Who would yield first?

"Unhand me and let me say my goodbyes," I ground out, "and then we will be on our way."

He made a noise of contemplation, tutting, before responding, "On second thought, I think I will take that dagger to use to clean my teeth the next time I go hunting."

Before I could even process what was happening, his intense gaze ignited with a spark of lighter blue, sending a chill down my spine. The spark wasn't natural–was it magic? I felt the icy tendrils spread from his hand, creeping up my wrist and enveloping my entire arm in a matter of seconds. The sensation of coldness seeped into my very bones, stopping at my shoulder as if it had been commanded to do so.

All I could do was stare in horror at his display of magic. I knew dragon's abilities came from an elemental deity, but there wasn't much knowledge in our books on the details of how it was used as drackya. Our singular librarian told me it was closely guarded information that the dragons ensured remained within their own lands. Naively, I'd assumed they could only use such power while in their beast form.

"Drop the dagger. Or I can shatter your arm from your body," he stated, seeming a mixture of annoyed and bored with my antics. "Your choice, dear wife. It doesn't matter to me if you lose a limb or two."

My lips pursed with unbridled fury.

"Tillie!" I called out, knowing I was outmatched in abilities with this shifter. "Don't fight them," my voice broke, "*please*. I will be okay."

It hit me as I spoke—I'd likely never see her again. I wouldn't exchange blows with Brenson tomorrow morning. I'd never have a chance to train Mira. A pit of despair opened in my stomach, threatening to swallow me whole.

Her voice grew distant as she yelled back, "No! Don't you dare give in, Siyana. Fight back! Remember who you are!"

My eyes pricked with tears as my face heated.

I dropped the dagger and my heart shattered as it clattered against the floor. It felt like an omission of my subservience, making me feel sick to my stomach.

I couldn't allow her or anyone to get hurt in their attempt to free me. If Tillie had heard of my marriage already, it was likely Brenson had as well, considering the generals had been at the meeting and would be appraising the commanders. I couldn't let him risk insubordination when there was no point.

No one could change my fate—save the elementals themselves.

"Now that's settled," my captor said with disdain before releasing the ice from my skin, warmth slowly seeping back as the blood flowed once more within. "You'll learn your place soon enough."

My heart swirled with fear and anger as I realized the true extent of my imprisonment. I liked to think that I could change the world, that I could be a voice and pillar of strength for women to see what we were capable of. At this moment, my dreams and desires tasted like ash on my tongue, burned to a crisp with the actions of these men.

I glanced back at my father as I allowed a single tear to fall from my eye.

"I'm sorry," he whispered, his head shaking as if in shock and despair—helpless.

I swallowed harshly, whispering back with the tiny

bit of strength I could muster in my voice, "I don't forgive you."

The room spun as I was suddenly picked up and thrown over the drackya's shoulder, his arm strapped over my body just below my ass with an iron-like grip.

"You're a brute," I spat, hitting his back with my fists. "Put me down!"

"But I'm *your* brute, dear wife."

The scent of him wrapped around me, suffocating me with every bit of him. Spearmint with a subtle under-lying hint of cedar. I couldn't escape his scent, his body, or his claim on me.

"Don't fucking remind me," I retorted as he walked down the corridor and toward the castle doors, stripping any last shred of dignity I held as everyone stopped what they were doing to watch.

I couldn't bring myself to meet anyone's eyes, embar-rassed and ashamed that I couldn't do anything to fight back.

Maybe I was only ever just a princess and not a warrior like I thought.

Chapter Five

SIYANA

My heart thundered in my chest as I rode away from my home, filled with churning emotions of anger, fear, and despair. The rhythmic clopping of the horses' hooves only amplified the turmoil within me, and I couldn't shake the sinking feeling that this journey would not end well for me.

As we left behind the familiar, rolling green hills of my lands and our glistening, white stone castle disappeared from sight, I could feel all hope slipping away. The realization that I may never see my home again weighed heavily on me, threatening to break my spirit.

Upon asking my captor if he had a blanket I could wrap around myself to shield me from the biting wind– considering he'd forced me onto the horse in a dress fit to be inside a warm castle– and him telling me to toughen up, I'd decided it was far past time to make his life as difficult as he was making mine.

"Stop right this instance!" he growled out as my horse let out a neigh, alerting him as I wiggled out of the saddle for the fifth time and dropped onto my feet with ease, despite having my wrists bound together with a coarse rope. After the second time I'd slipped to my feet to walk, he'd thought that would stop me.

I was proud to say it had not, despite the ground between our feet growing uneven as we cut through a rocky mountain pass.

"I don't even know how you're managing to do that in a dress," he whispered under his breath.

I'm so glad I was able to hear the whispered words, reveling in his annoyance. I was practically preening as he glowered at me, and I couldn't help but send him a wink.

"Till death do us part, dear husband," I taunted with a sardonic smile. "It's a lovely day for a stroll."

It was, in fact, beginning to turn into a frigid day that had my nipples pebbling beneath my gown, and a shiver began to work its way through my body despite the rays of sun peaking through the lush trees surrounding us. I couldn't let the weather force me into servitude just like he wanted, though.

I was more grateful than ever for my flexibility and agility from training with the sword, as well as my countless hours on horses as I explored the mountains around our home. If he wanted to force me to become his wife and ride all the way back to the snowy fortress in the north, I was going to make it the most excruciatingly long trek of his life.

Maybe if I was lucky, I'd freeze to death before we made it to the prison I was to call my home. If not, I'd settle for making this trip a blight on his memory.

It was clear from watching him on his horse for a bit that the beast within him was making the horse nervous, and the king himself had an awful seat. His ass was going to hurt from this trip, if I could drag it out as long as possible.

Hopping off of his large white and gray speckled horse, that stood about seventeen hands in height, he let out a heavy sigh and rustled through the large saddle bag. "Miserable wench," he muttered.

Glancing over at the beautiful black mare I'd been meant to ride, not walk next to in companionship, I whispered, "What do you think he's going to pull out of his bag of tricks next, girl?"

Her ear swiveled toward me as I spoke, before going forward once more, entirely focused on the king and his movement.

Neither of us trusted him.

I glanced at the king, wondering how he could make such a large horse seem small as I continued to walk forward with the reins in my bound hands. As I passed him, his scent enveloped me once more, and I scowled at myself for finding anything about this man appealing. Maybe I needed to stay ahead of him so the scent of horse dung wafted back onto him.

"Come on, you're going to make us late," I groaned dramatically, as if he was the problem here. "I don't know about you, but I'd like to get there before sundown."

Truly, this was marvelous work. Maybe he'd just send me home and be done with it.

"You're infuriating!" he shouted, drawing my head back toward him as he pulled out a long coil of rope from the depths of his bag. With quick, determined steps, he closed the distance between us, his strong hand gripping my arm with a painful force. I winced at the pressure and tried to pull away, but his grip only tightened. "Get on the horse," he growled.

It was honestly infuriating how handsome he was when I looked at the side of his face that was entirely human looking. His full lips drew my eyes to them each time he spoke, and I marveled at how they could look so soft as such a harsh voice spilled from them. The sharp lines of his jaw and cheekbones, however, matched the severity of his personality, and they were exaggerated every time he scowled and glared at me.

I let out a hum as if I was considering his demand.

The universe had done us all a favor with the curse, ensuring we couldn't be forever fooled by the fake charisma he'd used at the meeting this morning and a beautiful human face to pair with it. Those silver scales and calculating, slitted eye reminded me exactly who I was dealing with, no matter what tricks he pulled.

I let out a sigh and attempted to look compliant, even though every fiber of my being rebelled against it. "I still don't know how to get back up on my own," I argued, holding up my bound hands with pleading eyes. "You'll have to help me again."

I absolutely could have done it on my own–but where was the fun in that?

He tightened his grip on my arm, causing me to wince again. Each time I'd slid off my mare, he'd practically tossed me back on, and it seemed he was tiring of my antics more now than each time before.

The pulsating pain intensified as the stitches from this morning's injury protested against the strain. I gritted my teeth and refused to give him any satisfaction as a familiar warmth ran down my arm from the reopened wound.

His nostrils flared, as if scenting the blood instantly.

"Make that stop," he now demanded, taking a small step away and dropping my arm like it had personally offended him. "It will attract the beasts of the forest to this narrow pass."

I made a show of glancing around me before throwing my hands in the air in annoyance, "Yeah, I'll just go ahead and restitch the wound you tore open with the rocks and air around us! Great idea!"

His lips curled into a snarl as he shouted, "How was I supposed to know you had a pre-existing wound there?"

My voice rose to match his. "It wouldn't have mattered at all if you wouldn't have manhandled me like I'm cattle to be herded!"

A scoff of indignation worked its way out of him as he tilted his head and gestured at the mare. "You do have to be herded! You are the one that insists on getting off of your horse, or is your memory really that horrid?"

I swallowed the words on the tip of my tongue, hating that he had a point there. Instead, I deflected, "Why are we even on horses? We should be in a carriage befitting a king and a princess, if not just flying back, considering you can shift into a dragon!"

Save a horse, ride a dragon, or whatever–right?

He stilled at that, and the sudden silence wrapped us like the blanket I'd been asking for. We stood a few feet apart, glaring at each other until he finally spoke.

"You will never ride a dragon," he quietly seethed, training his serpentine eye on me as it began to glow. "Only those with a bond befitting a rider are given the honor of that, and you, dear wife, are not worthy."

It felt like the biggest punch to the gut, being insulted like that, and I didn't have the mental capacity to figure out why it impacted me so deeply.

Did I even want to be on the back of the beasts?

Feeling completely disrespected, I couldn't help but retort, "You act like I'd enjoy it. Your kind disgusts me."

"We are wasting time," he stated through gritted teeth before grabbing my hands slicked with the trail of blood that worked itself down my arm during our shouting match. I dug my heels into the hard, dirt-packed road as he dragged me over to his horse.

It wasn't lost on me that he managed to sidestep the carriage question.

"You can either be tossed over the horse on your

stomach, or you can sit," he stated dryly. "You have three seconds to decide before I decide for you, and my choice will be the least comfortable, I promise you that."

My lips pursed as I countered, "I think I will just get on my own horse," and tried to tug my hands out of his grasp.

His grip tightened as he let out a deep chuckle that sent shivers up and down my spine. "Oh no, you've had plenty of time to choose that option."

As his free hand reached for me and my stomach clenched in anticipation of the saddle digging into it, I swatted it away and snapped, "Fine! I will get on your horse."

He let go of my hand and in the span of a blink of the eye, a claw-tipped finger sliced through the bindings around my wrist.

So he could transform pieces of his body at will? The thought was unnerving.

Knowing that refusal would get me nowhere, I put my boot into the stirrup and hauled myself up into the saddle with a sigh. Upon getting comfortable and staring down at him, he cleared his throat and motioned me back with his hand.

"Surely you didn't think I'd be a gentleman and let you have the saddle after you made it so clear you wished to be anywhere but on your own horse? Move to the back."

I clenched my jaw and my teeth ground together.

How the tables were turning and consequences were

meeting actions. It turned out my ass was going to be the one unable to sit tomorrow.

I pushed myself up and worked my body over the cantle of the saddle before settling in with my legs widened to accommodate the thicker part of the horse's body. I eyed the ground with longing. How I truly wished to be walking now.

Holding up the rope still in his hand, he instructed, "Wrap this around your back and hold it until I'm in my seat."

One of my eyebrows rose in question but I did as he said. The horse let out a grunt as he hoisted himself into the seat, and suddenly I felt awful that the poor animal was having to carry both of our weight because of my antics.

"You know, I really do promise that I'll stay in my seat if—" I began, but was quickly cut off as he reached back for the two ends of the rope and roughly tightened it, making me huff.

My mouth widened in shock as I realized what he was doing. I scrambled, pushing away from him, but it was too late. My chest and cheek squeezed flush against his back as my body was tugged forward with the force, my hips tilted back with the saddle still between us.

The asshole had literally tied me to him.

My back and ribs flared with pain when I attempted to wiggle back and put space between our bodies, finding no slack in the rope to work with.

"Bastard," I ground out, hating him more than ever,

but a part of my body softened against him, seeking the warmth he had to offer in this frigid air. It was far more than any human I'd been in contact with.

"Wench," he shot back before clicking his tongue for the horse to walk forward.

Instantly, I was jostled with the way my body moved along with the horse's hips in motion, and my arms fell to the drackya's hips to steady myself. He didn't respond, which shocked me. I thought he'd snarl and tell me it was a disease to be touched by a human.

I thought fondly of my dagger he'd taken, wishing I'd left it sheathed against my thigh to be used to cut the rope at this moment.

"We will need to make haste if we are to avoid the first snowfall and the last minute hunting parties the beasts will take to prepare their bellies for it," he announced before the reins snapped against the horses neck, sending us into a canter as we neared the end of the pass. Trees beckoned to us from the end.

Although we were heading into the winter season now, we shouldn't be due for any snow for another couple weeks. The ley lines ensured stable weather patterns, and the only place that should have snow was the more northern territory of Andrathya, where it laid upon the mountainous peaks year round. Our people had specifically settled in the southern part of our lands long ago, due to the warmer climate that was more habitable for humans to exist within during the harsh winters.

Just as the thought crossed my mind, the smallest

drops of snow began to fall around us, coating the tops of the trees and open path cutting through the forest. As it settled onto us and melted, wetting my dress, I gritted my teeth and pressed myself further into his body as a new chill settled into my bones.

How was this possible? Were the ley lines growing unstable?

The tiniest of chuckles shook his body, the vibrations flowing into my own, and my brow pinched into a scowl as a thought occurred to me. If he had magic and control of ice, did he call the snow down on purpose to ensure I stayed close to him for warmth to further humiliate me?

To show that I needed him in some small way? Perhaps it wasn't the ley lines at all, but his errant magic.

"Don't ever say I didn't offer you assistance in your time of need, wife," he tossed out, as if hearing my thoughts.

I swallowed down what little pride I had left as I tucked my hands under his coat and encircled my arms around his abdomen in an act of self-preservation.

I guess it turned out that I didn't want to freeze to death, after all.

"You are truly a chivalrous drackya king," I muttered with all the faux sweetness I could conjure.

He chuffed, "You can simply say dragon king."

My brow knitted between my eyes, confused at his claim. "But you are a drackya."

"I still turn into a dragon and have the scales of one

on my being for you to see, do I not?" he retorted, a kernel of anger beginning to unfurl in his voice.

Perhaps I didn't understand their hierarchy and way of life, like I thought.

Sensing his annoyance, though, I pushed further, unable to help myself. "Still, you aren't a full-blooded dragon."

A deep howl echoed through the forest around us. *Wolves.*

"And you're insufferable, since we're pointing out the obvious now. Your presence gives me a headache," he muttered. "Be quiet, there are predators that will track the scent of your blood easily enough *without* your yapping giving away our location."

Why was he voicing concern over this when he was clearly the biggest predator here?

Chapter Six

SIYANA

"If I let you off to ride your own horse, will you be a good little princess and stay in the saddle? We need to move faster, and my horse needs a break from our combined weight."

He spoke quietly, and it was criminal the way the timber of his voice rumbled at this level.

I may despise him and everything he represented as a drackya, or dragon—whatever he wanted to be called—and he was at least half of the reason I was being forced from my home, but I was still a woman with needs and desires. While sitting behind his very human body in silence for so long as I concentrated on attempting to keep warmth flowing throughout my body, it was easy to forget those things when he spoke out of nowhere.

My silence seemed to perturb him and he goaded me, "Don't tell me you've already lost your bite, wench? That was far too easy. I like my prey to put up a bit longer of a fight."

It was on the tip of my tongue to tell him I wouldn't tolerate his condescending tone, but as he pulled the reins to slow his horse to a walk, my tailbone pulsed with pain. I'd give just about anything to be in my own saddle if it meant getting to our destination quicker.

I glanced back to try to see my horse through the small blizzard that had descended the closer we got to the peak of the northern mountains. The few rays of moonlight fighting through the gale glistened off her, confirming she was still with us. I couldn't help but marvel over how well trained these horses were, considering how she'd continued to trail behind without me leading her through the weather.

"Yeah, sure, whatever," I grumbled against his back, accepting the offer, but simultaneously soaking up the final moments of being pressed against such warmth. Considering his affinity for ice, I'd, for some reason, assumed he didn't have access to the fire you'd think of a dragon breathing, but the longer I was pressed against him, the more I pictured a literal belly of fire within him, stoking his internal temperature.

I hated to admit it, but being pressed against him had probably been the only thing keeping my body from giving into shock with the snow melting into me. It felt like my feet and nose were going to break off from the frigid wind, and the only thing that had saved my hands was being able to keep them under his coat.

As the horse came to a stop and the wind tossed my hair around, obscuring what little I could see, he had the audacity to laugh. "I thought you'd at least be on your knees thanking me for the chance to be away from me now."

Once again, I couldn't find the energy to snap back at him, focused entirely on how it felt like all of my joints had frozen in place. As the rope was released from around us, he glanced over his shoulder at me, the sliver of his dragon eye shone brightly in the dark. "Off you go, wench. I know you know how to do that after your blatant display earlier."

With a heavy sigh I prepared to swing my leg around the back, bracing my hand on the back of the saddle, but the second I sat completely straight for the first time since being tied to him, shooting pain ran up my spine and I swore my hips creaked.

"Fuck," I hissed, completely caught off guard by the pain. I guess at some point on the journey, everything had gone numb, being stuck in that spot for so long. "I might actually need help dismounting." The words felt like glue in my mouth, a sense of repulsion coming over me for even having to ask him for help.

His head turned forward and he laughed. "I'm not falling for that, wench. Come on, get off."

My eyes rolled at that, because of course my own bratty plan continued to backfire on me. I attempted once more to move, managing to get my left leg over the horse's hind leg, but as soon as I rotated it over its tail, my back seized up. The ground came rushing up to meet me as I fell from the horse, having just enough time and foresight to bring my arm up to break my heads' fall.

My breath rushed out of me on impact, and my head swam from the recoil against my hands. The bite of cold from the ground began to seep through my dress in mere seconds.

"Oh, you were being serious," he surmised, still sitting atop his horse, not moving an inch to assist me.

His nonchalant tone and lack of help, even now, sparked my own fire once more.

"Yeah, I was!" I yelled back through the howling wind as I attempted to push myself up to sit. Blinding rage flashed through my mind as he continued to simply stare. "You refused to let me prepare for this trip and had no supplies to help me during it! I'm freezing to fucking death over here and you *still* refuse to help me! What a generous king you are. Your people are so lucky to have you."

I practically spat that last part at him, feeling venomous in mood.

Rolling onto my knees, I pushed from my hunching position, placing one foot on the ground at a time as I attempted to find my balance. My body shook, and I wasn't sure if it was from the fall or the hypothermia likely setting in.

"I never claimed to be your knight in shining armor," he seethed, and it was clear I'd struck a nerve. "You are here to fill a role, and that is all. I don't need you or my people to like me, I just need you to obey."

We just needed to obey.

That statement told me everything I needed to know about King Takkar. His people didn't like him. I wasn't shocked, considering all I'd seen and heard today, but as a royal member of my own land, I couldn't imagine being so hateful to my people. Why was it so hard for him to show compassion or empathy?

The gentle brush of my horses' nose against my back comforted me as tears began to well in my eyes. I was thankful he couldn't see them in the dark, because I'd be damned if he saw how empty I felt right now.

Tears streamed down my cheeks, warming the skin they passed over on their way to my jaw, before the wind chilled it again. "You're a horrible person," I murmured, letting the wind carry my words away before turning to my horse and limping over to her side.

As I lifted my foot into the stirrup, his soft response had me stilling, the brokenness in his words shocking me more than the weather ever could.

"Yeah, maybe I am, but no one stops to wonder what made me this way."

The snap of his reins sounded and his horse took off, making me jolt out of my momentary stupor. Climbing into the saddle to the best of my ability, my horse pranced beneath me, clearly wanting to rush after them. Once settled, she took off with no command from me, allowing me to do nothing but focus on staying in my seat.

I squinted through the snow, glad it seemed my horse knew exactly where to go as we settled into a gallop, because I would have absolutely steered us in the wrong direction in this white-out.

Time passed by and I felt myself lulled into a pondering state of mind to try to distract myself from the harsh conditions around us. I couldn't allow myself to consider the way my teeth chattered so hard I felt like I was going to chip them.

Was there any excuse for the person he was?

Did it matter what was in his past that could have made him this way?

I wasn't sure how long I ruminated on those two questions, but eventually, my mind grew empty. My horse slowed suddenly as we exited the forest, and I slumped forward onto her neck at the sudden change in pace and inability to control my pain-filled body well. The only sound I could hear, alerting me to a stream or river closer by.

Water.

Wrapping my arms around her neck to keep me in the saddle, I turned my cheek to rest against her, finding some comfort in her warmth. What I saw would have taken my breath away if there wasn't already a rattle in my chest as I felt my lungs struggling to expand and fill with air.

A glistening castle came into view just beyond a

stretch of snow-covered ground before us. It stood tall, its stone walls blending into the white mountainside. The soft glow of moonlight reflected off the white walls and silver-framed windows, creating an ethereal ambiance. Each tower I could see jutting high through the air had some kind of large platform attached to it. After a too-long moment, it clicked.

So dragons could land there,

The whole scene had a dreamlike quality to it, like it was a moment frozen in time, serene and magical, as if the castle and the mountains were the only things in the world.

That's when I began to realize I was in truly bad shape—my vision starting to go dark and fuzzy at the edges.

"Please hurry," I whispered to my horse, but from the way her own ribs were expanding and collapsing rapidly beneath my legs, I could surmise that she was completely spent from the rough ride and weather as well.

Regret flowed through me as I realized it was my fault we'd been stuck out in these conditions longer than necessary.

My eyes fluttered shut as my fingers ran through her mane slowly. "I'm sorry."

Everything began to dull around me. The wind's howling quieted, the biting cold turned to blissful numbness, and my breathing slowed. My body began to tilt and I didn't have it in me to grasp onto anything to keep me straight. Gravity took me into its grasp, and this time when I fell, there was no pain, just mounds of soft snow to cradle me. I swore I saw flickering lights in the distance, but perhaps it was just wishful thinking.

Just as I felt my consciousness slipping away, something large clasped around my body, lifting me from the ground. My head fell back as my limbs dangled, and it took every ounce of energy I could muster to force my eyes open.

I had to be unconscious and dreaming, because there was no way a large, glistening, silver dragon claw was wrapped around me and carrying me through the sky toward the castle.

Right?

It turned out I also didn't imagine the lights, as we passed over a small town that was eerily quiet. Where was the music? The laughs from people sharing a drink with a friend?

It seemed as lifeless as I felt.

Unable to keep them open any longer, my eyes fluttered shut and I went entirely limp, giving up on caring about what was happening. It seemed I wasn't meant for this world much longer as the thudding of my heart in my ears began to slow.

My only regret was that I'd not been able to make a difference for my people. There were no other heirs to marry off. If I died now, the treaty would be broken, and war would likely ensue.

What a shame that no amount of training could have prepared me for my life to go in this direction. This morning, I'd been full of hope in meeting another woman who shared my desire to train with a sword, surrounded by protective love from Tillie, and filled with pride in how far my skill had come in sparring with Brenson.

Now? None of it mattered.

"Theo—you had one job after signing the treaty!" a man yelled, jolting my mind to try and hold my consciousness to listen. "Keep your new queen alive. Is that seriously too hard a task for you?"

If I could have forced my lips to move, I'd have smirked. The feeling of solid ground pressed against my body once more.

"I forget how fragile humans are," a familiar, deep voice rumbled.

So, Theo was the name of my husband and captor.

There was a scuffle of feet in my direction, but they halted when a yelp sounded.

"I was just going to carry her to her chambers, Theo! She needs to be warmed—now."

My body felt like it was vibrating as a deep rumble spread through the ground and into me.

"I can carry my own wife," he snapped, "and she will be staying in my chambers."

Yeah, there was no way I wasn't actually dreaming already. It seemed my consciousness was playing tricks on me, lulling me into an alternate reality where someone actually cared about my well-being, and that someone was my new husband.

As if.

Chapter Seven

THEO

Rivulets of sweat cascaded down my body, drenching my shirt and trousers until they clung to me like a second skin. Even after shrugging out of my coat, the heat in my chambers was suffocating. The fire roared relentlessly, casting an orange glow over the opulent furnishings that adorned the room. In all my years of occupying this room, the fireplace had served as mere decor, until now.

I swore to myself things wouldn't change when I brought my wife home, and here I was, less than two hours into her arrival, making a liar out of myself.

An undine dragon king, catering to a mere human.

As I gazed upon her sleeping form sprawled on my bed, my initial instinct was to call her a wench under my breath. But instead, I found myself mesmerized by the gentle rise and fall of her chest beneath the furs that Lucius had dropped off at my door as I got her settled.

I never thought such a derogatory term could begin to feel like a term of endearment, but she had a way of turning everything upside down.

Lucky me.

I'd need to find a new word of insult, and soon.

The thought had a scowl gracing my face as I turned to look out the balcony I'd landed on with her in my clawed grip earlier, fearful that I'd been too stubborn in my actions with her thus far, bringing her to the brink of death.

Lifting a glass of scotch to my lips, I took a deep draw from the burning liquid while contemplating the ways this arrangement could turn out.

I wouldn't weep if she died, but it would be a considerable inconvenience, to say the least. The humans didn't have another heir to offer me, and despite her father being a shortsighted fool, I didn't think he'd take fondly to my request for a replacement.

Setting down my empty glass, I shed my shirt and stepped out onto the balcony, letting the frigid winter air embrace me. A fleeting thought crossed my mind to close the doors behind me, for her sake, but I quickly dismissed it, annoyed with myself with how easily I'd fallen into caring for her.

You can't let her die, Theo.

I reminded myself of this fact repeatedly, ever since watching her fall off of her horse in the distance as she'd broken through the forest. It was absolutely the only reason I'd gone out of my way to ensure her comfort now.

I closed the doors.

As my body began to cool down and my eyes roamed over the icy tundra of my kingdom. The waterfalls were beginning to slow to a trickle as the rivers began to freeze. The town lay covered in a fresh heap of snow from the night, only visible by the torches interspersed throughout to help warm the water dragons who could no longer swim through the land. Normally the rivers remained just warm enough to remain free flowing with the ley lines magic, but in the harsh winter season, there wasn't enough energy to bolster our affinity powers *and* keep up with our environment. The worst of it would be behind us in two months time, returning to the perfect balance for both the water and ice dragon's that occupied Andrathya.

What was I supposed to do with this human if she recovered? She wasn't suited to our lands, clearly.

She was not what I expected from a human princess, though. No, she was strong-willed and fearless in the face of adversity, despite lacking any elemental powers or ability to shift into a beast like myself. They were foolish traits that would end in her death, as evidenced by our current predicament, and yet, there was something about her that resonated with the dragon within me, causing conflicting emotions to stir.

I had thought to keep her tucked away from the drackya, knowing her presence would cause a stir amongst the unmated ones. Desperate times were upon us, and no longer was my command keeping them under my rule. Over the recent years, more were defying me and heading into the human's domain, plucking the ones they'd felt a draw to in hopes of finding their mate.

Out of the hundreds of abducted women I knew of, none had managed to form a mate bond. That wasn't to say their souls weren't destined, but this blasted curse remained strong in causing them to be repulsed by our appearance and fearful of the beasts we were.

Rolling my head from side to side, the bones in my neck cracked as I tried to release the stiff joints. I ached to plunge into my ice bath, but all of my needs were on hold until I knew if the princess would live or die.

Siyana.

Her name was beautiful, objectively matching her exterior. She would be a feast for the eyes of my people, but they weren't the only ones to be cautious of. The full-blooded undine dragons nestled into the caves of this very mountain, and if they scented an unmated human amongst their territory in nesting season while their eggs were being safeguarded, she would be dead.

The only option was to keep her confined to my castle, preferably this singular wing of it.

"I see we have a visitor, Your Highness."

My nostrils flared as I took a deep breath. It was like the chosen representative of the full bloods knew I was thinking of my predicament with them.

"Yes, Alstrid. My human wife that I told you would be joining me."

As my chosen liaison for them when I was absent, he was privy to more knowledge than any other of his kind, but he was beginning to push my boundaries as of late–like a nagging grandfather.

"She is still unmated. When will you rectify that? The mated pairs will be restless if she comes near, as we spoke about yesterday."

"Alstrid," I sighed mentally, *"we are so far from wanting to touch each other willingly, unless our lives are on the line."*

That was perhaps a white lie on my part. Interest stirred within my human form upon seeing her in the council room when she stood and defied me in front of all the men. Again, it happened every time her feet plunked onto the ground as she slid off her horse, thinking she was accomplishing an act of defiance.

"You must win her over, then," he muttered with incredulity.

If I was being honest with myself, there was something that tugged at my being on a deeper level when I regarded her. When the tears had streamed down her face as she called me a horrible person, the need to defend myself and make her understand why I was this way had surged to the surface. Never before had I felt the need to do that, not since I'd killed off the side of me that had sought approval from others.

"Oh, must I?" I rebutted, *"You forget your place,*

Alstrid. I allow our open communication as a means to serve me, not the other way around."

My lips pinched as Sia's words from earlier replayed in my head. *"What a generous king you are. Your people are so lucky to have you."*

Rage boiled within my chest, blazing as strongly as the fire within my chambers. Little did she know, they *were* lucky to have me, considering the alternative was the king before me.

"Forgive me, your highness. I merely speak as a concerned subject. I will do my best to spread word of her arrival to the full-blood undines."

Despite his polite words, I sensed his deep aggravation before the line between us severed.

A huff fell from my lips. I was used to it. Actually, I was used to outright hatred from damn near birth, considering I'd inherited a cursed crown, and therefore all the blame from the undine for what my father had brought upon us.

I could have managed the hatred of my genetic association to my father, but to assume the weight of their blame when he'd taken his own life, in an attempt to escape the consequences of being the reason we'd all been cursed...My lip peeled back as a snarl rumbled through my chest, coming from the core of my dragon.

He was weak and pathetic. We were better off with his body burned to a crisp. He was as useless with a crown on his head as he was as ash floating through the world.

77

What a fucking inheritance.

I shook my head as I turned back to the doors and crossed into the room that had to be the same temperature as Salarya's kingdom. How the ember dragons flourished within the volcanic climate was beyond my comprehension, but I supposed they'd say the same of our frost-bitten world.

Instantly, my eyes were drawn to her as I neared the edge of the bed. Her dark tresses were strewn about the soft sheets haphazardly now, as if she'd been tossing and turning since I'd left.

A rumble of appreciation for the thought ran through me. Purely because it meant she was regaining strength if she was able to do so, not because I liked the thought of her wanting me close.

A heavy knock echoed through the room before Lucius cracked the large door open. "I'm turning in for the night, but I wanted to check in on our new queen. How is she?"

My dragon warred within my chest to take control as an overwhelming desire to protect her surged forth. His inquiry into her well-being felt like a slight to my ability to nurture her back to health.

I summed his large frame up, feeling like my chest puffed in response to his words. Would she find his dark hair more appealing, as it was similar to her own? Perhaps the shadow of his beard would draw her in, compared to my clean shaven jaw.

My chest began to rise rapidly as my breathing turned shallow.

I needed to calm down.

Logically, I knew I hadn't displayed the best ability to keep her safe today, so his inquiry made sense, but the animalistic need to fight off other candidates that could be vying to care for her needs...It was shocking.

It's because of your dragon's desires, not your own.

"Get out," I managed to say between clenched teeth. "Don't come back."

I needed to eat and sleep to restore my control over the beast. Never before had I been so at war with him, feeling like we were separate entities for the very first time.

Lucius' silver eyes widened in understanding before he lowered them to the ground in subservience. The pale blue scales on his forehead shimmered from the fire in the room as he retreated and closed the door behind him.

She's mine to take care of.

Apparently, I would need to keep all unmated drackya from being remotely near her, until I managed to regain my control. It was just a muscle I needed to train, considering the only women in our kingdom were older, mated pairs from before the curse set in. They only had eyes for their drackya, still.

I'd never known the touch of a woman, or felt the curve of their body beneath my own. It would be an adjustment to have Siyana in my personal chambers, as if she was already my mate. The beast within thought that was the case, having her scent in our domain.

I took a deep breath, noting the citrus, woody, yet floral aroma that had consumed the room despite the crackling embers of the fire also being present. My eyes closed as my dragon rumbled in contentment, knowing we were alone with her once more.

"This is going to be a fucking problem," I breathed out, still feeling the slight strain from the urge to go to her and mark her.

As my nervous system settled, I reopened my eyes once more and found her eyes–the very ones that reminded me of the glaciers my magic could create–trained on me.

Quickly, I took note of her tanned skin on display when the furs slipped from her shoulders as she pushed to sit and the swells of her breast peaked out. Her head tilted to the side as she took me in.

"Theo, is it?"

She was strong enough to talk—that was an excellent sign.

"You heard my name before passing out, I presume."

Her hair flew around her as she glanced around, taking in her surroundings. I found I much preferred it down around her like this, after I'd pulled the pins from it. As her gaze turned back to me and roamed my bare chest, a slender eyebrow raised. "Where are my clothes?"

There was a warning in her tone, and I understood the implication.

Folding my arms across my chest, I huffed. "I would never touch you."

Unbridled fury sparked within her eyes as she glowered and spat, "I'm glad to know you find me as equally disgusting as I do you. Now that that's settled, where are my clothes?"

The last part was a question, yet the strength in them made the demand clear.

I was too busy fixating on her calling me disgusting, with her misunderstanding of my words. I guess I should have added, without your consent, to my words, yet here we were.

Shoving down the rejection, I found my composure once more. It was of no matter, the marriage was for political gain and the betterment of my kingdom, not for me to lose myself in her flesh.

"They made great kindling," I offered with a nod to the fireplace they had been tossed into, smiling as her cheeks reddened.

Stripping her of the wet clothes was the only way to ensure I did everything I could to make her warm and give her the best odds of recovery. I had been clinical while removing them from her, only glancing and touching where needed.

Despite being a beast, I still had been taught manners from my mother before she died, and I wouldn't dishonor her memory by taking advantage of the situation.

It was cute, though, the way she woke up and instantly chose violence.

The thought hit me hard and I scowled. She was not cute, and she was clearly feeling better and needed to leave my bed.

"Did you remove them?"

Her ire was clear in the way she carefully articulated each word.

Heading toward my closet and plucking a long, white tunic from my wardrobe, I grunted in response. I tossed the material at her when I returned, before leaning against the stone wall near the door.

She quickly snatched the tunic before tugging it under the furs and going beneath them. Odd bits of her limbs stuck out as she struggled to put the tunic on under the weight of the furs.

Her attempting modesty was entertaining, considering drackya were open with such things in the shared bathing chambers. I allowed myself the faintest of laughs at her ridiculousness before she reappeared.

She quickly smoothed down the tangled hair that obscured her vision.

She let out a huff, likely to scold me for stripping her, but my hand went to the handle of the door and tugged it open. "As you said, we find each other equally disgusting. I didn't enjoy it. Now, get out. Your room is at the other end of the hall."

Her full lips separated as she stared at me in shock. It was only momentary, though, as she found her claws once more and attempted to surge to her feet as she threw the furs from her body.

She didn't make it far, stumbling like a newborn deer as soon as she tried to put weight on them. Still, despite her strength being far from recovered, she tried to keep going, throwing her hands out in an attempt to regain her balance.

It was honestly pathetic, and as I saw her knees start to give out, I crossed the short distance between us, catching her as she began to fall. The last thing I needed was her to further injure herself. It seemed she wasn't out of the woods yet.

She settled against my chest as her limp body dangled in my hold, and once more, a rumble came from my core as my dragon stirred.

Our eyes met, both wide but for different reasons.

Mine from embarrassment at her hearing that reaction, and hers from fear, as I'd seen the same reaction when I'd encased her arm in ice with my magic.

It was better this way. Her fear was something I could use to make her compliant to my rules.

"Let me down," she roared, her body wiggling in a weak attempt to break free.

I sighed in annoyance as I walked back to the side of the bed and held her out over it. "As you wish."

Dropping her unceremoniously from my shoulder height, I smiled in amusement as she let out a shriek.

"You bastard!"

Padding over to the other side of the large bed, I

settled in, giving her my back. I felt the heat of her gaze as I closed my eyes and muttered, "Go to bed, wench."

We'd see if she survived the night, and tomorrow we'd figure out how to keep her alive with the new dangers awaiting outside these walls.

For the first time that I could remember, I drifted off to sleep with ease as my dragon curled up in peace, feeling her near.

Chapter Eight

SIYANA

I'D FALLEN asleep with a scowl on my face and awoken to a similar one on my husband's face as I found him staring at me, his cheek still on his pillow with a large, muscular arm tucked beneath it.

My scowl had been due to how damn attractive his physique was and the way my body betrayed me in coming alive at the thought of him undressing me. Despite the roaring fireplace in the chambers, a chill had still crept in through the night, and I'd chided myself many times as the thought to scoot closer to him had crossed my mind.

The reason for his scowl? I hadn't a clue. Probably my ability to breathe, irritating him, if I had to guess.

"What could you possibly be pissed at me about already?" I managed to ask as the sleepy haze cleared from my brain. "Was I cursing your name in my sleep or something?"

Not out of the realm of possibilities.

I lacked my usual bite as the fatigue and exhaustion from our journey yesterday still lingered. It didn't help that I kept waking throughout the night, swearing that I heard screams echoing in the distance. It was highly unnerving, but each time I'd waited to hear it while alert, the screams never came.

As the morning light had risen during my last waking, I'd chalked it up to delirium. My body was exhausted and hallucinations were following me from my dreams to the waking world.

It was the same reason I still remained curled up on my own side, facing him, too tired to move without sustenance to combat my fatigue.

I quickly quieted the tiny voice popping up in my mind trying to tell me that wasn't the only reason why, and that the morning light streaming in from the glass balcony door reflecting off of his silver scales wasn't fascinatingly beautiful.

He didn't answer and I began to grow uncomfortable under the heavy weight of his silence. As I tucked the hair tickling my cheek behind my ear, I cleared my throat, trying to knock him out of whatever stupor he'd fallen into.

"Who did it, Siyana?"

His pointed question and use of my actual name caught me off guard as my brain scrambled to understand. My lips pursed as the wheels turned and I came up empty. "Who did what?"

The slitted reptilian eye of his narrowed as he inhaled sharply before letting it out. The deep timber of his voice rumbled as he clarified, "Who gave you the injury on your arm? It was clearly fresh, with how easily it opened under my grip."

His question was so far out of the realm of possibilities rolling around in my head that I simply laid there in silent shock as his arm bunched up, lifting to push his free hand through the mess of his bed-head hair falling into his eyes. His bicep flexed and the light did nothing to help hide the veins running through his forearm that bulged with his movement.

"Did you fall back asleep with your eyes open, wench?" he prodded as his hand came to lay flat against the bed once more. "Or are you taking a sudden vow of silence?"

It occurred to me at that moment, that we were just lounging in a bed together with very little clothes on, as if he wasn't a hulking brute who had conned my father into letting him steal me from my home and everything I held dear.

Apparently, I was pushing his patience with my non-answer, and he let out a sigh before pushing to sit up and look toward the balcony. With the movement, his abdomen scrunched, showing off each individually cut groove of muscle.

"Fine, don't tell me, it doesn't matter," he muttered in annoyance before moving on, "today we will begin training you to learn how to defend yourself properly.

Your attempt to hurt me yesterday was pathetic, and there are too many threats to your life lying in wait here."

My eyes narrowed and I murmured, "Bet you wouldn't be saying that if you didn't have the unfair advantage of magic, dragon boy."

His head turned ever so slowly until he looked at me and blinked twice. His voice was a low rumble as he asked, "Did you just call me 'boy?'"

Of course that's what his fragile ego fixated on. He may be part dragon, but he was full-blooded egotistical like any human man.

"I've yet to see any behavior that lends me any reason to think you a man," I answered with ease before closing my eyes and snuggling into the pillow. "Besides, I'm not well enough to do any training. I need to eat and sleep more to recover my strength."

A shriek clawed its way out of my throat as the warm furs were yanked off of me. A moment later, I found my body turned to lay on my back as a heavy weight settled itself above me. I knew it was him from the heat radiating into me despite our skin not even touching. I contemplated not opening my eyes to avoid him, but that felt even more weird than just looking at him up close.

Cracking my lids open, I found his face mere inches away. Up close, I could see a multitude of different colors of blue in his dragon eye, mesmerizing me as my inspection trailed to the scar running through the hard scale around it, before he blinked and sent me back to reality.

His voice rumbled, "This is *my* castle, you are *my*

wife, and that means you live by *my* rules. Tell me you understand, wench."

I swallowed hard and took a deep breath, letting my chest expand until it brushed against his briefly. His cold demeanor withered with the small contact, but as I spoke, his icy walls slid firmly back into place. "You may be my husband, but you will never own my mind. It is mine alone, and no amount of years here beneath your overbearing and belittling rules as king will change that."

My voice was soft and even, showing how little I feared him. If he wanted me dead, he wouldn't have shifted and come back for me as I found myself buried amongst the drifts of snow last night. He'd told me I'd never be worthy of riding a dragon, but him carrying me in his clawed foot felt awfully close.

What was he going to do if I continued to speak back to him? Eat me? Unlikely.

Despite the rumors of his cruelty and seeing a small ounce of it for myself, I was beginning to wonder if his bark was bigger than his bite.

My cheeks heated with warmth as he leaned in until his lips brushed against the shell of my ear, sending a shiver through my spine. "You seem too comfortable around me now, dear wife, seeing as your mental barrier just came down. Did you mean eating you in this form, or in my dragon form? Unclear."

He could read my mind?

Sheer panic flooded my nervous system as my eyes widened with the implication. I didn't think, reacting instinctively as I pushed against his chest in an attempt to get him off of me and away, as if space could prevent him from hearing me.

He was an immovable mountain, chuckling as he pulled back and traced his eyes over my face and down to where his thin tunic covered my chest.

"Looking a little cold this morning, wench, or is that your version of saying good morning?"

My mouth dropped open in horror as I glanced down and saw my pebbled nipples poking up into the material. "Get off of me!" I screamed, bringing my knees up and against his chest to try to give me better leverage for forcing him away.

Lacking my full strength still, I failed, and in a fit of rage went with the go-to. A crack echoed through the chambers as the palm of my hand stung with the contact to his too-perfectly-chiseled cheekbone.

His tongue ran along his top lip before he smacked them together, and his dragon eye flared with magic like it had before he'd turned my arm to an icicle. "Careful, wench, the fight is intriguing my dragon, and I don't think you want to fight him."

A split second later his body was gone and the chill of the room quickly settled into me in its stead. I quickly scrambled to pull the closest fur pelt to cover me and sat up, clutching it to my chest.

He strode over to the balcony, stepping out of the pants he'd slept in as he pushed the doors open, giving me a clear view of his firmly muscled ass. I did my best to picture a wall of ice around my mind, preventing him from seeing inside. The last thing I needed was him hearing that I didn't actually find him entirely disgusting. His back flexed as he twisted to glance over his shoulder at me, and I snapped my eyes up from his ass to meet his own.

"Can you make your way down the hall alone to your chambers to bathe and dress?"

I nodded instantly, unsure if I actually could, but wanting the chance to do something independently.

He stepped out onto the balcony and called out, "Stay there and I'll come get you to bring you down to eat breakfast shortly. Keep that mental wall up."

I only had a split second to revel in my victory of constructing a mental barrier before fascination overwhelmed me. I watched with rapt attention as his muscles elongated and more silver scales began to appear and cover every stretch of his exposed skin. Webbed wings began to grow, and thick legs bunched to launch into the sky as the full shift overcame him.

My mouth fell open as I quickly scrambled to my feet, using the bed to help push myself up. Gingerly, I walked over to the open doors and looked out into the beautiful blue sky dusted with a gentle snowfall.

His dragon soared through the air, cutting sharply as he banked to his right, flying up in the mountain range. As he turned and the sun hit his body, he was one giant ball of reflection, and it hit me how amazing of a defensive technique that would be, especially on a cloudy day.

My feet were glued to the spot despite the frigid temperature of the floor and the brisk air floating around me, pebbling every inch of my skin. I watched him soaring through the sky in a mixture of fascination and fear–that was the same person I'd just laid across from. It was one thing to know it, but an entirely different case to see it so clearly for the first time.

As he disappeared from sight behind the castle, I shook my head and turned back to his chambers. I gave the fireplace another glance, wishing I'd still had the clothes he'd burned, seeing as they were the only remaining tie to my home. Dwelling on it served me no good, though, and I walked slowly to the door and yanked it open, prepared to find my own chambers. Despite this being his castle, the concept of having my own chambers was appealing. A place that was mine to hide away in and not have to keep my mask in place.

I was a strong, fierce woman, and I wouldn't cower, but I also needed a safe place to mourn the life and people that had been ripped away from me with no time to process it. Both could be true at once.

Crossing the frigidly cold stone floor to the long black rug that stretched the expanse of the hall before me, I breathed a small sigh of relief at the minor buffer against my skin. I took my time scanning the large murals lining the hall and took in each name placard beneath them. Each previous ruling king and queen filled the space, and I noted the same white hair passed down from king to king, but as I reached the most recent, the image that had to be his parents, I noted that his navy eyes and sharp features had been handed down by his mother.

I found myself glued to the spot as I took in his parents, the king seated on a throne of ice and his mother standing behind him with a hand atop his shoulder. If Theo was the king, it meant his father had passed, but was his mother gone as well?

Despite it being a painting, there was a gentle and easy aura that radiated from his mother's soft smile and the wrinkled edges of her eyes that spoke of time and wisdom. I was drawn to her and marveled at the cold juxtaposition of the king's obsidian eyes that dared the viewer to oppose him. His closely cut hair gave him a much sharper appearance than Theo's, but I noted the waves from his mother's blonde hair matched his own. He was a seamless blend of them both.

"She was beautiful, wasn't she?" a voice asked, causing me to jump at the intrusion.

I covered my chest with my arms instinctively and took a step back as a young man came into view from the corridor just past the murals. His upbeat tone jogged a memory, and as I took in his large, broad build, it hit me.

"You're the other person who was there last night," I mused, recalling his words and smiling at it. "You chastised Theo for having one job in taking care of me. And failing spectacularly at it."

His dark hair fell forward over his shoulders as he took a deep bow at the waist before standing rigidly straight once more. His black tunic held the crest of a silver dragon on the breast, the same one that hung on the banners in the hall around us. "Lucius, Your Highness. Pleased to formally meet you."

His dimples broke through the shadow of a beard coming in, and his smile was disarming, matching his open energy as he regarded me with true respect. A part of me felt a trickle of guilt for branding all dragons as my enemies, when here one was, being as nice and polite as could be to me.

"Do you need assistance to your chambers?" he asked, tilting his head as he took me in.

I was surprised at the ease I felt around him already. It was easy to see his assessment of me was clinical, eyes never lingering for long in any one spot. "I was surprised to not see either of you in the dining hall this morning, as Theo normally rises before the sun. I wanted to make sure you hadn't taken a turn for the worse overnight."

Despite the comfort I felt, I shifted awkwardly on my feet as the cold still wrapped around my bare legs. "I appreciate your concern, Lucius, and it's lovely to meet you as well. My name is Siyana, but you may call me Sia."

He seemed to sense my discomfort as his mouth widened at the same time his silver eyes did. It was a testament to either my ability to quickly adapt, or my denseness, that I noted the pale blue scales running along his forehead last.

"I'm sorry, I didn't mean to catch you in such a state," he apologized as his eyes lowered to the ground.

"Do you want me to wait for you to get ready and show you to the dining hall?"

It was on the tip of my tongue to tell him that Theo said he would be back to do exactly that, but the rebellious part of my brain shoved that fact down. I didn't need to cower away and wait like the ever-dutiful wife.

"Yes, that would be amazing. Give me time to acquaint myself with the room and hopefully take a bath to freshen up after the journey yesterday."

With a nod and his eyes still on the ground, he retreated down the hall he'd appeared from.

A knot in my chest loosened at the thought of maybe having a kind soul around. Seeing as he was close enough with Theo to berate him without being killed or told to get on his knees and apologize, I gathered he likely wouldn't be an ally in my quest for independence while here. However, I'd happily settle for knowing there was at least one person I could speak to without wanting to gouge my eyes out with frustration, even if he was a dragon.

As I walked through the space he'd just occupied, I took in an appreciating breath and his scent lingered in the air. It was very much like the salty ocean air that bordered the northern portion of Andrathya, and in combination with his blue scales, I found myself wondering if he was aligned with the water affinity of the undine, whereas Theo was clearly ice. Either way, it was a lovely smell, and I wondered if they had bottles of perfume around that matched it.

Chapter Nine

SIYANA

As the warm, buttery goodness of the danish I'd chosen flooded my senses, the large double doors to the dining hall burst open, startling me. I'd had four already and was very much looking forward to a few more.

Theo stormed in, interrupting the question Lucius had been asking me about our food supply dwindling in recent years. I paused in my efforts to stuff myself painfully full of food.

"Morning, Theo!" Lucius called out, "I thought we—"

"I told you to wait for me!" Theo yelled, his voice booming through the empty room and cutting Lucius off. Thankfully, they didn't seem to have any staff here, or else they would probably be wishing to be in any other area of the castle right about now, just as I was.

Shrugging in response as he drew close to me, I lifted the danish back to my mouth and took a bite. In my plan,

I knew this would rile him up, but I never imagined it would pull this level of animosity from him.

His chest heaved with the ragged, deep breaths that filled the air around me as he closed in on my location. As I swallowed, his hand came flying out to smack the food from my grasp, knocking it to the ground.

"Hey, I worked hard on those," Lucius rumbled dejectedly from the other side of the oak table.

"Get out," Theo seethed in response to Lucius, unable to look back at the other drackya. No, his venomous gaze was meant for me alone to bear the brunt of his anger.

"Real mature," I muttered, glancing down at my fallen food. "Are you going to pick that up? Because I'm absolutely not, nor is Lucius."

Lucius' chair scraped against the floor as he let out a sigh and left the table, muttering, "Please leave me out of this," before the gentle groan of the doors closing sounded behind him.

A part of me felt really awful now for what I did. He hadn't known that Theo had told me to stay and wait for him, and clearly it was going to cause a big problem. It seemed I didn't know the depths of my husband's anger issues like I thought I did. This should have been a harm-less decision that mildly irked him and made him call me a wench.

As my eyes lifted all the way up to the towering drackya standing at my side, the war I saw in his gaze was unnerving. Not because he was angry—that I was accustomed to already. Even his annoyance was dismissible. It was the way he seemed to be looking over every inch of me that he could see with me seated, as if he was concerned for my well-being, that caused me pause.

"Theo, I—"

He cut me off, yanking me to my feet, causing my chair to clatter to the ground behind me. I didn't have time to breathe before his hands were on me, running the length of my arms as if the thin material of the dress sleeves covering me hid a plethora of new wounds from him.

"Theo—"

"Shut up," he snapped.

That was the perfect time to call me a wench, yet he abstained. This didn't bode well. He was truly furious.

His words were as harsh as his hands that traveled down to my waist and spun me around, continuing his inspection.

I whirled around, batting his hands off of me. "Stop it! I'm fine!"

His voice was thunderous as he roared, "Your well-being is my job as your husband, but how am I supposed to uphold that duty when you defy my direct orders, ones that are given to you to keep you safe in a land you don't understand?"

The irony wasn't lost on me, and a peel of laughter came from me as I threw my hands in the air. "That's rich, coming from the very person who didn't take into account my needs while traveling all day and night yesterday through the first winter storm of the season, that you supposedly knew was coming," I paused to take in a deep breath before continuing. "No carriage, no blanket, no cloak, not even any food or water! I almost died because of you! Now all of a sudden, when I'm in the safety of the castle's walls, with a dress lined with fur to keep me warm and food in my belly, suddenly I'm in danger enough to elicit this response?"

His lips thinned as he nodded and took a breath, seeming to deflate with my accusations.

"My actions are regrettable and showed me why none of your missing citizens ever returned. I might have made an error in judgment for your ability to survive in the wilderness alone. I will not do that again."

His words were like the rush of cold water that had flown from the bath in my chambers, chilling me instantly.

"What do you mean why none of our missing citizens ever *returned*?"

It was a hard turn in conversation, making the previous focus seem completely trivial now.

He ran a hand along his jaw, rubbing as he answered, "During our discussions for a treaty, your father mentioned none of the women my dragons stole came back. What he, and all of you don't know, is that after they failed to complete a mating bond, if the women survived that, I ensured they were given their freedom to return."

I stared at him, mouth agape at the stream of information hitting me all at once. Blinking rapidly, I lifted one hand for him to pause. "You're telling me that dragons were stealing our citizens in hopes to mate, and if they failed to do so, some of them didn't make it out alive?"

The screams I'd heard last night echoed through my mind, haunting me. Could that have been Leah? Even if it wasn't someone I knew, if they were a human, they were my citizens to protect—to stand up for.

He nodded, emotionless now, compared to just minutes before. "Yes. Sometimes dragons cannot handle the rejection from their soulmate. It blinds them with rage, because the bond can only be attempted once. If their mate denies them, they are now forced to live the rest of their days unmated. If it isn't their true mate that denies them, the humans are simply left alone in our lands by the dragon that brought them here in hopes of mating. That is when I'm alerted and ensure they get to the border of our lands without further issue."

Despair rolled through me as I thought of those poor women, slaughtered by the dragons that were supposed to be the ones who held them most dear, if the stories of fated mates were true. All because of this curse causing humans to be scared and repulsed. They'd stood before those beasts, torn away from their families and partners, and of no fault of their own saw the jaws of death coming for them. They'd never stood a chance.

Leah.

How could he allow them to do this, knowing many

had been killed, and that surely even more would be if the dragons were permitted to continue coming to pluck them from our lands?

I took a steadying breath as tears began to prick at my eyes, fighting the rage simmering within my belly enough to speak. "And *if* they survived that, you just sent them on their way to make that trek back to us? With no horse, no supplies, no anything? I just want to make sure I'm understanding your level of cruelty and carelessness at the expense of these women's lives."

He had the decency to look chagrined for a second before his head shook, clearing that from his face as he glowered. "How did you turn this into an interrogation of me ensuring other women's safety, when you clearly don't care about your own?"

I sucked my bottom lip between my teeth and bit down as I tried to find the words. "I'm only here in hopes that this marriage will allow me to help my people, Theo. Yet here I am, finding out I can't help any of the women who were unjustly ripped from their lives..." My voice cracked, "They're *all* gone. Hundreds of women. A woman who worked in my castle that I knew was taken just yesterday! How do I even know if she's made it to today?"

"I want you to focus on the fact that you can still help those that remain in your lands," he murmured softly, like he knew I was seconds away from exploding. "Think of the thousands you'll save if you help me break this curse. I clearly can't do it alone. The drackya are becoming harder to keep in line with each passing month–they are unsettled and distressed at the prospect of being alone while their mate is elsewhere, unclaimed." His chest expanded as he took a deep breath and looked at the floor before blowing it out. "It doesn't help that they hate me and the rumblings of a mutiny are beginning to stir. If we want to fix this, we have to act soon."

I had so many questions about the information he'd revealed to me, but I couldn't settle my racing pulse and thoughts enough to sort through it.

"I want to know about Leah," I demanded, "and I want to put an end to this. I want to know what you are doing to seek justice for the lives of my people that have been lost."

He stared at me, open-mouthed, as if it was preposterous to seek reparations. "What is it that you would have me do? They're beasts, Siyana. Don't let our human forms fool you."

A deranged laugh peeled out of me. "You think I'm not keenly aware of that? That we are just playthings for your people to pluck from our lives and discard or kill, if they don't achieve their desired results? This is not okay!"

His lips thinned and my nostrils flared in this standoff.

"They deserve to die," I whispered, uncaring of how callous I sounded. "A life for a life."

As his head reared back, I raised an eyebrow. "Tell me how else justice can be achieved, oh great *king*." I all but spat the title, mocking and making clear that he was not deserving of the honorific in the slightest.

His tone was much more even than my own as he responded, "I would have you wait to make such demands until we've broken this curse. To let us have a chance to repair what has been damaged between our people, without spilling more blood. It is not the answer."

There was a disgust deep within his eyes, and for some reason it hit me square in the chest. I was demanding people be killed. In such little time here, I'd suggested death as an adequate solution. Was there something in the air here that lent to such barbarous thoughts?

I hated to admit that the beastly king was more rational than me in this moment. That wasn't me. Nor could I allow it to become who I was. I wasn't a judge, jury, and executioner. I simply wanted to be the voice for my people, to ensure I found a path to a peaceful existence between our kinds.

"I can admit my hasty suggestion may have been made from the deep well of pain within me–pain that comes from the loss of my people. I'm aware that violence, the practice of an eye-for-an-eye, isn't the answer. I want you to promise that we will return to this conversation and seek justice for my people once the curse has been broken. I will stand for nothing less."

His head tilted as he regarded me, his dragon eye's pupil dilating with my words. "You have my word."

Despite not knowing if his word meant anything at all, I did know I wasn't in the position to be making demands, considering I'd been brought here as a pawn. I needed to play a long game of chess, to ensure I could truly help my people in the end.

I took a deep breath and forced myself to switch to the other issue that we should be able to settle with ease in comparison. "Lucius is clearly your friend or you would have harmed him, or at least reamed him out instead of me just now. All he did was show me the path to get food. You need to calm down. I already told you I wouldn't be controlled by you, and that includes being sequestered in a room."

"Calm down?" he parroted, mocking me as his voice dipped and a single brow rose. "You understand so little of my world, just as I do of yours, and you just placed a life outside of your own at risk as well. Climb down from your pedestal of superiority."

He crowded me, making me take several steps back until my back hit the stone wall harshly. His forearms came to rest on either side of my head, caging me in with his larger frame as he stared intently into my eyes.

"I went to your room and couldn't find you anywhere," he bit out. "A fragile human, lost and wandering around a land that's equipped and ready to kill her at every corner, and to make matters worse, another dragon's scent was mixed in with your own."

I opened my mouth, ready to argue once again that it was just Lucius, but his large hand clamped over my lips, stopping me. I let my unbridled fury shine in my eyes as I glared up at him and resisted the urge to knee him in the balls—for now.

"You had a choice," he murmured, lowering his head to run his nose along my neck. I resisted the urge to move, feeling like prey caught in the teeth of a predator. One wrong move and they'd snap. His breath tickled my skin as he inhaled deeply and let it out. "And you didn't choose me."

The weight of his choice of particular words hit me.

Had I...hurt his feelings? The very drackya who seemed to despise my existence other than the fact that I lived to serve a purpose for him.

"You're supposed to choose *me*."

I floundered, my mouth opening and closing repeatedly as he straightened back to his full height and dropped his hand to his side. There was a modicum of vulnerability in that statement, but when I didn't respond quickly enough, he whirled around, leaving me breathless with the rapid change of topic throughout this conversation.

"My dragon sees you as our wife, in every sense of the word," he explained with a gruff tone, keeping his back to me. "Even if I know it is an empty marriage to unite our people once more, in an effort to cease rebellions from stirring on both of our sides, he doesn't. He will kill Lucius if he continues to scent him on you."

A small gasp escaped me as I thought of his large dragon tearing into Lucius. While I knew the latter had his own dragon form, since I hadn't seen it yet, my mind still couldn't picture him as anything other than a frail human against Theo's beast.

Theo continued on, like he hadn't just spoken of such horrific brutality against a loved one, "My focus is firmly on finding a way to break the curse, but to do that I need you to listen to me, so I don't have to worry about you staying alive while you're here. I've already had to dismiss the majority of my castle staff to aid in that."

I was shocked to my core at everything he said since he'd stormed into this room. There was no space in my head to even be angry at his barbaric display of trying to claim me.

He walked toward the door, the soles of his boots echoing throughout the now-empty room. "Finish eating and I will be back in ten minutes to collect you and give you a tour of the castle, so that Lucius has no need to escort you anywhere, even if you don't wish for me to be with you."

As he left the room and let the doors thud closed behind him with a bang, I found myself slumping against the wall and sliding down until my ass hit the floor. Throwing my arms around my legs, I let my head fall onto my knees as I took deep, steadying breaths.

All of our missing women were dead.

The beast within Theo was incredibly real, and apparently thirsty for blood when it came to me.

We still had no clue how to break the curse.

Is there a way to prevent any of it?

"**Yes,**" Theo spoke into my mind, startling me so much that my head reared back and clipped the stone wall, making my vision swim with spots and a dull ache to throb in my ears. I groaned as his thoughts bombarded me. "**But that requires us to complete the mating bond, so that my dragon no longer feels threatened by other unmated dragons being near you. Now put your shield back in place. If I can break through so easily, so can others.**"

I slammed the imaginary ice wall back into place and let my head fall back to my knees as I rubbed the back of my skull.

What had I gotten myself into?

Chapter Ten

THEO

As the doors closed behind me, my eyes locked onto Lucius leaning against the wall nearby, clearly waiting to ream me out. Fury was etched into his pinched brow, and a narrowed gaze that promised wrath was trained on me.

"You're lucky I consider you a brother, Theo," he warned, "because my dragon is thirsting for justice with the disrespect you have shown me since she got here."

Planting my feet wide and crossing my arms against my chest, I mulled over his words. In a fight, I'd kill him with ease, so I felt no threat in that regard, but the memory of his scent all through Siyana's chambers had my muscles bunching and flexing as I attempted to control the rage simmering in my blood.

"Do you have anything to say for yourself?" he prodded, and I shrugged.

I couldn't help but let out a huff of breath at his attempts to rile me. It was bold of him. Even if I wasn't his king, my dragon far outranked him in terms of our power and size.

"You're treating her like she's your mate," he goaded, kicking off of the wall and stalking up to me. "But she isn't."

My upper lip peeled back as a snarl came from the depths of my dragon within, sizing Lucius up as a possible threat to my wife. He circled me and I resisted the urge to turn with him, not allowing him a chance to have my back exposed to him. I wouldn't show him that he was successful in making me uneasy.

"You said she'd be your wife only in the terms of a political arrangement, yet here you are, smothering her with your scent and sequestering her from the world she lives in now," he surmised before coming to stand at my front once more. His eyes traveled over me before landing on my face. He scoffed. "You're so down bad for her, brother. Admit it so we can figure out a way to win her over and put your pissy dragon to rest before blood is spilled."

Ice bloomed across my fists as I lowered them to my sides. Unrest swirled within my stomach as I forced the words out. "I don't owe you an explanation, as your king, but she means nothing to me," I spat. "I'm merely protecting her while she is here. As soon as the curse is broken and both of our sides are back to the way they were before my father's rule, I will break our contract and send her home."

A pang of sorrow slashed through me, as if my

dragon was physically clawing at my chest from the inside. I knew what was best for us, though. I merely felt this draw because she was the only option around. It would be better when she was gone and out of our space.

Lucius tilted his head at me and huffed, "So, you wouldn't mind if I took a pass at her after it's over, then? She's quite delectable and my—"

I didn't hesitate as I closed the distance between us and wrapped my hand around his throat. I tightened my grip as I walked him back to the wall, enjoying the way he gasped as his eyes bulged.

He would never touch her.

The desire to be rid of him overcame me as I pictured him trying to court *my* wife. My nostrils flared as my bones cracked, and I struggled to contain the shift that was threatening to overcome me.

Lucius wheezed as his hands tried to desperately pry mine from his throat, with no luck. I reveled in his desperation. He wasn't strong enough for her. She deserved the best. Someone who could protect her from all threats, and he would never be able to protect her from *me*.

My eyes zeroed in on his lips forming the silent words I was preventing him from uttering.

"Yield. I yield."

His submission knocked me from the haze of my quest to make him see his place in the food chain. Releasing my grip on him, his hand instantly went to the red skin around his throat, rubbing at it as he took in deep, gasping breaths.

I shook my head, wondering what his intentions were to purposefully incite violence from me.

Glancing down at him as he bent over slightly, I murmured, "That was stupid, Lucius. Don't do that again."

He laughed before going into a coughing fit as he straightened up to look at me. After clearing his throat for a few seconds, he answered, "Sure was, but I got the confirmation I was looking for, and you should have too. Your dragon isn't going to give her up, no matter what logic you try to convince yourself of. There are only two options here: bond with her or kill any unmated drackya that looks her way. Either way, she won't ever be leaving to return home."

My lips thinned as I blocked out his words. She'd go home as soon as the curse was lifted. It was clear she didn't want to be here, and I'd never accept a mate who despised our kind the way she did.

"Enough," I commanded, turning on my heel to walk down the hall. "Make yourself scarce for the next few weeks. I can't promise to reign my beast back in again."

He called out at my retreating back, "Theo! You can't run this castle with no staff while she's here. There is too much to be done, and you cannot do it all while also trying to find a way to break the curse with her. Allow me to find mated drackya to take over a few positions in the meantime, at the very least."

My feet came to a stop and I glanced over my shoulder. "Fine. Mated staff only. For the ones I severed from their positions, see that we find them a new job outside of the castle. I don't need to give them further reason to incite a coup or make an assassination attempt. When she's gone, they can return."

When she's gone.

Immediately, my dragon surged to the surface and scales ran along my forearms, shocking me. I'd never had such little control over myself or my dragon. I prided myself on not being like the others beneath my rule that couldn't rein the beast in. I couldn't allow her to be the reason I unraveled and showed such little restraint now.

I clenched my fists before forcing them to relax, repeating the movement over a few times as I took deep breaths.

You cannot afford to show that she is your weakness.

Even if the desire to protect her was from my beast, the others wouldn't see it that way. They'd think of her as the perfect way to get me to bend the knee to their demands, if only they could get their hands on her.

The thought struck me. Perhaps keeping her confined to our wing of the castle wouldn't be enough. I couldn't be with her at all times, that much was clear. Yet I had duties as the king that must be attended to. That exact reason was why I'd not been able to find the time to dig into the curse enough as is, though. Something had to change if I was hoping for a different result now, with Siyana here. Time was of the essence.

Here I was, thinking things could continue as they were, yet I was giving commands to empty the castle and completely change the staff, thinking that wouldn't raise suspicion.

"Disregard what I said, Lucius," I breathed out and locked eyes with him. "Bring the regular staff back in two days and don't let them know that I requested their leave in the meantime. I name you Counsellor in my absence. I need to focus all of my attention on breaking this curse so I can have her gone, for her sake and mine, as quickly as possible."

His brow pinched as he stared at me in shock before quickly recovering. "Of course, Your Highness. I'm honored. Can I ask where you both will go in the meantime? Also, I will do my best to cover the scent she's left behind to avoid questions, but you know that if they get a single whiff, rumors will swirl."

My hand lifted to pinch the bridge of my nose as the semantics of leaving my post, even for a brief time, overwhelmed me. Was this even the correct choice? This was becoming far more complicated than I'd anticipated. I shook my head and held up a hand to wait as I opened my connection to the elder dragon I needed answers from before I made the final decision.

"Alstrid?"

His answer was swift. **"Yes, My King?"**

"If I were to need to reside in one of the dragon

caverns for the time being, with my wife, is there an alcove that would be a far enough distance from the nesting dragons?"

His scoff of incredulity sounded loud and clear before his response. **"Such a space doesn't exist."**

I felt a 'but' lingering, and waited for him to add onto his response.

"Is this a dire circumstance?"

"Yes. We put all of the drackya and my wife at risk if we stay here. I must hide her presence. It's become clear to me that I didn't take every scenario into consideration before bringing her here."

"I told you that you need to mate her," he murmured, with a tone of arrogance I didn't appreciate.

Annoyance bled through in my response as I retorted, *"And I already told you that isn't an option, Alstrid. Now answer my question. Is there an alcove we can occupy?"*

A heavy sigh echoed. **"I will make it so, Your Highness, though it comes with risks that we cannot fully eradicate. Are you sure it is safer here than within your castle walls?"**

Was it? I was beginning to admit to myself that, for the first time in my rule, I wasn't entirely sure of my decisions.

"I'm not sure, but I almost killed Lucius twice today already," I admitted begrudgingly. *"You know of the delicate control I have over the unmated drackya, already. If they find out she's my weakness*

while she remains my wife, yet unclaimed as a mate and open for others to stake a claim..."

He grumbled. **"A precarious position, indeed. I had only been focused on the risk to her safety from the full-blooded dragons, but it seems we may indeed be the lesser evil of the two right now. Give me until tomorrow morning and I will shift a few of the alcove assignments around."**

While I may have been regarded as the king of all of the undine, full-blooded dragons and drackya alike, I found our relationship less strained when I appointed Alstrid to be a point of contact. The full-blooded undine took better to commands from one of their own, even if they were being handed down by me, through him.

The mental connection severed and I turned to face Lucius fully. "We will go stay within the mountains for now. Perhaps while we are there, I will think of a better plan, but you're correct in saying I can't keep a handle on my duties and keep her safe at the same time. The castle must continue to operate as is while we focus on breaking the curse. It's likely the search will take us out of our territory, as is, so enacting you as Counsellor is for the best."

His dark hair fell forward as he dropped his head and lowered his eyes in deference. "I will do my best in your stead."

I hummed my agreeance as my feet began to pace back and forth. Dropping all formality, I asked, "Am I doing the right thing, Lucius?"

A huff of surprise came from the only being I would consider a true ally. Halting my pacing, I glanced at him, waiting for his answer.

His shoulders lifted in a shrug as his head swayed back and forth. "I think we're in uncertain times, Theo. But you haven't been able to find the answers on how to break the curse in the span of your short rule thus far. It could be your best bet to look outside of the castle for the answers."

I mulled over his words, finding myself agreeing with them before he tacked on, "However, I am not of the royal bloodline. They may see this as an opportunity to finally take over the throne while you are gone. You know that only your dragon is revered as the authority due to the fear you strike into their hearts. I will do my best, as I said, but we must be honest about what you may come home to at the end of this."

Indecision plagued me, and the urge to soar through the sky overcame me. I needed to just exist within the clouds and feel the snow on my scales. It'd done the trick earlier as I'd tampered my overwhelming desire for Siyana while in my chambers, but I couldn't leave her again. I'd naively thought her safe within her chambers then, but this conversation, and seeing her rebel against my word to stay put, had truly highlighted just how wrong I'd been.

"I have to take the risk," I muttered as my mind conjured the image of an overrun castle and the drackya who found himself foolish enough to sit upon my throne. "Either we find a way to lift the curse and establish peace and prosperity to ensure my rule continues, or we find mutiny at our doorstep anyways."

Lucius took a deep breath and nodded. "Let's hope it doesn't end in my death while you're gone. I will prepare horses and supplies for your journey into the mountains."

"There's no need for the horses," I grumbled, thinking of how long and arduous the journey would be for the creatures. They'd barely managed the journey yesterday as hard as we'd pushed them. I'll have to swallow my pride and take her myself.

He raised a brow, clearly thinking I was unable to do exactly that. "You're going to let her ride your dragon?"

I waved him off. "Just gather food and supplies that she can carry. Try to prepare enough for a few weeks, but I can always hunt for more food as needed. The animals will be scarce heading into the winter months now, though."

Lucius chuckled and turned to do as I asked, but I stopped him. "Do you think he can fit me tonight?"

His dimples flashed through his trimmed beard as he grinned. "I hope I remember this moment forever. The fearsome undine dragon king, asking if the saddler can fit him in for an appointment to allow his human wife to ride him."

"Don't make me strangle you again," I deadpanned, earning a laugh in response from him.

Just this once, I vowed to myself. *Just this once will she ride me.*

Chapter Eleven

SIYANA

"What do you mean the tour is cancelled?"

My voice was filled with shock, considering he'd just told me that was the plan as of an hour ago. What really threw me off, though, was the way I watched his eyes scan up and down every hall before we walked down it, and the way he scanned the sky outside of every window for the briefest moment as we passed.

Despite his earlier diatribe about how my being around other unmated drackya could prove disastrous, this felt different. Somehow bigger than I could possibly understand. And it was deeply discomforting.

"Theo!" I snapped, not appreciating being kept in the dark, though I still managed to keep my voice low. My body was suddenly tense and ready to parry an attack at any moment with his behavior.

It was obvious he was on high alert, and seeing as we were in his castle and he still felt the need to be on the defense, an uneasy feeling had quickly settled in the pit of my stomach.

His hand on my lower back as he guided me back to our wing would have normally been the first thing I corrected before moving an inch, but I'd be a liar if I didn't admit it made me feel a modicum safer. Something about the warmth of his hand and the possessive touch had me under some delusion that he would actually protect me if something were to happen.

He ushered me up the steps that finally led to our wing at the corner of the castle. "Hush, wench."

From the little I'd seen, there was no one around the castle to hear us, but it wasn't worth arguing with him about. Our footsteps were light and quick as we walked down the hall of portraits, but as my eyes snagged on his mother once more, curiosity got the better of me, causing me to break the silence again.

"You look like her. Are the two of you close?"

His steps faltered briefly before his hand pushed on my back, guiding me forward again. "She's dead, so I'd hope we're not close."

Despite the brisk nature of his tone, I didn't sense any actual animosity in his response. Just deflection.

I, too, was a big fan of using dark humor to cope.

"I didn't mean physically," I murmured as I glanced at him out of the corner of my eye. The tiniest curve tilted the corner of his lips before it was gone.

So it seemed we couldn't have productive, mature conversations, but morbid jokes were on the table. Got it.

I wanted to ask what happened to her, but it was clear he wasn't ready to dive into it, if the non-answer to my first question was any indication.

Focusing on the warmth that flowed over me as he opened the door and pushed me through, my toes curled in delight. It seemed he'd come back to his room after his flight, considering the large bed was made and the fireplace had been renewed with fresh wood thrown in, crackling merrily in greeting. Thankfully, the dresses in my chambers fit well, despite being a few inches too long. They would keep me from freezing to death in this icy tundra, where fireplaces seemed to be a rare commodity.

His hand fell from my back as he closed the door behind us, and I made my way closer to the blazing warmth. I rubbed my cold hands together, using friction to my advantage before settling into one of the armchairs.

"The last time I saw her in that dress was my seventh birthday."

The sudden admission was personal, and also unnerving as I glanced down at the navy material pooling on the floor around my feet. Yeah, because wearing your deceased mother-in-law's gowns was entirely normal. I suppose it made sense, considering Theo didn't know my sizing and couldn't have prepared a wardrobe for me prior to my arrival.

I knew I couldn't demand much, given my situation, but perhaps if I inquired nicely about where I could retrieve my own clothes, he'd take pity on me. Being without money or anything of value had a sense of vulnerability, something I wasn't used to, settling in.

Glass clinked together behind me where he stood at his collection of alcohol. As the sound of his drink splashed into his chosen cup, I asked, "Could you pour me one as well?"

A hum was all I received in response before his heavy steps drew closer. A glass full of amber liquid was presented as he stepped around my chair. Our fingers brushed against one another as I closed my hand around the glass, and I stilled at the contact. It wasn't as if it was the first time we'd ever touched—but as our eyes met and neither of us moved, I could say with the utmost certainty that it was the first time the semblance of even a single butterfly took flight in my belly.

I cleared my throat and averted my gaze to the beautiful crystal as I brought it to my lips, shattering the moment. The alcohol burned a path down my throat as I tipped the entirety of the contents into my mouth, suddenly feeling the need for liquid courage.

I couldn't stop the coughing fit that overcame me. Whatever this was, it was far stronger than anything I'd consumed before. There were hints of cinnamon and honey on my tongue in the aftertaste, but it was hard to focus on that as my throat constricted and my eyes burned.

"First time you've had bourbon?" he asked, amusement clear in his tone as he settled into the chair across from me with his hand on one of the curved arms and his glass atop the other.

I shifted uncomfortably beneath the weight of his stare that was suddenly fixated on my lips as my tongue swept over them. Coughing a few more times, I held my hand to my chest as if I could somehow will them to stop with the motion.

"No," I croaked out, shaking my head, "I actually drink this to hydrate myself during sparring sessions. Very smooth. I just had a tickle in my throat."

Either the world was coming to an end or he actually cracked the smallest smile for the second time in the span of ten minutes. Of course, it was gone and replaced with an icy mask of indifference in the time it took me to blink, but I'd not imagined it.

Suddenly, my eyes slammed shut as a piercing pain slashed into my brain. "Fuck!" I muttered, holding my free hand to my temple. "Son of a bitch, that hurts."

A rumbling laughter floated through the air as I forced my eyes open once more. "Well, perhaps the alcohol loosens your lips, wench, but I'm glad you're able to keep your mental wall in place still. I had to be sure before we dive into the logistics of the remainder of your stay here."

Either I was an extreme light-weight, with this bourbon hitting quickly, or my brain hadn't heard him properly. "The remainder of my stay?" I parroted. "Wouldn't that entail, I don't know, the rest of my life, considering we're married?"

His eyebrows slanted and the skin between them pinched as he seemed to ponder either my words or his own before responding. He seemed rather uncomfortable as he took a long drink from his own glass instead of responding. He lowered it from his lips for a second but then shrugged and downed the rest as I had, albeit with no coughing fit.

Show off.

"So, I think it goes without saying that I don't understand the needs of a human and I haven't taken into consideration the fragility of your species," he began as he lowered the glass to the side table between us.

My brows rose in a 'well you don't say,' look.

"Could you refrain from giving me that very attitude that makes me want to throttle you for a few minutes?" he quipped. The corners of his lips turned down as his reptilian pupil constricted to the skinniest slit. "My dragon finds your attitude appealing, but I don't."

My head tilted as I forced a smile. "Could you refrain from saying things that spark my attitude? You could fix the problem right at the source."

He rubbed a hand over his scaled eye before dropping both hands to clasp together between his long legs. "Despite my carelessness with the lives of the women that were stolen by my people, I don't actually want to see any humans perish. That includes you."

My face and tone went flat. "But I'll believe it when I see it."

His lips thinned and his nostrils flared as he took a

deep breath. With narrowed eyes trained on me, he muttered, "That's what I'm getting to if you'd stop interrupting me."

I offered a shrug. "Sorry, it seems to be a favorite hobby of mine since I have nothing else to focus on now that I'm trapped with you."

He leaned forward, putting his weight on his forearms that rested on his knees as he glowered at me, the intensity making my throat constrict. "If you would shut your insufferable mouth, you'd hear that I'm going to end our marriage once we've ended this curse. You'll return home and be free of me."

My throat was suddenly dry, and not a single word floated through my mind as I stared at him, mouth agape.

"I'm..." I faltered as the wheels in my brain processed his words. "You want a divorce when this is done?"

He nodded before grabbing his glass and standing. "Do you want another?"

I lifted my glass to him in answer.

As he poured us another round, I found myself shaking my head, trying to make sense of his announcement. "Our marriage is a way to mend the terse relationship between our people and unite Andrathya once more. How will we be united, if we aren't you know..." I stammered.

"United?" he offered cheekily, making me scowl.

I huffed. "Yes."

The idea of going back to my life wasn't an offer I thought I'd ever have on the table. When Theo had thrown me over his shoulder and forbid me from saying goodbye to my loved ones, I'd had to quickly come to terms with the fact that I wouldn't ever return to my home. Now here he was, offering my freedom, so quickly after whisking me away.

There had to be a catch. It was too good to be true.

As he offered my now-full glass back to me, I couldn't help but throw his words from yesterday back at him. "Don't tell me you've already lost your bite, Theo? Did I already wear you down? That was far too easy. I like my prey to put up a bit longer of a fight. "

He glared at me from above the rim of his glass as he took a sip. Lowering the glass to rest between his hands, he muttered, "I'd be a liar if I said this was entirely for your benefit, wench. We both want to return to our lives before. All we have to do is find a way to break the curse and we can be done with one another."

While his words weren't cruel, and they did ring true, my chest constricted nonetheless. Perhaps it was just the alcohol.

We can be done with one another.

Yes, that's what I wanted. I took a sip and nodded in agreement before giving him my attention once more. "Alright, but how are we to ensure the unity remains, assuming we can lift the curse?"

If anything would come of this short-lived marriage, it would be me ensuring my people were safe and out of harm's way when it came to the beasts he couldn't keep in line. I wouldn't settle until we accomplished that, even if it meant rotting away in a wing of this castle for the rest of my life.

"We haven't required a marriage between our people in all of the generations before us," he offered with a shrug. "My kind want to mate for life. I need to find mine, and I can't do that if I'm married already. Eventually, my dragon will force me to try to bond with you, as he already thinks that is where this is heading. As you know, it doesn't end well when the bond doesn't work, due to the human not being the correct person. I think we'd both like to avoid that particular scenario."

Once again, he was purely stating the facts, but a spark of rejection and the stark reminder of women from my kingdom being slaughtered by the dragons soured my stomach. Perhaps this wasn't what I pictured for my life, and I hadn't asked for any of this, but in the short time since meeting Theo, I'd not had to fit into the role of crown princess, heir to the throne of Andrathya.

I'd simply been Sia—the witty, stubborn, and opinionated woman who had always resided within me, nestled away for the simple facade of politics. While I might not love the position I'd been forced into, the thought of going back and fitting into the same old mold as before wasn't as appealing as it should have been.

I mean, it was my life, after all. I'd have my family and friends. I'd be able to take over the throne and rule justly for my people. I'd be able to bring positive and much-needed change to our world. My eyes fell to the ever dancing flames stroking against the burning wood as I sat back in the chair and pulled my feet up.

I'd have to be above reproach once more. The head of the kingdom couldn't afford missteps. I—

"Do you agree to my terms?"

His question startled me out of my thoughts.

He was offering me exactly what I wanted yesterday, so why was I hesitating now?

I took another sip of the bourbon and nodded before slamming the glass down a little too hard onto the side table. It was just the alcohol making my thoughts fuzzy. This was for the best.

"Sounds like we have a curse to break. Tell me everything about it, so we can be done with this."

Chapter Twelve

SIYANA

"Don't bother trying to keep pace with me," he warned as I told him to fill my glass again after he brought the entire bottle over to his side table. "My metabolism burns it off much faster than a human's. You won't prove anything to me by having another, besides that you're too stubborn for your own good, which I promise I'm already well aware of."

"I've taken care of myself for a long time now," I argued, not appreciating his implications. "If I wanted to impress you, I'd do something other than drinking myself under the table." Both his circular human pupil and slitted dragon one widened at that comment. No, he most definitely wasn't wondering what I meant by that, right? I shouldn't have said it. Switching gears, I tossed out, "Besides, the liquor is keeping me warm, and who knows when I'll have a chance to have it again, considering this marriage will be short lived."

"I won't be cleaning up your puke, but be my guest," he murmured, an air of arrogance swirling around him as he leaned over to refill my glass. It seemed as if some of the tension and animosity we'd felt around each other had evaporated with the revelation of our impending divorce.

Could we work together in the meantime? My guard would remain up, but perhaps a truce would assist us in making progress.

I resisted the urge to scowl at him, just barely, instead choosing to focus on the task at hand—gathering information. "I need you to start at the beginning. Where did this curse originate, and what do you know about breaking it so far? Our history books don't cover the topic, and those who were alive when it happened refuse to speak of it, despite our town being full of gossips. I need to understand it in its entirety."

His broad shoulders heaved with a deep inhale before he stood and let it out. I noted trickles of sweat streaming down his temple as he glared at the fireplace. Clearly, it was only burning for my sake, and while I was enjoying basking in its warmth, a part of me felt bad that he was agitated and uncomfortable in his own chambers.

"You can kill the fire, if that would help you settle in for this conversation," I offered just as he turned to glance at the bright light streaming in from the balcony. From this angle, it showcased the black tunic stuck to his wide back, drenched through with sweat and showing his muscles bunching as he placed his glass up on the mantle.

"I have a feeling we're going to be here for a bit and that there isn't anywhere else we can go, considering your cagey behavior on the way back from the dining hall."

He glanced back at me and I quickly averted my gaze from my perusal before forging on, "Don't think I forgot about that weird behavior from earlier. I want an explanation for that as well."

"Will you perish if I snuff out the fire? I fear I don't truly understand what you can withstand."

Something about his question had me chuckling with genuine delight, which caused his brow to pinch in confusion as he waited for my answer. He was being so serious. The undine king, unaware of the limits of a human body–it was as ludicrous as it was humorous. But then, I suppose there was more than enough that I still didn't understand about his people and their way of life. The thought was all the levity I needed to bring me back to the moment at hand, though I couldn't help but still chuckle.

"No, I won't *perish*," I breathed out between laughs as he shook his head and ran a hand through his hair, pushing back the damp pieces from his face. "Put out the fire and I will let you know when the cold becomes overwhelming."

Relief seemed to wash over him, his shoulders sagging as he bent down. Holding a hand in front of the fireplace, shards of ice came flying out of it, piercing the wood. He let out a curse as he crouched down fully, balancing on the balls of his feet. I watched in fascination as the ice quickly melted within the grips of the fire that licked mercilessly against it, and Theo tried again. This time when he lifted his hand, a steady stream of snow blasted from his palm, coating the entire area. Steam began to fill the room as it melted against the embers and the fire began to dim.

It was the most dramatic way to put out a fire that I'd ever seen, and it became abundantly clear that he'd never done this before. I let out a sigh and shifted to my feet, feeling the buzz of the bourbon washing through my veins as I stood and ambled over to where the iron poker sat, clean of the grim of soot and clearly unused. I felt his eyes on the side of my face as I knelt down onto my knees and placed my hand on his, pressing down lightly to get him to stop.

"You're actively fighting against the fire," I murmured, poking the pieces until they fell and the heap of wood no longer remained.

With the damp logs still sizzling and the flames slowly tapering out, he admitted, "You're lucky that starting the fire was easy. I'd never had to do that before either."

I couldn't help but joke, "All this for little ole me? And they say an old dragon can't learn new tricks."

Glancing over at him, I choked on a laugh as his lips thinned. "I'm two years older than you, Siyana. I am not old."

I brought my hand up to cover my giggles and slowly but surely, a small laugh fell from his own lips. I was enraptured as soon as the sound hit my ears. It was rich and deep, with a vibration that seemed to fill the space. The way his scales bunched up as his smile grew was odd to see, watching the edges shift over one another with ease.

Before I could think it through, my hand lifted in the air, reaching out to touch them. How could they move so seamlessly, considering their rigidity? His smile fell as soon as he realized what I was doing, but he didn't stop me. Silently, I traced the tips of my fingers along the edges of the scales, and his eyes widened with the contact.

His serpentine eye sparked with that bright blue magic I'd grown to know meant his dragon was present.

"Hi there," I murmured as if the beast could hear me, concentrating on the rough ridges within each scale but marveling over the pliable skin between them. It was much rougher than our human skin, but I could see how it could absolutely be pierced by a blade, unlike the seemingly impenetrable scales. "So your scales can shift over one another as a defense mechanism to protect the skin. How fascinating. Is it like that all over your body?"

A low buzz had settled into my mind at some point, and my fingers tingled with the prolonged contact.

My gaze wandered, and as soon as I saw his very human eye gazing at me, it was like I was sent hurling back to reality. I snatched my hand back, gasping as I realized what I'd done.

I'd just freaking pet the king of dragons. What had gotten into me?

He cleared his throat, pulling back to push to his feet, clearly just as shocked as I was. "So, now that I can focus without feeling like I'm suffocating from the heat, we should begin our discussion."

I blinked at him a few times, still confused at what had come over me. "Yeah, uhm, okay."

Taking our seats again, I remained quiet, waiting for him to begin. I couldn't bring myself to look him in the eyes, so I settled for staring a hole in the plush gray rug beneath his feet.

"The year I was born, my father had an affair with a woman outside of our lands."

My heart was racing as I tried to focus on his words, completely taken off guard by the severity of them. Instantly, my eyes snapped up to his and I found him gazing out at the sky through the glass doors behind me.

"Apparently, I was a difficult baby."

The opening to make a sarcastic quip about him being difficult was there, yet I couldn't think of anything I'd rather do less, for once.

He shrugged and grabbed the decanter of liquor that was already half empty, plucking the lid off and placing it back on the table. "At least, that's the excuse my father used to defend his deplorable actions. My parents had drifted apart and he found solace between another woman's legs. Only, he hid his identity from her, concerned that she would demand access to our money, or worse, attempt to become the queen and disrupt our lives."

How Theo managed to speak of this as if it was a storybook he was reading from spoke to the deep issues I assumed he was likely still struggling with. His suddenly monotone voice was so unlike him, and I wondered if it was the only way he could get through sharing this—just brushing past how incredibly fucked up it all was and explaining it all as fact.

As he drank directly from the bottle, I grimaced. Yeah, this had to be awful to discuss.

It was on the tip of my tongue to tell him to stop, to prevent him from reopening these festering wounds, but I held back. As hard as this likely was for him, I needed to know the details. There might be a clue somewhere in the mess of this fucked up history.

Resting the bottle on his knee when he was done, he focused on wiping his mouth with his sleeve next.

"He's a fool and didn't realize the woman would find him, searching for answers about the man she met in the woods and sparked a connection with, thinking she had found the love of her life when she stumbled upon him."

I groaned, seeing where this was going and not wanting my suspicions confirmed. However, there was one thing that bothered me. Why was this woman randomly wandering through the northern territory of Andrathya? It wasn't exactly known for its views or welcoming environment.

His head lolled to rest against the edge of the wing-back chair. "Upon realizing that not only was he married and a king, he was also a beast at heart. The woman was rightfully scorned, but it seemed she and my father might have been more alike than she wanted to admit, because she wasn't entirely forthcoming about her identity either."

His eyes slid from the sky behind me to scan over my face. "She was a witch, or at least a descendant of one." My mouth fell open as a million questions peppered my mind, but he kept pushing on. "She at least possessed magic potent enough to lay a curse on my father's kind, so that no one like him would ever be able to deceive a lover again. A piece of their beast would be on display at all times, and she meant it to scare off anyone who might dare be tempted to lay with us. She cursed our kind to die out with us, leaving us unable to find a willing, true mate."

He was quiet for a few moments, seemingly letting me digest that.

"I thought witches were a thing of myth," I breathed out, settling on the first thought that came to the surface. "The old texts say they were the female descendants of the elemental gods, having affinities for magic in the same way the male offspring, the drackya, do. Is that true?"

His lips pursed. "That is what we were taught, but, save being able to ask an elemental ourselves, I suppose the creation of beings is hearsay this many centuries later."

A thought hit me with his wording, and I leaned forward in my seat, a spark of excitement running through me. "Has anyone ever been able to converse with the elemental gods? If it was a witch that laid the curse, surely the creator of witches would be able to break it, right?"

He spluttered and looked at me like I was insane for even asking. "Siyana, why would the gods bother to talk with any of us?"

Not allowing him to deter me, I rebutted, "Well, do you have any better ideas? Did your dad ever tell you if the witch said anything about how to break the curse?"

"No," he answered briskly as his hand tightened on the edge of the bottle, "he didn't bother to tell me much before he killed himself years later, unable to handle the shame and hatred he received as a result of the curse, taking my mother with him."

I leapt from my chair, unable to contain myself. "He killed your mother?!"

Rubbing his eyes with his free hand, he sighed. "He may as well have. When a drackya and human complete their bond, part of the magic from our dragon is shared with our mate. It allows their lifespan to stretch far beyond that of typical humans. But when their drackya dies and that magic source is snuffed out..." he trailed off, leaving me to fill in the blanks.

"So her mortality caught up with her after he was gone," I surmised as he took a drink. My feet carried me back and forth in front of the near-dead embers in the fireplace. "Fuck, Theo...that's a lot."

I stopped pacing and stared at the drackya before me, no longer seeing him simply as the dragon king, or the reason I was torn from my home for the first time. I was simply seeing Theo, the child who had to grow up too quickly and take on the mantle of king from his fucked up father. Stuck with the responsibility of having to break the curse, when it should never have been his burden to bear.

"I had to take over the throne when I was thirteen," he admitted hollowly, gaze going back out to the sky as he seemed to lose himself in thought. A long moment passed before he sighed, shoulders slumping slightly as he continued, "As you can imagine, the hatred from our people is heavy, considering it is my father's fault the curse was given to begin with. That hatred has fallen to me in his absence. I suppose it has to be directed at someone."

"Hey," I whispered, finding my voice softer than it had ever been with him. My heart was splintering as more of his life was revealed. "Don't say that. You don't deserve their hatred. It sounds to me like you've had it the hardest due to your father's horrid actions. Not only are you cursed like everyone else, but you lost both of your parents, *and* you have to shoulder a responsibility that is too heavy to carry alone."

His haunting words came back to me. *No one stops to wonder what made me this way.*

"Well, I've done a shit job since taking the crown, according to my people," he admitted before his jaw clenched tightly. "I'm nowhere close to understanding the curse or how to break it, and here we are, twenty-seven years later, still stuck. The patience I've asked them to have has all but dried up, and they've begun to take matters into their own hands—hence them snatching humans from your lands in a desperate attempt to find a mate."

I scoffed, "Yeah, because that's smart. Terrify the women before hoping they'll pledge their life to you as a mate."

Snagging my drink, I gulped the bourbon down as the cold began to settle back into my bones, much quicker than I anticipated. Thankfully, the liquor warmed my chest and heat spread across my cheeks.

"You don't understand, Siyana."

Every time he used my full name, it felt wrong, as if I was a stranger he was being formal with. But I supposed that's exactly what I was. Here he was, baring his life story to me, yet he didn't know me at all.

I lowered my glass to my side and met his eyes. What I saw had my knees trembling. There was a deep hunger in those navy depths that made me want to shrink away, once again feeling like prey.

He pushed to his feet and stalked toward me, and all I could manage was to not step back and show the fear building tightly within my chest. Suddenly, he was crowding my space like he had in the dining hall, forcing me to tilt my head back in order to maintain eye contact.

"Dragons mate for life," he whispered, causing the skin on my arms to pebble as a chill went down my spine. "It begins to drive us crazy. Knowing our mate is out there, yet being unable to claim them, it drives us into a frenzy eventually. The older we get, the less time we feel we have to satisfy what the beast within needs."

My lips were suddenly dry as I croaked out, "And what's that?"

His head tilted as his dragon's eye sparked and zeroed in on my lips. "To claim our mate. To breed them. To worship them. To not understand where one soul stops and the other begins once the bond is complete."

My breaths grew shallow and rapid as my heart rate spiked. I swore my heart had drifted into my ears at the way the steady beat whooshed within them. His closeness was doing things to me, or maybe it was the alcohol finally kicking in. Things that shouldn't be possible were rising within me, considering I despised his kind. Yet his scent and warmth wrapped around me in a comforting embrace that I was beginning to get used to, and I found my own eyes tracing his lips in return.

The words were falling from my lips before I could even stop myself.

"And why are you so sure that I couldn't be yours?"

Chapter Thirteen

THEO

THOSE FEW WORDS from her lips were testing my restraint in a way it had never been tested before. My dragon wanted out, and he wanted her.

My fists clenched before forcing themselves open as my talons slid out on their own accord. I was quickly losing control over my shift, as the overwhelming need to put her words to the test roared to life within me.

Her wide eyes looked hopeful, and confusion warred within me. Already, my feelings for this human were something I was trying to actively sort through. I'd come to the conclusion that she'd be safer and happier away from me once this curse was broken and the alliance between our people was restored.

Was I wrong?

Did she not hate me?

A growl rumbled through my chest as I resisted the urge to run my nose along the soft skin of her neck, breathing in her tantalizing scent. Already, she was beginning to smell like me. Like she was mine.

Could the elementals be laughing as they watched us in this moment, knowing we entered this marriage for political reasons, but were somehow two halves of each other's soul?

My jaw ticked as she raised onto the tips of her toes, eyes completely focused on my lips. Every single part of my body became rigid as she approached, her intention clear as day.

It was like time came to standstill as mere inches stood between our lips, my body somehow acting of its own accord, lowering to meet her halfway. I felt the warmth of her body radiating toward me as her chest brushed against mine and her hands came up to wrap around my neck.

My hands glided over the small of her waist and down the swell of her hips before my fingertips pressed in.

Fuck, I wanted to let my beast out and test her. She had shown she was strong and stubbornly fearless. Could she withstand the weight of the curse and not run away as she looked into the eyes of my dragon?

Could she want me...for me? All of me?

Just as her breath fanned across my lips and her eyes closed, I recalled her words. That my kind disgusts her. That she felt the same when I said I'd never touch her. The way her hatred had burned so brightly in her eyes the entire journey from her castle to mine.

It couldn't be her.

Grabbing her hips tightly, I veered my head to the side of her face, resting my lips next to her ear. We couldn't do this. I couldn't let my restless desire to find a mate put her in harm's way. Not when this wasn't how she truly felt. No one could change that quickly.

I'd rather her hate me and realize she was better off far away from me. Far away from all of the beasts lurking in the shadows of my lands. Let hate fill her heart once she finished her duties to her kingdom in this marriage, if nothing else than to protect her.

This was a contract for an alliance, and we needed to keep that in mind.

My beast lashed at the bars of the cage I kept him tucked away behind as I forced the words out. "This is just the alcohol loosening your tongue and a spoiled princess not enjoying the fact that I'm denying her as an option. You told me that my kind disgusts you, and I told you I'd never touch you. Let's not make liars of ourselves, wench."

I pulled back just in time to see the haze of lust clearing from her eyes, and a spark of shame burned across her cheeks. I took no enjoyment in seeing her fall onto her feet and glare at me with the intensity of a million burning suns. Her small hands pushed roughly against my chest, attempting to move me away from her. She couldn't accomplish that herself, but I took the steps back anyway, allowing her the space to move away.

My head fell as she demanded, "Put the fireplace back

on. I'm cold and we need to discuss how we are going to begin our search for a way to break this curse. The sooner, the better."

A blood-curdling cry sounded from my dragon within, filling my head with a piercing rage as I lifted my hands to my temples.

Hush. She is not ours. Would you rather kill her while proving that point?

As I dropped my hands and turned to glance at her curled back up in her chair, staring a hole into the ground, my shoulders sagged. Even if I couldn't have her, the brief time of not being at each other's throats that we'd just shared within this room...I wanted more of that. I wanted more of her smiles and laughs. I wanted more of her coming to my defense and feeling like someone wanted to carry the weight of my burdens with me.

"Are you going to light the fire, or should I go back to my room?" she snapped, refusing to meet my eyes.

Her offer to put out the fire had been purely for my comfort. Now that I'd offended her, I wasn't surprised at her recension of that small act of kindness.

It was better this way.

As my eyes scanned over the damp logs within the fireplace, I murmured, "I'd need to locate more wood. I can't use these now."

Glancing back at her, I watched her shoulders pull back and her chin tilt up as she glared at me. "Fine. Let's finish this conversation quickly, so I can go to my chambers. Why were you acting cagey on the way back here, and when can I expect for us to begin searching for answers?"

My lungs expanded with a deep breath and I moved to sit back in my chair across from her. An itch was spreading across my skin as my scales burned to come out, the itch to let the shift overcome me damn near overwhelming. I needed this conversation to be over so I could lose myself amongst the snowy mountainside.

"As I mentioned before, there is civil unrest with my people, and I'm afraid my word alone cannot keep them in line. Having you here may draw their focus, and I cannot defend you if they decide to assemble into a mutiny. I may be the strongest drackya here, but even I can be defeated by numbers."

The admission wounded my pride, but after shutting down her advances in such a callous way, this was the least I could do. It was an attempt at honesty. She deserved that, at the least.

She sucked her bottom lip between her teeth, nibbling on it as she seemed to mull over my words. The action drew my focus, and I had to clear my throat and tear my gaze away.

"So, tomorrow we will be heading into the mountains with the full-blooded dragons," I shared, eliciting a small gasp from her as her eyes widened and focused on me. "We must be respectful of the nesting dragons present as they protect their eggs, but an elder dragon is currently moving them around to provide us with an alcove that should give us some protection, compared to being within this castle. The dragons are loyal to me as their king and aren't blinded by the mating haze that's come over the drackya. They will help to protect us, and from there, we can work on your training and our next steps for ending the curse. You will be riding my dragon to ensure we get there quickly and safely, so dress for extreme weather."

She composed herself quickly, nodding and pushing to her feet. It was strange to not hear a sarcastic quip in response to my commands, considering I'd told her she'd never be worthy of riding a dragon, yet here I was telling her she would.

This was exactly what I'd wanted, though. Distance and clarity between us and our roles here.

Her hands smoothed along the front of the dress as she asked, "Is that it for now? I have problems within my own kingdom to figure out so that when I go home and take up the throne, I can implement new strategies."

Take up the throne.

I closed my eyes and silently cursed her father. That bastard allowed her to think she would be the next ruler, as heir to the throne. From my letters with him, it was clear that was not his intention. It crossed my mind to just tell her that, but I wasn't exactly in her good graces and worthy of being trusted. Not yet. And maybe not ever.

"Hold on," I murmured, crossing to my desk near the bed. Rifling through the manilla parchments I'd saved, I noted the dates on the tops of them until I found the first from her father.

This would be the proof she needed to see exactly what her father meant for her. The items he offered me that I hadn't taken him up on, mainly the opportunity to not only be the king of my people, but theirs as well through this marriage. I had no desire for such things, considering he demanded we reside within their human castle if I agreed to his terms.

I'd rather burn within the fire elemental's domain for eternity.

"What's this?" she asked, brow pinched as I approached and offered the letter.

"I take no joy in giving this to you," I warned, knowing her mind would go there without prompting now that she felt scorned by me. Like I was kicking her while she was down. "I owe you these answers, considering you will be going back there when our marriage is done. You deserve to know exactly what you're going back to, on the off chance your father tries to arrange another suitor for you."

Those words tasted like ash from the fireplace had settled on my tongue, and I bit down on my lip, hard. How had it not crossed my mind until the words had come out that he would likely marry her off to another after this was over?

The guarded look I'd grown to know well from the fiery wench came back as she gave me a curt nod and strode toward the door.

"Siyana?" I called out, causing her to pause as she pulled it open. "For what it's worth, I'm sorry."

She didn't bother looking back at me or responding, and the door quickly shut behind her. A roar came from within me as I gave in to the beast, who fought to take over the moment she was gone from my sight.

I stripped my clothes off as I raced toward the balcony, not wanting to destroy my chambers again if I didn't get into the sky in time. As a teen, the shift had hurt as I learned to master it, but now it felt as natural as breathing. The world shifted as I grew wings, the wind calling to them as the blizzard raging outside consumed me. My vision became sharper with both eyes acclimating to my advanced sight as a dragon. The scent of the salt from the ocean bordering our lands was accentuated as I launched into the air and rolled through it, finding the current that offered the least resistance.

Somehow, I didn't manage to go very far, instead only wrapping around the side of the castle and to the other end of the building, where I could easily catch a glimpse of Siyana within her chambers. The snow would obscure me from her view, but not her from me.

As my wings beat through the gale of the storm, whooshing in time with my beating heart, I zeroed in on her small form as she crumpled the letter in her hands and threw it into the blazing fire. Despite being encapsulated within the stone walls and far from my ears, I still heard the anguished scream that came from her.

It shocked me that such a sound could come from a

woman as small as her. It spoke of grief, hatred, and the need to get vengeance. I knew that scream intimately, because it sounded the same as my own when my mother died. Only I would never have the chance to seek the vengeance I craved.

I hoped that in letting her return to her home, she could claim hers, having all of the information needed to aid her at her fingertips.

Pride swelled within me as I pictured her slamming the doors open in her home castle and letting her father finally hear everything she thought. The demands she would make. The fire within her that dared to burn anyone who denied her. I wanted her to refuse to take no for an answer, to never allow her father or anyone else to ship her off to the next best suitor as he had shipped her to me.

I wanted her to take the throne and be my equal, running her own castle, not by marriage but by her birthright.

She paced around the room for what felt like hours as I made loops in the sky, watching her, unable to tear myself away. As the sun began to set and the fire within her room began to dwindle, she threw herself onto the large bed, face first.

Drawing closer to the window, I watched as her body trembled, the sound of her sobs wrenching through the air. It was a risk to be this close. If she lifted her head, there was no doubt she'd see a hulking dragon within the blizzard staring at her. Two navy eyes sparking amongst a sea of white, unable to look away.

She curled up on her side, giving me her back. A deafening cry tore its way through my throat and into the sky, my beast aching to tuck her against it.

We'd destroy anyone who made her feel this way.

No. It wasn't my place to be that sort of protector for her.

As she began to turn, I launched up above the castle and away from her sight.

The truth was, she didn't need me to be her champion—she was strong enough on her own.

Chapter Fourteen

SIYANA

SOMETIME THROUGHOUT THE night I'd awoken to only the embers of my dying fire providing a minute amount of light and warmth, compared to the roaring fire that had lulled me to sleep. I hadn't the desire to go to Theo and ask him for anything, even something as small as more wood for my fire. The shame I'd felt in his denial still burned brightly within me, but the fight I'd usually hold on to was nowhere to be found due to the contents of my father's letter.

The way he'd offered *my* throne to Theo. My fucking birthright.

My sleep was far from peaceful as I'd forced myself to try and rest more, but waking fits disrupting me throughout the night. Upon my most recent fit, I noted that even the embers of my fire had died out. The shivers running through me and my chattering teeth must have been what woke me this time.

"Shit," I breathed out, feeling pain in my lungs from just how damned cold the air had turned. Tossing the heavy covers from my shaking body, I dropped my feet onto the floor and stumbled, finding the surface slick with ice. Throwing my hands out to find my balance, I squinted, trying to see what had happened with the help of the little bit of moonlight streaming in from the glass windows next to my bed. The snowstorm was still raging beyond my window and the wind howled, buffeting against the window and rattling the panes. A shiver ran down the length of my spine–the atmosphere in the dark room was eerie, just off enough to leave me feeling unsettled.

A loud crack sounded through the room and my heart leapt into my throat. My head snapped in the direction of the sound, eyes landing on a dark corner near the fireplace.

"It's just one of the logs cooling, Sia," I tried to reason with myself, but I still felt the skin on the back of my neck prickling with some preternatural sense of danger.

Taking tentative, small steps over the icy floor, I drew closer to the fireplace, crossing the small sitting area situated in the middle of the room. I cursed Theo for taking my only weapon from me, suddenly desperate to feel the cool hilt of my dagger pressed against my palm.

Just as I swore, a large figure swam into view from the shadowy darkness, with two glowing, silver eyes snapping open. My breath caught in my throat, the fear piercing my chest leaving me momentarily stunned.

Was this another drackya?

From the slit in their left eye, opposite of Theo, I'd wager that it was.

"Who..." I stammered, taking a step back, "who are you, and what do you want?"

I could barely sort my thoughts as my heart beat frantically in my ears. My chest seized with pain from the arctic temperature in the room and the panic that was quickly overtaking me. I had no means of defense, and if my iced-over floor was any indication, it would seem that this drackya also had an affinity for ice like Theo. Even when I'd had my dagger, it'd done me no good against his magical abilities, rendering me useless back in my castle.

"I'm your future mate, little rabbit, here to pluck you from the clutches of the weak king."

His words had me tearing down my mental walls and screaming for the one person I needed most in this world right now.

Theo!

A scream ripped from my throat as the drackya lunged toward me, and I tried to run. My feet slipped on the floor, my entire body going down hard as he tackled me, his weight making me incapable of slipping out from under him. I tried to kick him, but being chest down, pressed against the icy floor, left me without the leverage needed to put real strength behind the move.

His musky breath surrounded me as he sniffed my

hair and groaned. "Such a delectable little rabbit to feast upon. I was enjoying watching you sleep, completely vulnerable and ripe for taking."

I threw my head back and relished in the loud crack of his nose crunching with the force of impact.

"You fucking bitch!" the drackya hissed as his hand wrapped into my hair and yanked back. Lancing pain burned across my scalp, pieces of my hair tearing free with the force the drackya used. "I hope Theo didn't break you in yet, because I want to be the first drackya to make you grovel."

Theo! Someone is in my—

Before I could finish the thought, my door groaned before splitting completely in two. A snarl ripped through the air as the drackya on top of me was suddenly gone, his weight removed from my body, giving me the space to suck in a greedy breath. I scrambled to my hands and knees, crawling toward the bed as furniture crashed to the floor behind me.

I smelled Theo's scent in the air, and tears welled in my eyes. He was here. He would protect me.

"You picked the wrong fucking woman," Theo roared before the room went deathly quiet.

Adrenaline coursed through me, but I couldn't bring myself to turn around and see what happened. If Theo was killed and the other drackya tried to claim me, I'd go down kicking and screaming, but I knew my chances.

Maybe I should have taken Theo more seriously when he offered to train me. It was too late now.

A large hand clamped down on my shoulder and I whirled, letting out a snarl as I swung my fist around. I made contact and felt all the knuckles in my hand crack. Splintering pain wrapped around them and I whimpered.

"Fuck, wench, you pack a punch."

Theo.

My entire body collapsed with relief as I cradled my hand to my chest. Warm tears poured down my cheeks, the adrenaline still waging war in my mind. I was safe. I was okay. Now if only I could convince my wildly beating heart of that.

A sob broke free despite my best efforts to contain it, and seconds later I was wrapped tightly against his chest. I breathed him in as his arms cradled me and his hand ran through the back of my hair.

"You're okay, wench. I've got you," he murmured, the deep tones of his voice vibrating through me with how tightly he held me. "He's dead. He won't hurt you."

"I couldn't do anything," I admitted through shaky sobs. "I wouldn't have been able to fight him off. He would have..."

"Shh," he answered, cutting me off. "You held him off long enough. I'm proud of you."

I wasn't sure how long we were on the floor with me practically sitting in his lap, wrapped around him as he rocked us back and forth. Eventually, the tears faded and my adrenaline turned to shock, and I sat completely still and silent.

"I'm going to move us to my chambers, is that okay?"

His question broke through my mind, replaying the scene from earlier on repeat and all I could do was nod against his chest. He gathered me in his arms and pushed to his feet with ease, not jostling me in the slightest. Folding into his warmth, I buried my head against his neck as his steps crossed over broken pieces of the furniture and door, the wood crunching beneath his weight.

Lucius appeared in the doorway and I felt Theo's chest puff out from beneath me. "Get out of my sight right now if you want to keep your heart in your chest, unlike Olivander."

He'd...ripped the heart out of that drackya?

"Understood, sir. I'll clean up the mess."

I was thankful they didn't clash and that Lucius stepped to the side quickly. My mind couldn't handle any more panic and fear, and despite how little I knew of Lucius, I didn't want to see him harmed, especially not for my sake.

Theo's long strides had us in his chambers within a minute, and instantly, I felt my muscles loosen at the comfort I felt within the space. I *shouldn't* have felt that way, considering how little time I'd spent here and with Theo in general, but he'd just proven that I could trust him. That I could depend on him, even if it was just for my safety.

"Hold on, beauty," he murmured as he placed me onto the bed gently. I fought my instinct to keep my grip on him, instead loosening my arms as my shoulders curled slightly inward. My eyes locked in on his form as he crossed the room to stoke the low-burning fire in the fireplace, adding fresh wood until it roared to life once more.

Reaching blindly, I grabbed the blankets, pulling them up to my chin before dragging my knees up to my chest and resting my head atop them. When Theo turned back around, my lips parted in surprise at the sight of the massive red mark on his right cheek.

I'd done that. Fuck.

"I'm so sorry," I began as he grabbed the half-drunk bottle of liquor from earlier and crossed to the bed.

He sat on the edge near me and offered the bottle to me. "Take a drink. If you broke the bones in your hand from that punch, I need to set your bones, and it's going to hurt."

I swallowed hard at the thought and brought my mangled hand up, wincing at the sight of it in the light. Punching Theo had been like smashing my fist into the stone wall, and it finally set in just how weak I was against the drackya, despite all of my years of training with Brenson.

"I want you to train me when we have down time," I whispered, dragging my gaze from my crooked fingers up to his face. "I want to learn to fight against you. If you're the strongest, I want to face you."

I swore something akin to a purr rumbled through the room, and his dragon eye sparked. "My beast would love nothing more."

He held the bottle out once more, but as my fingers wrapped around it, he didn't let go. "For the record, wench, I'm not sorry you punched me. Your instincts did what was needed, and I won't ever care if I'm caught in the crosshairs. Always choose yourself."

The last time I was in this room with Theo, my heart had hardened toward him, icing over like a pond in the peak of winter. This time, something about his words warmed my heart, thawing it in my chest and leaving me with a feeling of gratitude toward the drackya that I hadn't imagined possible. The letter from my father came to mind as the thoughts took me down a rabbit hole.

"You seem to have my best interest at heart," I muttered, snagging the bottle and taking a healthy swig. "Even if your way of showing it is demented as fuck at times."

His chuckling response floated through the air, making my toes curl as I soaked in his grin. Motioning for me to take another sip, he gently took my wounded hand within his large ones and gingerly inspected it.

I winced and downed more of the bourbon, praying to the elementals that it began to at least slightly numb my senses, and quickly.

"I need to set two of them," he explained and I took a deep breath, nodding in answer.

My entire body seized up in preparation.

"I need you to relax, or this will be a hundred times worse," he warned, sensing my fear. "Tell me about the loved ones you wanted to say goodbye to. The woman who was fighting the guards to get to you seemed to love you fiercely."

The thought of Tillie had my body instantly easing and a smile taking up residence on my face. I missed her, despite it only being a couple days since I'd been so unceremoniously ripped away from her and the rest of my life in Andrathya. We'd never gone so long apart from one another.

"She's my cousin, but truly, I consider her a sister," I began.

Snap.

It was like a bolt of lightning flashed through my finger before a pulsating pain set in after. My throat constricted, a strangled cry catching in it. My breath froze in my chest as the pain radiated from my finger outward, arching up my arm. If I didn't already know how it would go, my gut reaction might have been to punch Theo.

"She seemed like she wanted to kill me when I caught her gaze," he offered, distracting me once more as his fingers moved deftly to the other broken one on my hand.

It was harder to stay relaxed this time, knowing that he would do it unexpectedly and now understanding the severity of the pain following the setting.

I focused back on Tillie, letting my love for her fill my chest. "She isn't interested in combat like I am, but there's a tenacity and fire to her that would ensure she found a way to put you in the ground."

"Then it's a good thing you'll be returning to her, for my sake, right?" he joked, but somehow the reminder that I would one day leave here and return to the castle I was raised in made silence settle between us.

"Yeah," I muttered, raising my brows. "Things will definitely be easier for you when I'm not around."

Snap.

This time I couldn't hold back my single shriek of pain. I rocked back and forth on the bed, cradling my hand to my chest now that he was done.

"For the record, wench," he said, drawing my focus to those haunting eyes that seemed to want to devour me, "easier isn't always better, I'm coming to find out."

I wasn't sure what to say back to that, feeling like every conversation we had gave me severe whiplash. The only thing I knew with certainty after tonight was that I could trust him to protect me until I went home, and maybe that just had to be enough for now.

It seemed he was content to also remain in silence, and eventually we both laid in bed, facing opposite ways. It was insane just how differently I felt laying next to him now. I wasn't cursing him out in my head, furious for being here at the behest of men who hadn't considered my wants or needs.

This time, all I felt was gratitude.

As the fireplace crackled and popped, radiating growing heat as it ate away at the wood, I swallowed my pride. "Theo?"

His voice was thick with the haze of sleep, his tone huskier than usual as he asked, "Yes, wench?"

I didn't hesitate, knowing I owed him so much more than these words. "Thank you for saving me."

This time his voice was clear and rang through the air with certainty.

"I told you that you're mine to protect."

Despite everything in me that should be terrified after being ambushed in my chambers, his words allowed me to close my eyes and not fear for my life, drifting to sleep.

Chapter Fifteen
SIYANA

"YOU KNOW, I'm a little tired of you acting like it was entirely my fault that you almost died. You were the reason our journey lasted so long, thinking you were proving a point by getting off your horse continually."

I ripped a piece of the cold jerky off to chew on as Theo checked through the supply packs that Lucius dropped off at some point during the night. There had been a new set of clothes for me that was better suited for our journey, consisting of thick, fur-lined pants and a matching vest and coat to wear over a tunic Theo lent me. The look was completed with new leather boots. I'd wondered how the sizing on all of the items had been so perfect, and then promptly felt a bloom of heat pricking my cheeks and chest, remembering that Theo had undressed me from my wet clothes my first night here.

Pausing as I lifted the meat to my lips, I frowned. He had a point. A point that I wasn't going to confirm. I may have trusted him to protect me, but that didn't mean I was going to roll over and be a sweet little princess for him. "I think we should focus on the future and not keep bringing up the past."

I popped the savory, smoky meat into my mouth, chewing as Theo's head swung around, eyes narrowing to pierce me with a glare. A shiver ran through me at the intensity he always seemed to carry around him like armor. I was finding that it didn't strike fear into me, anymore, though. After last night...

The memory of the drackya atop me and the thought of Theo ripping his heart clear from his chest had my stomach souring. While I'd have preferred to never feel that level of fear in my life, something good had come from it. I wasn't sure if I'd call what was brewing between the king and me a friendship, but there was at least a new level of comfortable tolerance between us. Our banter was more friendly and good-natured instead of the pointed, sharp attacks against each other of before.

"You're kidding, right?" he retorted before closing up the packs. "You literally were the one that just brought it up, saying how maybe you wouldn't die on this journey now that I'd thought to get you proper clothing."

I hid my smile behind my hand and finished chewing.

One thing I knew with absolute certainty now was that Theo wasn't my enemy. I couldn't speak for the rest of the drackya, but I knew in my heart that at least this one was okay. Lucius was tentatively on the list as well, but I didn't know him well enough to confirm just yet.

"So, did you say goodbye to your friend?" I asked before hopping off the bed and wrapping the meat back up in its cloth.

He reached out to snatch the food from me, mumbling, "That food is for the journey, yet you're already snacking."

I slammed my heels together, saluting him. "I had to ensure the food wasn't poisoned for His Majesty. I'm happy to report it is perfectly safe and quite tasty."

His cold demeanor cracked and he smirked at me, shaking his head and freeing the longer white strands he'd tucked behind his ear in the process.

"Has anyone ever told you that you're a little odd?" he asked before heaving the large packs to the balcony.

Relaxing from my salute, I shrugged my shoulders and thought about it. "Nope, but there are only two people in my life who would ever know I was anything other than a perfect princess."

Glancing back at me, he countered, "Make that three now."

It was a simple statement, but it hit me square in the chest that he was right. Tillie and Brenson were the only people who knew me–the real me–for the entirety of my life, up until now. In my efforts to be the opposite of the perfect little wife, I'd simply just shown Theo the real me.

I nibbled on my bottom lip, unsure of whether I liked that fact.

"Anyways, what friend would I say goodbye to?" he asked in confusion, making my mouth part and my brow pinch.

"Uhm, Lucius, obviously?" My voice was tinged with disbelief. How could he not know who I meant?

A rumble sounded as he seemed to ponder my words, his brows slanted, and his eyes fell to the floor. Wow, he really had no idea.

"I suppose he'd be the closest thing I have to a friend," he offered tentatively before looking at me once more. "I don't think I've ever had a friendship like you have, though. Lucius and I wouldn't fight to say goodbye as you and Tillie did."

I groaned and rolled my eyes while crossing my arms against my chest. "You're kidding, right? Lucius has continually shown up to help you and me in the short time I've been here. Maybe you guys don't exchange lovey-dovey words, lamenting your friendship, but actions *do* speak louder than words, Theo."

His nose did an adorable scrunch as his head reared back slightly. "I mean, he does call me brother a lot, I guess?"

My chest expanded as I took a deep breath and slapped my hand across my forehead, rubbing at the skin there. "You're so clueless, Theo, it's actually crazy. Not everyone in the world is out to get you, despite what your upbringing has conditioned you to believe. It's okay to let people in when they've proven their loyalty."

He hummed as his hand came up to rub at his jaw. "Who is the other person in your life besides Tillie?"

"Don't think I don't see what you're doing, changing the subject off of yourself," I stated, pursing my lips. "But to answer your question, the other person is named Brenson. We grew up together, and he was the only one willing to teach me how to use a sword and train me. He's one of the commanders in our army now."

Instantly, Theo's dragon surged to the surface, his pulsating blue eye locked onto me. The veins in his neck and forehead bulged and his fist clenched at his side making my core tighten. "And this man...is one you were fighting me to say goodbye to before we left?"

Was he...jealous? No, that wasn't not possible. The drackya had literally denied my attempt to kiss him yesterday, as much as I tried to black out the memory from my mind. A part of me was relieved when I thought about it, because I had been heavily under the influence and not thinking clearly. If I was being entirely honest with myself, his words at the time weren't completely wrong, despite the callous way he'd said them. It did hurt to be rejected so completely, as if I wasn't good enough to be his dragon's mate, even if I didn't want that. At all.

I turned to grab my heavy coat from the bed as I answered, "Yes, I guess you could consider him my Lucius. He's shown up again and again to help me, and he's like family. He's the one who gave me the cut on my arm you asked about."

As I tugged the coat on, I jumped with the answering

growl to my admission. After pushing my hands through the sleeves and fastening the buttons down the front, I turned on the heel of my boot to see what had ruffled the dragon's proverbial feathers.

I found Theo pacing back and forth on the balcony with his hands clasped behind his back. "He hurt you, yet you still care for him? Why?"

It had never been as clear to me as it was now, how little Theo knew about love and friendships. It actually made me feel a sense of sadness for him.

"Calm down," I breathed out as I approached the prickly king. "It happened during a sparring match when I wasn't paying attention. He didn't wound me with the intention of making me suffer. It was my own fault."

His pacing came to a stop with my words, but as his eyes trailed up my body before landing on my face, I shivered from the wrath exuding from his tense frame and calculating eyes. "I'd like to meet this Brenson one day."

Men.

"Alright dragon boy, let's get going," I said, clapping my hands together with a bit of excitement. Now that I wasn't pissed at him anymore, my joy was palpable.

It was time to ride a dragon.

His lips thinned as they turned down in a frown and he regarded me with disgust. "I am not a boy. Stop calling me that."

I couldn't help but wink at him. "As soon as you stop calling me a wench."

He had nothing to say back to that, so for now it seemed that we'd just be a dragon boy and his wench.

Well, not *his* wench, just a wench.

Theo began to remove his tunic and I quickly averted my gaze, giving him privacy despite the urge to peek. I focused on the room, wondering if I'd ever return here.

"Are you sure you'll be able to get this saddle and the packs onto me?" he questioned for the umpteenth time and I bristled.

"Theo, I'm far more capable than you think! I can do this."

Those were officially my famous last words. An hour later, I stood at the front feet of the massive silver beast who was stomping around in annoyance, it seemed. I could hardly imagine how much more insignificant and small I'd feel around a full-blooded dragon, considering the drackya were slightly smaller.

As it was, I barely came up to the bottom of his knee.

So it seemed that I may have underestimated his height and my ability to climb him while carrying the heavy saddle at the same time. The only help I had to propel me up the steep slope from his tail to his rump was from the protruding, gleaming silver spikes that ran down his spine to the tip of his tail.

"Stop looking at me like that! And stop all of your stomping while you're at it!" I yelled, dropping the saddle to the ground as my arms shook from the exertion of hefting it for the past hour. "I'm trying my best here,

167

and you're not making it any easier with your little temper tantrums."

A slitted tongue snaked out of his large mouth in my direction, and I glared. This wasn't what I pictured at all when I'd thought of what it might feel like to stand at the foot of a dragon while I'd been sparring with Brenson. I thought it would involve a lot more fear and a whole lot less silent bullying from the beast in question as it lost its patience with me.

"Did you just stick your tongue out at me?" I asked, popping my hip out as I placed my hand on it.

I felt him prodding at my mind and I let my walls down to allow him access. Lowering my mental walls while still at the drackya's castle wasn't ideal, but how else could he speak to me in this form if not in my mind? He'd yet to try to do this the entire hour I'd been struggling, so I'd been left to simply yell at him and try to interpret his movements and sass.

"Are you giving up, wench?"

I threw my hands in the air. "If you would just stretch your back legs out more, I could make the climb up your tail with the saddle, but it's too steep to not use both hands to hold onto your spikes as is. I already told you this!"

A large huff of air came from the dragon, quickly becoming a steam cloud that blew around me.

"Don't give me that attitude. I swear you're trying to make me fail on purpose."

A rumble came from the dragon then, his large body shaking with his apparent mirth.

"Did you just laugh at me?" I asked in shock, staring up into the eye I had grown used to seeing in his human form, the scar that marred his face apparent in the rough skin around the eye in this form as well.

"Well, it has been amusing to watch you slip and fall onto your ass so many times in a row. As I seem to recall, you don't like being in saddles, anyways."

I gave him my best unamused look before walking right up to his large head with both hands on my hips. "Can we consider us even now, about me not staying in the horse's saddle? I promise to stop bringing up how you definitely almost killed me on our journey here."

His large head tilted, and I was painfully aware of how similar the movement was to how he reacted to me in his human form when he considered my words. A rush of wind and snow chose that moment to blow against us, causing me to lose my balance at the gale-force strength of the gusts rolling in. Soon enough, my outfit wouldn't keep me as warm, if the blizzard that seemed to be roiling to life in the clouds kept up.

I threw my hands out to balance myself but found myself hitting a warm, scaled foot that moved to stop my fall.

A heavy sigh of exhaustion fell from me as I pushed off of his foot.

"Thanks."

"Pick up the saddle and climb up. I will lower

myself further onto the ground, just steer clear for a moment while I move."

Relief poured through me as I grabbed the leather saddle and stepped back. His muscles bunched as he first lowered his front half onto the ground before plopping down on his backside. The large tail curled around him until the tip pointed directly at me. I squinted through the snow and nodded as the path I needed to take seemed much more manageable now.

Quickly I ambled up the flat part of his tail, hauling the saddle in one arm while using my hip to carry the brunt of its weight, considering my other hand was still tender from the bones Theo had set the night before. As I started my ascent up the back, I slowed my pace and took calculated, sure steps to ensure I didn't slip as I moved higher. Without needing any of the spikes' assistance now, I made it up rather quickly, beaming with pride as my feet finally met the larger scales of his back.

"I did it!"

"You remember the instructions from the saddler for where to hook it in?"

"Yes, dragon boy. I read it over until I had the directions memorized."

Keeping to the flatter stretch of scales around the spikes along his spine, I made my way across his back to where his saddle was sized to fit in front of his shoulders. I saw the smooth area the saddler had mentioned and rushed to drop the saddle down. My shoulders and biceps ached from how long I'd been lugging it around, and I was happy to be rid of it.

The saddle fit in place perfectly, with the pommel sitting just behind a large scale that curved upward. It would apparently protect me from the wind coming directly at me if we had to fight against the gusts. Anything strong from the sides, though, and I'd have to hope that the leg straps would stay in place and my hands wouldn't slip from the pommel.

Yanking the long straps that were rolled up and fastened to the edge of the saddle, I slid on my butt to get down to the top of his shoulder where the saddler had left a small cut to fit into the correct scale. Fastening the anchor around it, I used the strap to help me climb back up and then moved to the other side. Once those were in place, I had to run back down and grab our supply packs. Tossing those over each shoulder, I was heaving with my attempts to get air into my lungs by the time I reached the saddle and clipped the tops of the bags into the designated area on the back.

"I think we're good to go. The saddle is anchored in and our supplies are fastened."

I wasn't sure if he'd fallen asleep while waiting for me, but he startled at my words and lifted his head from where he'd been resting. Craning it around to look at me out of the side of his eye, he nodded after a few moments of glancing over my work.

"Get in the saddle and let me know when you're strapped in."

Lowering myself into the seat, a thrill ran through me. I strapped my feet into the boot-like areas and fastened them all the way up to my knees. Supposedly these would keep me in place if we had to roll upside down and I lost my handle on the saddle, but I wasn't too keen to test them out. I moved on to the lap belt that looped around from the back of the saddle and to just below the pommel.

"All set!"

"Siyana?" he questioned in a serious tone that had my smile faltering.

"Yes, Theo?"

"Do not ever tell anyone I let you ride me."

I cackled at that. *"Oh, I'm going to tell everyone. All my friends will be—"*

He cut me off, his words thick with dry sarcasm, **"All two friends? Don't act like you're so popular all of a sudden."**

Before I could retort that I at least had more friends than him, he suddenly launched us into the air. I scrambled to get a grip on the pommel with my one good hand as gravity hit me like a brick wall, wanting to force me back down to the balcony.

The wind whipped my hair back, and tears pooled in my eyes before being quickly whipped away in the wind as I squinted. My calves were pressed tightly into him, and I swore a layer of skin on my face was being peeled away from the force of our ascent.

Then suddenly we were floating and my body loosened up instantly. Opening my eyes fully, I craned my head around in every direction, taking in as much as I could through the blizzard. From this vantage point, I could barely make out a cluster of buildings just on the other edge of the field I'd passed out in that first night. That had to be where the other drackya lived. I couldn't count the number of buildings from this height and with the snow blinding me, but from the sprawling around was easily twice the amount of land that the castle took up.

Theo's wings flapped as we glided through the air with ease, banking to the right as the mountain his castle was etched into came closer.

"We're going to travel along the mountainside before taking a steep trip up. I'm going to keep you down here where you can breathe a bit easier for as long as I can, and I'll warn you before we have to make the quick ascent into the alcoves."

I nodded as if he could see me, too busy committing this moment to my memory, hoping I'd never forget the feel of such weightlessness and the sense of being one with the sky.

"It's beautiful."

"Yes, it is."

My cheeks heated, and it wasn't from the frigid temperatures biting at my skin.

Chapter Sixteen

SIYANA

By the time we made it into the alcove, my face and hands were practically numb from the cold. At this elevation and nearness to the ocean, the temperatures were far colder than anything I'd experienced up to this point in my life. However, there was something soothing about hearing the waves crashing against the jagged mountainside, as long as I didn't picture falling out of our alcove and down into the icy depths waiting for me at the bottom.

"Lay my clothes out for me, please, I'm going to shift back."

I'd just finished unhooking the saddle and bringing it off him, which was made incredibly difficult with how stiff my joints were. Fumbling through the bags, I tugged out what appeared to be trousers and a tunic. Turning over my shoulder with them in hand, I yelped at the sight of Theo—naked.

For some reason, my instinct was to throw the clothes at him and slap my hands over my eyes.

"I told you I was going to shift back, wench," he said, amusement rich in his tone.

"I thought you were going to wait until after I had the clothes out for you!" I exclaimed in defense, as if I'd been caught red-handed doing something wrong.

I heard the rustling of his clothing and spread my fingers ever so slightly to peek through. Just to see if he was done, of course. While I'd seen his stunning physique on display, with his naked torso and the curve of his muscled ass, what I hadn't seen prior was the gift between his legs. His fingers quickly tied the trousers in place and I dropped my hands, feeling comfortable with the remainder of his nudity.

Whoever his mate was wouldn't be disappointed in that department, to say the least.

"Your kind cares far too much about modesty," he rumbled before tugging his tunic over his head and tucking it into his pants. "Have you never gazed upon a man's nude body before?"

It felt like a loaded question, but considering I didn't need to worry about presenting myself as a wholesome princess my father had likely painted me as in the letters I hadn't seen, I answered honestly. "If you're asking if I've seen a cock before, the answer is yes. I just felt wrong glancing at you without permission. I'm not without manners."

His jaw ticked with my answer, and he brushed past

me without a word as he moved to our supply packs. I watched with my arms crossed against my chest as he lugged them onto his shoulders before grabbing the saddle.

"Let's go," he demanded, somewhat harshly, "this alcove has a tunnel that leads into a more enclosed space that should better protect you from the temperatures. Alstrid gathered supplies for us to be able to build a fire within."

It felt like such a startling change of conversation that I just stared at his retreating back as he walked down the small crack that led into the mountainside. I'd somehow missed it entirely upon my first inspection.

Pulling my hands to my mouth, I attempted to warm them up with my breath as I followed him into the mountain. Darkness swallowed me whole, and I was forced to place a hand on the rock wall to guide me the further in I went. The chill of the rock seeped into my fingers, stealing the little warmth I had managed to breathe into them.

"Theo?"

When he didn't answer, panic quickly rose up within me as I had a flashback of my dark room as the strange drackya's eyes stared at me. My throat constricted and my knees trembled.

"Theo?" I called out, louder this time, unable to hide the quiver in my voice.

A warm hand touched my own that rested on the wall, and I startled, feeling on edge.

"Sorry, wench, it's easy for me to forget that you don't have the same eyesight as me," he admitted from the dark void in front of me before his eyes sparked with his magic, illuminating the space enough to see a small outline of his face.

Still feeling a little rattled, I cleared my throat and wrapped my arms around myself. "It's okay. Can you guide me, though?"

"Of course, give me your good hand."

I offered it, and the second his fingers wrapped around it, my nerves settled and the knot in my chest loosened.

"I should have gotten you gloves as well," he breathed out with a hint of frustration biting at his words. "I'm sorry. I keep managing to fuck up. We will get you warmed up in the hot springs within the mountain. The ley line runs through it, bringing warmth to the mountain for the water undine to exist comfortably despite the cold the ice undine require."

The thought had me practically on top of him as he guided me through the tunnel, an eagerness to submerge myself within the hot water overwhelming me.

Soon enough, the tunnel opened up in a large cave that had a massive fire roaring within it in the corner. The fire itself was nothing more than a heap of uneven logs and odd kindling, but it did the trick, chasing away the worst of the chill in the air.

As soon as my eyes adjusted, I dropped Theo's hand and helped take a pack from his shoulder. We made quick work of setting up an area to sleep with the blankets we'd brought and the brush that the dragon who'd been communicating with Theo had left for us. It wouldn't be wildly comfortable, sleeping atop tree branches, but if it meant we were safe for now, it would have to do.

When he finally seemed satisfied with our bed, I was practically prancing around in excitement. Giddiness poured through me as I asked, "Can we go to the springs now?"

While it was warmer here than in our initial landing spot, I felt like my bones themselves had been frozen during our journey, and I was thawing as fast as a glacier.

The fire reflected from the scales on his cheeks as they pulled up with his smile. "Yes, wench, we can go. I need to lay some ground rules for the duration of our stay here first, though."

He held a finger up. "First, you don't leave this cave without me. There's a massive tunnel system here that the dragons frequent. Any other time of the year it would be dangerous, but right now, it would be lethal if you ran into any of the nesting mates. This is when their young will start to hatch, and their territorial instincts are immense."

I nodded, completely understanding the rule. However, my mind wandered, trying to picture a dragon egg and a baby hatching from it. How big were they? Did they come out with scales?

His voice snapped me from the thoughts as he ambled on, holding up a second finger. "Second, keep your mental barrier up at all times. You haven't yet trained in mindspeak and don't know how to keep the connection open to only me. Lucius heard you yelling for me last night with your projection."

So that was why he showed up when he did. I grimaced. I really owed him an apology with how often I seemed to put him in danger.

"It's okay," Theo stated, "no human is ever trained until they have a mate bond established. It makes it far easier to feel the connection between their dragon and them and to use it as a base to work with."

A third finger popped up. "Rule three. If you break rules number one and two, don't blame me for your death."

My jaw dropped and I spluttered, "Theo! That is not funny."

He shrugged. "I beg to differ. With your track record, I felt it pertinent. Let's get going. I doubt the fire has warmed you up too much yet."

He held out his hand and I quickly took it, following him down a large tunnel connected to our temporary new home. It was definitely big enough for Theo's dragon to fit in, so I had no doubt this was the path that the elder dragon had come to bring us the few supplies he'd left.

"How many dragons live here?" I asked, shocked at the way my voice echoed in this area. I lowered my voice instantly. "And do they ever come down to mingle with the drackya?"

Our footsteps were the only sound for a bit as I awaited his response.

Finally, he said, "It continues to shock me, how little we know of each other's world, when before I was born, our people coexisted. The curse truly had its intended impact, separating us."

When he worded it that way, a tinge of sadness crept up within me, which was odd. I'd always struggled to picture how the cohesion of our worlds had ever occurred, but after spending some time with Theo, I was beginning to see glimpses of it.

"Let's wait to continue this conversation until we're in the springs. I don't want our voices to startle any unsuspecting dragons, despite Alstrid alerting them to my visit," he explained, leading me down a new direction as the tunnel curved.

The scent of salt and ash hit me as a draft of wind swept down toward us.

We walked in comfortable silence for a bit, and as the sound of rushing water grew, so did my excitement alongside it. I felt the ground beneath us slowly slope down, and the air grew thicker and warmer as we descended.

"All of the water undine have been barred from using the springs until we are done, and the ice undine would never come down here," he announced, dropping my hand as we drew closer to the pools of water. They were illuminated from the smallest crack above them that let a stream of light into the cavern.

I came to a stop, suddenly feeling horrible that the dragons had been prohibited from using their own territory because of me. "Maybe we should go back to our cave. I don't need to be here. This is their home and I'm intruding."

His head whipped around quickly, eyes narrowing on me. He took slow, calculated steps toward me as he clasped his hand behind his back. "Careful, wench, that almost sounds like your heart is softening toward our kind."

I opened my mouth to say I still saw the dragons as separate from the drackya, considering they weren't the ones who had kidnapped our citizens and killed them, but he took me by surprise as his hand lifted to run his fingers along my cheek.

"Besides, I think you forget that I am their king," he rumbled, dropping his hand to my neck, "and therefore, you are their queen."

My mouth was suddenly dry, but I forced out the words rolling around in my mind, "Until you divorce me."

The moment was shattered, and his hand dropped as if my skin burned him.

"Get in the water, wench," he murmured. "I'll wait nearby but give you your privacy."

His footsteps echoed until they slowly faded away and I could no longer see him. Feeling crestfallen, I stepped closer to the pools as I considered the odd crossroads Theo and I seemed to find ourselves constantly at, in regards to our marriage and the undeniable draw that we clearly both felt. I could deny it all I wanted, but that didn't make our draw any less true.

After it had finally clicked in my brain that he wasn't my enemy, I was beginning to see that all the reasons we clashed so much were because of our similarities. We were both too stubborn for our own good, guarded, and didn't want to bow to anyone.

I mulled that over as I stripped free from my restrictive clothing, shivering as I quickly made my way down to the rocky, natural steps that led into the spring. My eyes searched the area, curious as to where Theo was waiting and wondering if he was truly giving me privacy or if he was watching me still.

My nipples pebbled at the thought of him seeing me, but the feeling was also accompanied by a hefty dose of uncertainty. Would he even like my body if he was watching?

A hiss came from me as my foot met the water, and I jerked it back. I wasn't sure if the water was truly that scalding, or if it was the severe cold biting at my extremities. Slowly, I allowed myself to adjust and waded into the water inch by inch until my hair pooled around my shoulders, floating around me like inky tendrils in the warm water.

My muscles loosened as I glided through the water and a soft moan came from me at the relief I felt. The remainder of the chill I'd been feeling on my nose and cheeks began to fade as the steam billowed around me. I dropped my head back, letting the rest of my hair soak before running my hands through it. There was a silky softness to it, and I wondered what minerals were present in the springs.

As I allowed myself to truly look around, I noticed the most subtle, light-blue streaks etched into the ceiling. They seemed to pulsate with energy and my mouth fell open in wonder. Was this the ley line, visible to the eye?

As my feet landed back on the smooth rock bottom, I scanned the depths of the water, looking for more evidence of the magic, considering Theo told me it ran through the springs. But as I looked around, I caught the briefest glint of silver scales and Theo's dragon eye in a shadowed recess.

He'd been watching me, openly.

I found it didn't actually bother me at all that he'd broken his word to give me my privacy.

Was it possible that neither of us actually found the other disgusting after all?

Chapter Seventeen

THEO

FUCK, my little wench was really testing my restraint. More so, she was testing the hold I had on my dragon. The line between my logical human brain and the feral need of the animal within me was becoming precariously thin with Siyana in my life.

I hated to admit just how quickly she'd infiltrated my mind, especially when I had to accept that she never chose this life for herself. I'd forced her to be by my side, and that would never equate to finding my true mate.

My taloned hands curled into fists, ripping into my skin in a desperate attempt to ground myself with the pain. I wanted to give into the pleasure that threatened to drag me under from the sight of the supple curves of her body glistening in the water.

Perhaps I was taking advantage of knowing she had deplorable vision within the cave, unlike myself. Curiosity had won over to see what she was doing, though, and as I saw her body floating within the gently bubbling water, I'd attempted to avert my gaze. For all of five seconds.

I shouldn't have stared for as long as I had, but the swell of her breasts and tanned nipples pointing toward the ceiling had been too tantalizing to ignore. I'd told her I'd remain near, and she knew of my excellent sight.

Had she truly taken me at my word to give her privacy? Perhaps it made me a brute to disregard the promise, but then again, I'd already told her I was her brute.

As her body suddenly shifted and was submerged as she stood, her head snapped in the exact direction I'd come to sulk in, wondering if she'd go home and marry this Brenson she seemed so fond of when I dissolved our marriage contract.

I slammed my eyes closed, knowing there was no way I could contain my dragon from sparking the magic that danced within my eye, giving away my position in the depths of shadows. The beast was here to stay, at least until I could find a way to release this pent-up energy rolling through me like a midwinter storm.

Hopefully she would glance away, considering whatever drew her eye a fluke, and I could resume my perusal.

A few minutes passed before I dared to open my human eye. Instantly, my hardened cock—that I had tried to calm down with a few deep breathing exercises in the last few minutes—was back and harder than I'd ever experienced. A groan escaped me at the sight that awaited my hungry eyes.

Her hands cupped her breasts as water droplets rolled down the swell of them. My mouth went suddenly dry as her fingers tightened around her nipples and twisted them between her fingertips. Her eyes remained trained on the exact spot I still occupied. Slowly, she waded back until she bumped against the rocky steps normally used to exit the water. Instead of turning and walking out, she dropped her hands and slowly lowered herself to lay back against them, lifting her feet to rest on the lowest step.

I swore she winked as she spread those sinfully long legs and watched me from between them.

*Was she...*I shook my head, trying to clear the thought. No, she wasn't doing this for me. *Right?*

One of her hands snaked down from her breasts, trailing a finger down her abdomen to nestle within the center of her pussy. Slowly, she made circles around her clit and her head tilted back as her legs opened even further, giving me a look at the glistening center I wanted to bury my tongue in. A soft, needy moan echoed through the cavern, and I swore it was instantly and permanently etched in my memory. It was the most spellbinding sound I'd ever heard, and I never wanted it to end.

As her head tilted back up, allowing her to gaze at me once more, I found that I could no longer keep my other eye closed. I wanted to see every minuscule detail that she was offering me with my dragon's superior vision. Her fingers delved inside of her, setting a pace I took note of, before her other hand came down to resume the swirls of pressure from the pads of her fingers on her clit.

Pain pulsed through my cock with the need to release within her. To breed her and mark her as mine, so that no other dragon or drackya would ever question who she belonged to. I wanted her so full of my seed that it slowly dripped down those pretty thighs as she walked next to me, reminding her that my cock would be the only one she ever needed to satisfy her.

She wouldn't need Brenson's or whoever's cock she'd claimed to see before.

I watched as her body tightened and her head dropped back again, her cries of pleasure growing in volume and quickening.

I wanted to wrap those legs around my shoulders and learn every inch of her pussy until she was trembling, realizing that I could give her everything she needed. She needn't satisfy herself.

She'd see that not only could I protect and provide for her as a mate, but that I could devour her.

My feet began to move on their own accord. I could go down there now and prove it...*No.* I forced myself to still.

My lips parted and a growl rumbled through my chest as my beast suddenly surged to the surface, detesting the restraint that I only barely held onto. My bones begin to shift, cracks and pops sounding as I felt the demand to give in to the dragon.

"Run," I groaned quietly through the haze of futile resistance.

I couldn't possibly protect her from what was coming. I should have recognized the surging possessive need to not only devour her, but dominate her. I'd been too lost in the shock of seeing her openly tempt me to recognize the direness of the situation.

She had no idea the danger she was tempting.

My dragon was determined to claim her, right here and now, by initiating the bond. She'd reciprocate or she'd die. My beast was too prideful to let her leave and find a different mate.

She was *mine*.

Just as I lost myself to my primal urges, her cries of pleasure reached a crescendo and I watched as she relaxed, pulling her hands from her pussy as it spasmed.

A roar shook the cavern as I leapt into the open air before I could destroy my nook of the cavern with the shift. My wings snapped open, carrying me with ease to the springs. Despite the heat licking at my scales and making them shift with disgust of the steam billowing around them, I was focused on the way her face shifted from one of pleasure and shock to horror as I drew closer.

My wife.

My mate.

She was waiting for me.

As my large feet landed in the water, spraying her, she tried to push herself up the steps and away from me. Her mouth and eyes were wide as I watched the rapid rise and fall of her chest.

"Theo?" she called out, her voice shaking as she did.

My name on her lips instantly earned a rumble of approval as I lowered my snout to her chest. I inhaled the scent of her arousal and felt the wild stir within my chest to begin the bonding.

A blazing blue tether appeared within my mind, and I pictured it reaching out to meet her own.

I saw the moment she felt it as she gasped and gently lifted her hands to settle against my snout. Her voice was barely a whisper as she leaned her forehead to rest against the smaller scales there, "I don't understand what I'm supposed to do. I thought you said I couldn't be your mate."

I felt her mental walls lower despite me telling her to keep them firmly in place while here. I instantly surged into her mind regardless, not caring who in the moment might hear our exchange.

"I was an idiot for saying that. You're mine."

She pulled back to gaze up at me, and a look of fear sparked within her dark blue depths. "But if I'm not your mate...I..." she trailed off, glancing away as if it was too hard to get the words out. "I don't want to die."

Hearing her soft, broken words spoken aloud broke through the mating fog clouding my mind for a brief moment.

How could I force this on her right now? What was I doing?

Her fear was palpable and spoke to her not being ready for this type of commitment. She'd reject me and I'd be faced with the immense, near impossible, battle of holding my dragon back from meting out retribution for the emotional wound her choice would inflict.

Any chance of her being my mate would be stripped away. Even if she was mine, truly, if she rejected me now, we'd be fated to forever walk this world separately, unable to attempt the bond again.

Her hands on my snout began to tremble as tears formed in her eyes. "Theo, please tell me what to do. Do I accept it?"

Her words were like an ice spear to my chest, gouging through my scales and through the thickened hide of my skin, all the way to the large heart that beat within.

Every decision I'd made since realizing a soft spot for her had developed within me was to keep her safe and give her a chance at a life in which she was in control once we broke this curse.

If I went through with this, it erased all of that and placed her in direct danger from me.

I had to reign myself in long enough for her to escape.

"Leave, Siyana. Leave this cavern and return to the alcove we landed in. We cannot allow my dragon's urges to put your life needlessly at risk. You belong with someone like Brenson, not me."

I felt her shock reverberate through the mental connection, but it was quickly overcome by a feeling of rejection and pain. Her lips pursed as the tears rolled over her cheeks before they dropped to join with the endless water of the spring.

"Why are you so jealous of Brenson?" she screamed. "He is just a friend! Someone who has only ever supported me and wanted me to achieve my dreams."

I snorted at the implication as the sound of his name on her tongue drove my rage to new heights.

"Jealous of this water that enveloped your body instead of my hands? Yes. Jealous of the tendrils of sunlight that dance along your flesh? Yes. Jealous of the air that enters your lungs, filling you so completely there isn't room for anything else? Yes."

Her pupils constricted and her chest rose with a sharp inhale.

"Jealous of a human? Never. But that is who you belong with, Siyana. Humans."

"Stop fucking with me, Theo," she seethed, pushing herself back and up onto a step. She climbed to her feet and shot me a look that promised retribution. "You keep giving me glimpses into a life where maybe this could be more than a mere contract. That maybe this arrangement could be for more than just the well-being of our people. That it could be about *us*."

Her words should have made it easy to put the beast away. The anger and betrayal she was feeling couldn't have been more clear, but all the diatribe did was cause a renewed surge from the beast within me to show her that

I could be all of those things for her. That we were more than that.

Leave, now.

Her bottom lip was sucked between her teeth before she bit down and shook her head. "The most fucked up part was that I actually let those glimpses convince me that maybe it was worth staying here, to figure it out, when the curse is broken and behind us."

My head jerked forward as a chuff fell from my parted jaw. I managed to pull back before my snout could slam into her and knock her onto her ass to stop her from leaving.

To her credit, she didn't even flinch this time. She simply gazed at me with a bitterness that had my dragon stomping the water, hating that I was causing her to reject us, now, in this moment. Somehow I'd never found her more beautiful, standing firm in the face of a snarling dragon while naked and vulnerable, tucking away the fear she'd felt just moments before.

"You are going to live a very lonely life, Theo," she murmured before turning and giving me her back. "You don't have to be this way, you know."

"This is who I am. Nobody said you had to like it."

A heavy sigh came from her before her shoulders rolled back, pinching her shoulder blades together. "Enjoy the prison of ice you've locked your heart within. I hope you get everything you deserve."

This time her words hurt my soul, not just my

dragon. I'd opened up and shared more with her than anyone. I'd shown her that she was melting away my walls with the fire of her own soul.

Yet it didn't matter. All I needed was for her to leave, now. Yet despite her words claiming she was done–with me, with the situation, with us–her feet remained stuck to the steps of the springs.

Was she waiting for me to deny her words—to fight for her and this bond my beast was still projecting to her?

I had to put her life above the glimmer of hope she'd inspired within me for the first time in my own wretched life—that I wouldn't be stuck alone to bear the weight of my burdens. I'd felt a spark of friendship kindling between us, and despite what I needed to do now, I'd never forget the kindness she'd shown me when her own walls were down.

You confuse me for someone with remorse. Leave.

And just like that, her walls were slammed back into place, sending me flying from her mind as silence descended in its place.

She rushed from the water and quickly grabbed her clothes. I dug my talons into the ground, anchoring myself into the mountain itself to stop me from chasing her.

As her body disappeared from my sight down the path we used to get here, I let out a roar so loud that it shook the stalactites of limestone from the ceiling, making them fall and crash off of my scales and into the bubbling water surrounding me.

Hatred and self-loathing pooled within my mind for how I'd hurt Siyana, and for once, my beast and her were in unison, both making it clear that I'd betrayed them with my choice.

Magic spewed from me as I lost control of the dragon, filling the room with ice instantly. What was once a steaming cavern was now an icy tundra, glittering like the quartz deposits on the ceiling did.

My prison of ice.

Chapter Eighteen

SIYANA

"STUPID FUCKING DRAGON," I muttered as I trailed my hand along the rough wall to try to find my way through the pitch black tunnel system. "Or drackya —whatever."

Why had I even considered reaching back out to him in the bond when I'd felt the tug on my soul? I had known him for mere days, and despite him proving he wasn't just the arrogant, cold king that I'd first met, we were nowhere near that level of commitment. We hadn't even kissed, yet when I'd felt the weightless, floating sensation take over me, like I was somehow going to float away into the sky with him if I only said yes, it'd felt... right. A warmth had enveloped me when I'd thought of accepting the bond, as if the future was wrapping me in a tight embrace, welcoming me.

My lips pursed and I came to a halt, letting the

resounding silence wash over me as I attempted to get my erratic heartbeat under control.

But then he'd told me to leave.

A chill ran down my spine as wind blew through the tunnel, making my wet hair feel like icicles running down my neck and the side of my face.

I'm just as stupid, thinking there was a chance.

As my hand slipped from the wall and curled into a fist at my side, I forced myself to take in a controlled, deep breath. I held it for a few seconds once my lungs had expanded to the point of pain. Blowing out slowly, I tried to picture the negative emotions being expelled alongside the breath.

What's meant for me will be.

I will not fault myself for wanting to find a connection, it's only natural.

Theo did us both a favor by putting a stop to that, considering the possible outcome.

As my lungs emptied, I still felt the raw sting of rejection, but the overwhelming anger was beginning to subside. Logic was beginning to stake a place in my thoughts once more, and I knew that even if by some miraculous chance Theo and I were mates, I wasn't ready for that commitment. Or that connection.

Suddenly, it felt as if the mountain itself was moving as the floor beneath my feet vibrated and the tunnel shook. Small bits of rocks pelted the floor as I heard a deep, menacing roar from not too far away, it seemed. I spun, trying to make out from what direction it was coming, but it was echoing and reverberating through the space around me, making it impossible to pinpoint the exact location.

Fear spiked within me as only darkness stared back at me.

That wasn't my—*no*—that wasn't Theo's dragon.

I'd come to know the sounds he made from our journey here, and there was a distinctly higher pitch to this one.

All I knew was that I needed to get back to our designated alcove, now. I threw my hands out, desperate to feel the wall again, but a sick feeling twisted my gut as I realized I had no idea what direction I needed to go in now, after spinning around.

"Shit," I breathed out, instantly feeling that frantic heartbeat return.

Despite finding the smooth wall with my left hand, I felt no joy in the discovery. Another ear-splitting roar had me throwing caution to the wind and running with my hand against the wall as the ground trembled beneath my feet. The dragon sounded closer this time.

I'd given up on squinting early on in my trek back to our temporary shelter, but I found myself attempting again. I was desperate to see anything that would make it seem like the fire we'd left blazing was anywhere even remotely near to where I was.

My fingers dipped along the seemingly random gouges I could feel growing in number beneath my fingertips. I risked taking a moment to stop and examine the length and depth of them with my hand. I hadn't noticed these along the walls that had led us from our shelter, but it was entirely possible that they were here when Theo had led me through the dark.

I reached up and around the area until I felt like I had a good grasp on the mental image it was producing. The only logical thought I could come up with for them was that dragon scales had rubbed against the walls as they walked through, or that a fight had occurred and a dragon had been slammed into the wall, indenting the rock.

Either way, I was entirely screwed if I ran into a full-blooded dragon, and my already low confidence in my choice of direction was suddenly sinking to zero. It was too late to change course now. I needed to find a defining area and work my way from there. If I turned back now, I could get lost even further into the mountain. Every single bit of it was a risk.

I continued at a brisk pace, and the warmth that had lingered from the spring was beginning to seep out of my body and through the furs I was wrapped in. I may not have been any closer to a fire to stay warm, but after what I thought was around ten minutes of not hearing any dragons, it seemed as if I'd chosen the right direction necessary to survive. I'd at least be safe until I could figure out how to get back.

Would Theo come find me?

The thought alone had my face twisting with the utter annoyance that now bled through me.

No, Sia, you can figure this out. You aren't a damsel in distress.

My shoulders rolled back and I continued on. Eventually, I was rewarded with the faintest golden glow reflecting in the distance. A squeal of joy worked itself out of my mouth, despite my efforts to stay quiet, and I ran toward the light.

Only as I drew closer to it, the floor suddenly dropped with a sharp decline. My foot slipped from under me as I tried to plant my feet into the ground to halt my hurried pace. My tailbone vibrated with shockwaves of pain as I crashed into the ground, slipping down the slope. I scrambled, attempting to grab onto any crevice with my hands, but to no avail.

All too soon I was sprawled on the suddenly flat ground with the breath knocked from my lungs. A groan escaped me as I pushed off the floor with my hands to sit.

Where am I?

My eyes dropped to the padding beneath my hands and my mouth dropped open. An array of moss, leaves, and branches were laid out across the entirety of the floor around me, and as my gaze traveled out further, I suddenly saw why.

I was in a dragon's nest.

Eggs the size of my body were lined up in a semicircle around a blazing fire that showed no signs of going out anytime soon. Warmth radiated from the opposite side of the room from me, emanating from the biggest bonfire I'd ever laid eyes upon. Heat licked at my face as I pushed to my feet and walked closer to the eggs, absolutely mesmerized by the different colors and sizes I could see in the flickering fire light.

Gazing around, I took note that there were ten eggs in total, with the majority ranging in shades of deep blue. However, my feet carried me to the two eggs at the end of the line, furthest from the fire. They were such a light blue that I'd thought them white from far away, but upon closer inspection, they glimmered with ice surrounding the hard shell.

Baby ice dragons.

The thought had the corners of my lips tugging up as I imagined little versions of Theo blasting each other with ice.

I knew I shouldn't be here, and I most definitely shouldn't reach out to touch the eggs, but there was something about the bigger of the two eggs that drew me in. It felt similar to the innate draw my heart had felt when Theo had reached out, offering the bond. I couldn't stop myself from lifting my hand and resting it on top of the egg, the height of which reached my forehead.

Instantly, it began to shake and I gasped as light began to spark from within the egg, reflecting in the most beautiful way with the ice surrounding it. I attempted to lift my hand from it, but found myself stuck. My jaw clenched as I wrapped my free hand around my wrist, trying to use extra force to remove my hand. I dug my feet in and huffed with the force and pain that came with it. It felt as if my skin would tear off if I pulled any harder.

The glow from within began to grow, becoming a blinding white that had me lifting my free hand to block my eyes from it. I squinted, trying to peek through my fingers as a warmth began to spread from my palm and up my arm. I couldn't see anything, but I gritted my teeth as the feeling moved up my shoulder and into my chest, becoming unbearably hot as it grew.

Searing pain etched itself above my right breast and I let out a scream of pain just before the shell exploded around me. I yanked my previously trapped hand away as I stumbled backward, falling onto my ass as the glow began to die down.

As my eyes adjusted back to the fire-lit cavern, I gasped. In place of the egg was a blue baby dragon, sitting on its hind legs with a shimmering blue tail wrapped around its taloned feet. A large, round head tilted my way as their milky-white eyes gazed down at me and a burst of love exploded in my chest.

He was so cute, and somehow I *knew* it was a he.

Tiny ice spikes protruded from the edge of his neck, curving toward his back, and more ran down his spine, sticking straight up.

His mouth opened as he chuffed at me, and the tip of his tail flicked around, as if he was agitated.

"What is it, honey?" I asked, getting the courage to get back on my feet and stand eye-level with my new friend.

Could this baby dragon kill me? Probably, but I could think of a million worse ways to die than being mauled by the cutest creature I'd ever laid eyes upon.

There was still a level of trepidation that had my chest clenching with nerves as I walked closer. He let out another chuff and shoved his head forward as I closed the distance between us. The force knocked me back a few paces, but I laughed as the thick skin between his eyes pulled together, like he was confused as to why I was suddenly away from him.

He pushed off his back feet to stand and wobbled as he took shaky steps toward me. I couldn't help but lift my hands to cover my mouth as awe overcame me. I had seriously witnessed a baby dragon being born and now taking his first step.

As he got to my side, I let out a cheer of encouragement, "You did it, buddy! Great job."

His eyes widened and a purr rumbled from him. Just as I thought my heart couldn't take any more of his adorable personality, he plopped back down onto his butt and leaned against my side, resting his head against the side of mine.

Tears welled in my eyes as I gently tilted my face to rest my cheek against his. Never in my life had I ever experienced such a profound moment, and truly this would be one of those memories I bursted with joy to tell to anyone and everyone who would listen to me.

However, what felt like a sacred moment was broken as the other icy egg began to wobble.

"Oh!" I gasped as my friend pushed back onto his feet and took tentative steps over to his sibling's egg. Cracks began to form, but this time, there was a lack of glowing light or crazy energy radiating toward me. The call I'd experienced as the first dragon hatched was noticeably absent this time.

Slowly, pieces of the egg began to fall off as tiny limbs broke through. Before long, a head burst through the top. It was identical to my little friend's, and as the rest of the shell fell away, I realized that they were actually twins. The only difference between the two was that this new dragon seemed slightly smaller.

A delighted smile lit my face up as the two dragons touched snouts and huffed out air. My friend used his nose to help the smaller one stand, supporting her belly as her hind legs flexed.

My vision became blurry as the tears began to really spring up before slipping down my cheeks. I brought my hands up to brush them away, not wanting to miss a moment of this.

As I moved, though, the smaller dragon's eyes snapped toward me and a warning snarl echoed through the space.

My joy shriveled up at the tiny noise and I immediately took a few steps back as my sense of self-preservation kicked back into gear.

"It's okay," I whispered, holding my hands up. "I'm not going to hurt you. I'll go now."

The small one's jaws opened and a loud trill came

out, as if they were trying to roar but couldn't produce the noise yet. It would have been cute if she didn't follow it up by snapping her jaws in my direction as I continued to slowly retreat.

Shockingly, the bigger one lifted his head from her belly and nipped at her side, as if telling their sibling to knock it off. He turned to look at me and chuffed.

Okay, maybe he wouldn't let his sibling eat me. That was comforting.

Just as I began to let myself breathe and think of life after I escaped the nest, the room shook with the force of a rumbling growl. I was hesitant to give the babies my back, but I had to confirm if the sound was as close as the warning bells in my head were telling me it was.

I turned slowly on my heel, inch by inch, until my eyes landed on the behemoth navy dragon that had their head hanging down into the nest, silver eyes trained directly on me.

Mommy was home.

Chapter Nineteen

SIYANA

"Okay, I know it might look like I'm trying to steal your babies, but I promise I'm just a dumb human that got lost and maybe was a bit too curious when I saw your beautiful eggs." My voice teetered on the edge of panic at the end, my tone hitching higher and higher as I spoke.

For a moment, the mother only blinked at me, unmoving otherwise, and I remembered suddenly from my studies that dragon's could understand humans.

Maybe she was a fan of my self-deprecation?

That hopeful thought was short-lived. Seconds later, she was surging forward into the nest, jaws wide as her eyes sparked with the energy of magic I was growing well accustomed to. I didn't know what magic water dragons were capable of, but I knew it was more than enough to take out one measly human if they so desired.

On instinct, I sank to the ground and wrapped my

arms around my body, tucking my head down as much as I could.

This was it. This was how I died.

For a moment, I contemplated reaching out to Theo to tell him I was going to die and that I forgave him for telling me to leave, for the good of us both. It was strange how looming death could, in the blink of an eye, make one realize how trivial their prior issues were.

Maybe I was too sensitive, or felt too deeply, but I wouldn't change that for the world. What I would work on was listening better, and not hearing what my brain twisted words into—to think before reacting so quickly.

I didn't want him to blame himself for my death, though, so I shut down the idea of calling out to him. I'd made the choices that led me here. Hopefully, he'd never find my remains and he'd think I'd just left Andrathya.

I squeezed my eyes shut and held myself tightly. *Please let this be over quickly.* I didn't want to feel what was certain to be an insurmountable amount of pain.

The ground shook beneath me, and I knew she'd be upon me any moment. My stomach tightened into an iron fist, and I screwed my eyes even more tightly together, unable and unwilling to face the literal jaws of death baring down upon me.

Suddenly, everything was still.

Had it happened so quickly that I truly hadn't felt an ounce of pain? Had I gone to the afterlife so swiftly? Would the elementals see me fit to experience Elysium? Or had my soul been deemed unworthy?

I prepared myself to face the gods, but as I lifted my head and my eyes opened, I was met with the sight of the same nest surrounding me. What was truly shocking, though, was the baby dragon standing in front of me with his wings out, as if shielding me from the mother.

A hiss sounded, and his scales lifted near the ice-ridge down his spine. The dragon I assumed was his mother had a wickedly sharp-tipped tail flicking around, danger-ously close to us. I surged to my feet, barely resisting the sudden urge to get in front of the baby.

She wouldn't hurt him, would she?

I blinked rapidly, confused by the situation, and unsure whether I should get my hopes up about being left alive for the time being.

The baby dragon began to glow again, and once more, the searing pain above my breast appeared. I tugged at my fur coat, opening it and yanking down my tunic, needing to see why I was in pain there.

"What the..." I breathed out, trailing off as I tried to make sense of the mark on my skin.

A light blue circle was etched into my skin, and as I dipped my head to look closer, I could see what was a dragon that seemed to be curling around to almost eat its tail marked above my breast.

My hands flew to my temples as the walls of my mind were attacked and ripped apart with ease. Pain seared behind my eyes and a deep throbbing began throughout my head, leaving me breathless as I struggled to grapple with the pain.

"You are weak and unworthy of being bonded to my offspring."

"What? Bonded?"

My eyes were squeezed shut as I fought through the waves of nausea that began to roll through me in combination with the pain. Somehow, I got the impression that vomiting on the floor of the cave wouldn't endear me to the already infuriated voice in my head.

"Look at me when you are speaking to me, human."

It hit me then that the rich, commanding voice was a dragon. They were speaking to me as Theo did.

A moist snout bumped against my face and I opened my eyes, squinting as the room spun around me from the attack on my mind. Disorientation in the face of a grown dragon was high up on the list of things I didn't want to ever feel again.

On instinct I reached out, placing my hands on the baby dragon who'd bravely stepped in front of me, protecting me with his life. The sides of his face were rough, but much softer than the skin I'd felt on Theo's. It must harden as they age, I reasoned. This certainly wasn't the time to be thinking such things, but my mind couldn't seem to latch on to the fact that I was in imminent danger.

The baby's wings were now tucked at his sides, and he gave his back to the looming threat that was his mother. I didn't like how exposed it left him, guilt gnawing my insides raw at the thought of being the party responsible for any harm that came to him. I stumbled around him as I dropped my hands to my side. Lifting my arms out at my sides to make myself a bigger target, I planted my feet in front of him.

I attempted to reach back out mentally as I'd done with Theo, but was met with a block, so I settled with yelling out, "Will you hurt him for protecting me?"

Her pupils narrowed to slits as she brought a large foot up before slamming it into the ground. I tried not to focus overly much on the way my legs trembled in response to the earth-shaking stomp of her massive, clawed foot. Her talons dug into the ground, the screeching sounds of rock being gouged through stinging my ears.

"Do not insult me. We protect our young with our lives."

I kept my arms up, despite feeling him nudge at them from behind me.

"I'd also give mine up for him," I answered, lifting my chin and trying to muster all the false bravado I could find within myself. "I owe him that, now."

Her large head jerked back and a chuffing sound came from her, over and over, like she was laughing.

"You owe him far more than that, rider. He awoke at your presence, sensing the soul he found worthy of a bond. Your lives are now intertwined."

Her large eyes blinked before her massive head swung down to sniff at me. I'd thought Theo's dragon large, but as she loomed over me, I realized I wasn't even tall enough to reach above her ankle. The undine shifters must have far advanced magical abilities over the full-blooded undine dragons to even stand a chance in a fight.

I tilted my head back to look up into her eyes. "I don't understand. I've not heard of a human in Andrathya bonding to a full-blooded dragon. How did this happen?"

She shifted her nose to the left of me and I watched her long tongue snake out to lick at the baby behind me. Dragon spit bounced off my face and I flinched, waiting to see if it hurt me in some way. When I realized it wouldn't, I barely resisted the urge to wipe it off, disgust filling me. Who knows what had been in her mouth recently. A deer or a bear, perhaps.

I dropped my arms, sensing no animosity from her other than her finding me wholly inadequate. The baby dragon I was supposedly bonded to now wobbled out to stand under her large head. She cleaned him off, seemingly ignoring me for now.

I took the moment to glance around, remembering the tiny spawn that also hated me. Sure enough, the smaller baby was wobbling toward us, seeming weaker than my friend. I moved toward them, wanting to help, but once more, it hissed at me.

"She is angry that she was born early and is weak because of it."

"Was she born early because of me?"

"The connection as twins is strong, and she

didn't want to be without her brother, but now that you are bonded, she will have to be."

Remorse filled me as the smaller twin hobbled by me. I watched as she plopped down under their mother's head, seemingly exhausted from her short trek across the nest.

The mental block I felt in my connection to the mother disappeared before she spoke once more.

"Fret not, they will be able to communicate with each other as we are when they come of age. They just have not developed the skill. It won't matter how far they are from one another."

Guilt gnawed at my heart from stumbling upon the nest and awaking these two babies before they were ready.

"Is there a way to remove the bond? I don't want to rip him from his—"

She snapped her head up as I spoke to her mind, narrowing her eyes on me as her jaws opened, revealing hundreds of sharp teeth. The lead weight of fear dropped in my stomach, threatening to pull me to my knees until I was prostrated in front of the mother dragon.

"Are you saying my offspring isn't good enough for you now?"

My hands snapped up as I reasoned with her.

"No! I just don't know anything about being a rider, as you called me, and I don't want to take him from his family! I feel like this was a mistake."

A whine sounded from my bonded as he turned his white eyes to stare at me, like he could sense my feelings.

"Buddy, I'm sorry," I pleaded, finding myself a lot more comfortable with the big feelings of animals than those of humans. It was only days ago I was considering asking Tillie to stop crying. How far I'd come in such a short time, at least with the upset baby in front of me. "You are worthy of the best human out there. I just don't know how to take care of you."

Here I was, wanting to wrap my arms around this dragon until he made happy trilling sounds again. I'd grown soft.

"His name is Kaida and his sister is Katla. I am Sinda. If I am to guess, you are the new queen?"

Kaida. The name felt right, and as I gazed at my dragon and the sadness radiating from him, I knew I'd never be able to walk away from him. He was mine. And I was his.

I walked over to him and ran my hand along his cheek, loving the way he leaned in to my touch and closed his eyes. "Hi Kaida, my name is Sia. Do you want to figure this out together with me?"

A trill of happiness sounded and I laughed, already shocked at how easy it was to sense his emotions. I wished more than anything that we could speak, but for now, I hoped our bond would allow me to know his needs.

Glancing back at his mother, I nodded.

"Yes, I am the new queen."

She stopped licking Katla and regarded me once more. **"I was bonded to the previous queen. Perhaps you will live up to her and become worthy of Kaida."**

She had to mean Theo's mom, right?

The thought had me reeling with shock, and then it hit me how profound of a loss that must have been, if they were bonded. It had been mere minutes since I had bonded with Kaida's, and already I couldn't imagine the pain of losing him. Nor could I imagine how much worse it must be for the dragon, who would live for centuries without me if I were to die young.

"I'm sorry for your loss."

Her large body settled as she sank to the ground, and instantly Katla got up and wobbled to curl up against her mother's chest. Meanwhile Kaida settled onto the ground next to me. I glanced down as a tickle ran along my ankle and smiled as I found the tip of his tail wrapped around me possessively, or as if he didn't trust me to not leave him.

"Thank you. She was everything I could have asked for in a rider. Regal and beautiful. Strong yet soft. When our souls touched, it was instant, like you and Kaida, it seems. She didn't deserve what that foul king did to her."

I felt the immense sorrow in Sinda's voice, aching at the loss of a woman I'd never met, yet seemed to mean so much to those I was now meeting.

While I didn't want to pry, this could be a chance we

wouldn't get again. I wasn't sure of Theo's knowledge or relationship with Sinda, but I had to try and gain information, anything that could help bring an end to this curse damning the drackya and the women of my kingdom in turns.

"Did she ever tell you of the witch who cursed her husband and all of the drackya? Did she ever mention that she might know how to break it?"

Sinda's chest swelled as her eyes glowed and sparked with magic.

"I don't know, but if I could get my jaws on that witch, I'd tear her apart limb from limb, slowly. Why she had to curse an entire species of drackya instead of just killing the king is something none of us will ever understand."

My shoulders drooped as the excitement of possibly getting some answers fled like a rabbit into the underbrush in the face of a predator.

"But, if you are seeking an answer, you should go to the elementals' domain. They have the power you are looking for."

Dread and pride swirled within me in the strangest combination. On one hand, I was thrilled that perhaps I was on the right track of thought with the elementals, but also, they were sentient beings. I was just a mere human asking for help. They could, and likely would, strike me down for wasting their time. Would the reward ever be worth that big of a risk? Yes, I decided in an instant. Yes, if it saved more women and released Theo from a curse he did not earn yet shouldered the weight of daily.

"I thought the same, but I don't know how to reach them; and if we do, would they even help us?"

Her rumble shook the ground beneath my feet as her head settled down on the ground.

"You would need to cross into the forbidden lands. It is rumored if the gods deem you worthy of entering their world, a portal will appear. If you aren't, they take your life to feed their own energy, in retribution for seeking them out."

Instantly, my dread swelled to new heights, completely snuffing out any ridiculous pride I'd initially felt for my idea.

"You mean Sanctum?"

In the center of Edath, bordering all of the kingdoms, was Sanctum. The territory was a neutral ground claimed by none. I heard tales of many disappearing from each kingdom and never being seen again, but the myths I'd heard were that there were sirens within, calling out to lone travelers and drawing them into the mists that covered the land there.

Perhaps the sirens were truly the gods.

"Yes, now take a seat or lay down. The twins will need to sleep deeply to gain strength after their birth, and you cannot leave until Kaida has awoken."

I glanced down at my dragon and smiled before gently lowering myself to lay next to him. Reaching out, I ran my fingers along his cheek, needing to feel just how real he was as I questioned if this was all a dream and I'd really been killed by his mother.

He purred and tightened his tail around my ankle.

Who would have thought the denial from a drackya would lead me to finding the bond I sought in a full-blooded dragon?

Chapter Twenty

THEO

THE TIPS of my wings scraped against the walls as the tunnel narrowed, but I refused to collapse them, needing to get to my wife as quickly as possible. Maybe I would be forced to give her up at the end of this, but for now, she was mine, and I was the reason she was now in danger.

There was a dragon blocking her mind from being reached, and I didn't know which. Whoever they were, no matter their size or power, I'd have them cowering beneath my wrath if they harmed a single hair on her head.

My warning growl ripped from me and through the tunnels as I followed her scent.

I'd been so obsessed with not allowing my dragon to claim her that I'd sent her right into the jaws of another, but this time it was a full-blood. There would be no hesitation from them, no possibility of her being a mate to them—she was the enemy to them all. Nothing more. Nothing less. She was simply a human encroaching on their territory, despite the announcement that a human queen was here. Without a bond to me, she lacked the scent of a true dragon queen. Any dragon worth their mettle would question her, even if she claimed to be such.

The only thought keeping me sane in my search through the endless tunnels and alcoves was the knowledge that she was alive since I could still sense her mind, even if I couldn't reach out to it. I didn't understand the looping route her scent had led me on, but now that it was growing stronger, I was confident that I'd found the tunnel she'd gone down.

"Alstrid!"

The elder dragon once again didn't answer, likely meaning he was in a deep, restorative sleep. He would be of no use to me, so I did something I swore I'd never do and opened my connection to all of the dragons within the mountains, asserting my dominion as king and forcing myself into their minds.

"All undine dragons, hear me as your king. If you are in the presence of a human woman with tanned skin that has a warmth to it like the sun, bright blue eyes like the peaks of our mountains, and the size of a baby dragon in height, you may not touch her. That is my wife and your queen. If I

find she has been harmed by whoever is shielding her mind from me, I will destroy you."

I didn't make that threat lightly. The trust between dragons and drackya within Andrathya was a tense thing, and it had taken a very long time to come to our current terms of coexistence. Many generations of drackya had passed since the shaky peace had been established, and I bore no excitement over possibly being the king that ended it with my use of power and threats.

I was overwhelmingly hit with responses, some calling me a fool for disturbing them and others swearing they didn't have her. A rumbling growl grew in my throat, frustration tearing through me as viscerally as the guilt that gnawed on my insides. If something were to happen to Siyana before I found her, I alone would be responsible.

A light appeared at the end of my tunnel and hope flared within me. Siyana had to have gone toward the light, hoping to be able to see.

"Calm down, young one."

"Sinda?"

"Yes, I have your human here."

I couldn't help but correct her, *"You mean the queen?"*

Sinda scoffed into my mind. **"She has yet proven to be worthy of such a title, and I don't think I need to remind you that she won't be recognized as queen until you have a bond with her."**

It was because of the bond I knew Sinda had with my mother that I held my tongue at her attitude. She'd never see me as an adult–and likely never would–having been present for my birth and her own lifespan being more than quadruple that of mine.

"Where are you?" I demanded to know.

She didn't need to answer, because a second later I descended into the nest that was covered in Siyana's scent. My eyes instantly closed in on her small, unmoving form curled up next to a newborn ice dragon. They were surrounded by a thick wall of ice. My heart thundered in my chest as my mind swirled with what felt like a thousand questions all at once.

Why was she laying down in a dragon nest? Had she been harmed?

I landed to the side, unable to get as close as I would like when Sinda was taking up the majority of the nest. I wasted no time in shifting back to my human form and running to Siyana's, needing to feel the steady thrum of her heart beat for myself.

As I drew closer, my hand lifted and ready to dismantle the ice wall with my powers, Sinda hissed.

"They are bonded."

My feet faltered, pulling me to an abrupt stop a few feet from Siyana, and I glanced at the towering undine I'd spent much of my childhood with. A replica of the baby near Siyana lay at the chest of Sinda, making me do a double take between them. She'd had a rare set of twins.

"How is that possible? Undine dragons rarely

bond with humans. My mother was the first in hundreds of years, as you well know."

"Do not speak to me in such a tone. Of course I know that. I'm just as shocked as you, if not more so. My Kaida hatched early in her presence. It is not ideal, but it has happened and cannot be reversed now."

My hand dropped to my side as I looked at their sleeping forms from within the ice once more. His tail was curled around her ankle, and it seemed she'd fallen into the quickening with her hand on his cheek.

A surge of jealousy coursed through me from my dragon. Rationally, I knew the bond wasn't the same as what she could be for me, but the thought of another dragon having any claim on her was sending waves of rage through me.

Self-hatred pooled as I remembered this was my fault. I'd felt her fear of the bond but also her tentative hope that it would work, and yet I'd denied her, forcing her from me until I could get a handle on my beast. Now she'd drawn another dragon to her.

"Did you tell her what to expect from the quickening?"

"No. I merely told her to rest next to him and that she wouldn't leave until he woke. It wasn't a lie."

"So you conveniently left out that she wouldn't be leaving because she would fall into a magical hibernation?"

A big gust of air brushed across my body with Sinda's heavy sigh. **"She didn't need to know, and Kaida had already fallen into it!"**

"Humans are fragile, Sinda, or have you forgotten?" I demanded out loud, unable to contain the fury her careless decision stoked within me. I'd already almost lost Siyana once to carelessness such as this. "She needed to feast in advance, so that her body has the reserves to carry her through this! Not to mention the near-freezing temperature she's encased within!"

Sinda surged to her feet, towering over me, yet I didn't flinch, keeping our gazes locked. I stood by every word I said.

"Don't you dare ask me if I know how fragile humans are. My bond to your mother still wasn't enough to save her after your father died. I wonder every day if there was anything else I could have done."

Her words served as a balm to my fears and I dropped my head.

"Young one, I would have prepared her if there had been time, but Kaida initiated almost instantly, and she had to join him. Their scenario is not one I've seen before, but my twins are special. They are seers."

My head jerked back up as I glanced at the dragon who'd chosen my wife.

If that were true, that would make them an unusually powerful pair, with his powers and her claim to her throne. She truly wouldn't need me when our marriage dissipated. All she had to do was return home with her dragon and demand what was rightfully hers.

The thought twisted my stomach into knots. While I knew she could stand on her own without me, I'd never considered that there would be a dragon in place of me to support her.

A cry sounded in my mind as my dragon wailed, feeling the loss of the one he wanted to claim.

"I will watch over them for the duration, if you need to leave."

"No," I quickly said, rejecting the idea. My eyes traced over the rise and fall of Siyana's chest and the way her dark hair pooled around her as if she were suspended in water. "She is mine to care for, still. I will wait here until the quickening is complete, and after that, I will train Kaida to protect her, for when I am not around."

"You plan on leaving your queen?"

Sinda's incredulous tone had me sighing as I prepared for the incoming judgment.

"Save it," I said, lifting a hand up toward her as I continued to gaze at the bonded pair, who were cementing their connection. "It's for her own good."

A blast of water hit the side of my body and I stumbled from the force of it, spluttering as it went up my nose until Sinda saw fit to stop the barrage. I glanced over at her, lips thinned and nostrils flared. "Was that truly necessary?"

"I did it for your own good. How did you not know that?"

I lifted my hand and wiped off the remaining water before squeezing out as much as I could from my hair. "That's not the same thing and you know it. I forced her into this marriage. We will find a way to break the curse, and then she will go back to her life as princess of Andrathya."

Exhaustion crept into my bones as the mental and physical toll of the last few days finally caught up to me. I didn't have it in me to have this argument. Not truly.

"Did you ask her if she wanted to go home?"

"Sinda!" I exclaimed, whirling to face her. "The odds that she is my mate are practically none. I won't risk the wrath of my dragon if a bond doesn't work."

"And if she is your mate?"

My words were sharp, speaking to the pain I felt at the thought, as I countered, "And what if she denies me, still, forgoing our one chance?"

Perhaps I was the one who wouldn't be able to handle her rejection, not my dragon. Maybe what I'd been doing all along was hurting her before she could hurt me with her choice.

Sinda's front leg lifted until her talon knocked me back onto my ass. "Silly boy. You have much to learn about love. Sleep now. I sense your exhaustion. I will watch over you all. Perhaps when you all wake, everyone will have more clarity. And sense."

Sinda was the only dragon I'd entrust to watch over

not only myself, but Siyana as well. I was sending a thank you to the undine god for ensuring this was the nest she stumbled into. The results would have been disastrous had she found herself in any other nest, with any other dragon.

I didn't bother arguing, knowing I'd need my rest as soon as Kaida and Siyana came out of the quickening. Not only would I have my hands full of a sassy, head-strong woman, but I'd also be responsible for a baby dragon that I would need to turn into a battle-ready guardian. No doubt Siyana would treat him like a baby and fight me every step of the way.

As my head lay against the ground and I gazed at the two of them, I couldn't hold back a chuckle. I'd never pictured myself as a parent, but the thought of raising Kaida together, at least for the time being, had a new kind of warmth radiating in my heart. Thinking of him as a child to take on seemed to settle the beast within me.

My eyes closed and I attempted to give myself over to sleep, but I tossed and turned, unable to. Worry for Siyana's well-being in such a state gnawed at my mind. Each quickening was different from what we knew, and there was nothing I could do to wake her up from it if her heart began to slow.

Eventually, I gave up on sleep and settled my racing thoughts by simply watching over her. What I wouldn't give to see those eyes open and look up at me.

I bit down on my lip as I thought back to how

haunting her gaze had been only hours earlier. Would she continue to look at me with such distrust and hurt?

Would she even give me a chance to remain at her side with another dragon completing a bond with her, even if it was different from the one my own beast ached for?

None of my questions mattered if she didn't make it through the quickening.

Chapter Twenty-One

SIYANA

My head throbbed with a dull ache and my vision blurred as I opened my eyes. I tried to sit up, but my body felt heavy and foreign. Panic set in as I looked around, trying to piece together where I was.

Icy wind bit at my skin as I took in the landscape. The tundra stretched endlessly in every direction, the only landmark a majestic castle of ice looming and glittering in the distance. As I took in my surroundings, I noticed a small, blue baby dragon lying beside me and startled. Its spine was tipped with glistening spikes of ice, and its milky white eyes were fixed on me.

Was I going to be its dinner? It seemed rather docile, the way it slowly rose to its feet and stretched out languidly. Their snout rose and swung to sniff at my face, and I went completely still as flurries of snow danced around us.

Once satisfied with their inspection, it seemed, they

let out a soft, almost melodic growl and jerked their head toward the castle. I knew that we were bound together in this strange, frozen world. I wasn't sure how I knew that, but it just felt like a statement of fact in my mind.

What I couldn't recall as my brain whirled, was how I'd gotten here, and even worse...who I was.

A wave of fear washed over me as I struggled to piece together fragments of memory that remained just out of reach, teasing me to find a path to tether them back to me.

I blinked rapidly as I slowly rose to my feet, lifting my hands to block some of the glaring light reflecting from the castle and directly into my eyes. It seemed like the only logical option was to head in that direction, considering there seemed to be an endless embankment of snow every other direction I looked. So, why did my stomach fill with dread as I took a step forward?

The warmth of my companion pressed into my side, reassuring me, somehow. I lifted a hand to rest on the side of his neck, careful to stay away from the spikes that gleamed there, threatening to impale me if I didn't use caution.

We began our trek toward the castle, but as its impressive size began to grow bigger and closer, my boots began to sink through the snow as it built up around us. Each step demanded exhausting exertion, my feet dragging through the mounds. Soon enough, the drifts were up to mid-thigh and I could barely feel my limbs through the tingling coldness that had settled into them. The fluffy snow was beginning to turn to slush around me, seeping into my bones and leaving me trembling with big, body-shaking shivers.

I wasn't sure when my hand had lifted from the dragon, but as I glanced to the side for help, I found myself suddenly alone. How was that possible? Had I gone in a different direction?

It was as if I'd fallen into some kind of trance, so hyper fixated on the endless stretch of snow surrounding me and moving through it, that nothing else existed.

"Help!" I yelled as fear constricted my lungs, realizing I'd strayed too far from my friend.

Could they even help me? They seemed far too small to fly and I didn't want them to be encapsulated and stuck like I was. *Shit.*

The slush began to harden, becoming immovable blocks of ice encompassing my entire lower body. I slapped my hands on the slick top of it as I desperately tried to lift my feet but felt the strain of the tendons running down my hips to my knees. If I pulled any harder, I was going to seriously injure myself.

Stay calm. Panicking won't help you.

It was easier to tell myself that than to actually force myself to practice it, and after all of a few seconds of forced deep breaths, I gave up. My heart slammed wildly in my chest, as if it was trying to escape from me, the same way I was trying to break free from my prison of ice.

A roar echoed loudly through the air, and my head

swung around, trying to place what direction it had come from.

That was no baby dragon.

I saw death coming for me as the snow parted and large jaws opened just twenty feet away. A maw filled with rows of razor sharp teeth promised to make it a painful, albeit quick, passing into the afterlife.

I didn't want it to end like this. Sure, I wasn't aware of who I was or what my aspirations and dreams were, but I had to have some, right? Had I had enough time to accomplish them? Did anyone out there love me enough to miss me when they realized I was gone and never coming back?

As the shimmering metallic blue of the dragon's massive body became clear, I knew I only had seconds left. If their jaws alone weren't the cause of my death, surely my end would come from the curled talons–that seemed to be the size of at least half my body–that were hanging eye-level with me. The dragon's wingspan took my breath away, and as the shadow of their body cast over me, I shut my eyes, prepared to say goodbye.

Shockwaves rolled through my body as a large crack rang out and the ice around my body splintered. My eyes snapped open just in time to see the large dragon lift back off of the ice before pulling their wings in and dropping like a stone. Their weight shattered the ice around me with finality, and I just lifted my hands in time to block the shards from gouging my eyes out, though searing pain in my cheek and jaw signaled I hadn't escaped unscathed.

"You're injured. I'm sorry, but I wasn't sure how else to help you escape. This body feels foreign to me, and I don't know how to use all of the magical energy I feel racing through me. I didn't want to risk tapping into that right now."

My hands shot down to my sides as I glanced up at the only other creature near me.

"Did you..." I stuttered before taking a moment to blink and wipe away the blood trickling down my face and neck with the sleeve of my coat. "Did you just talk to me?"

Their large head lifted up and down before craning down to my height. Familiar milky-white eyes stared deep into my soul, and it clicked. This was my friend from earlier, but how was that even possible?

"Yes. I couldn't speak to you earlier, but somehow by the time I'd realized we'd been separated and I found you, the ability seemed to open like a bridge between our minds."

I stood there, in complete stupor, staring at the dragon. The voice was distinctly male, but the deep timber of it was jarring when I thought of the small baby he was what felt like mere minutes ago.

The dragon blinked those two large eyes at me, and I noticed a film that passed across their slitted pupils like a second shield beneath the lid. How fascinating. Even more so, I realized how quickly my fear had been replaced by tranquility when my brain connected this large dragon to our small friend.

Why did I trust him so implicitly?

"What's your name?"

"Kaida, and you can speak back to me with your mind, instead of trying to yell through the wind."

The thought of speaking into a dragon's mind seemed unreal, but I couldn't recall if I'd ever even met a dragon before Kaida. Perhaps this was normal and I was severely behind the curve with my lack of knowledge.

I brushed off the ice that stuck to my coats and stomped my feet to try to get the blood flowing back through them as I attempted to project my thoughts to him. *"So, Kaida, do you know where we are, or better yet, who I am?"*

His head swung from side to side. **"Please don't yell."**

I grimaced and lowered my mental projection–well, at least I hoped I had. *"Sorry."*

He seemed to settle as he gazed down at me with unblinking eyes. It occurred to me that perhaps I should have found Kaida's gaze unnerving, considering I had no idea *why* I trusted him. **"That's better, and no, I don't know either of those things. I do, however, feel a draw toward that castle. Perhaps we will find an answer there."**

My legs seemed to burn as tingles ran from my feet all the way up to my hips. Stepping forward gingerly, I was able to keep my balance, but a shuddering tremble passed through my limbs from the exertion demanded by our harsh environment.

"I don't think I will be able to walk there until I find a way to warm myself. I don't know how long I was walking through the slush before it turned to ice. Time seems like an odd construct here, like something that I can't wrap my mind around."

Steam puffed from his snout as he breathed. **"Can you climb up my tail to my back? You can use the spikes to pull yourself up. I can carry us to the castle if so."**

My eyes traveled across his tail and up toward his back, a sense of déjà vu enveloping me. A part of me felt like I'd taken that exact path before and the memory of holding onto silver spikes hit me hard.

So I had been around dragons before. Why couldn't I recall this?

The skin between my eyebrows furrowed as I shook the questions that began to build from my mind. I needed to focus on the present.

Kaida's tail flicked around to lay at my feet and I stumbled toward the tip, eyeing the sharp points of his spikes. As soon as I attempted to lift my foot enough to step up onto the smallest part of him, my hip creaked with resistance. After multiple attempts, including trying to pull myself up with my hands on his scales, I heaved out a heavy breath, defeat hitting me square in the chest.

"I can't do it. My body isn't cooperating."

The ground shook as he launched suddenly from it,

the force from his wings sending a tidal wave of air over me, nearly knocking me to my ass. A whirlwind of snow flurries followed his sudden movement, and I reached up to shield my eyes from the sudden onslaught.

"Don't move. I'm going to attempt to grab you with my claws."

Fear spiked within me, making my chest clench with the lack of confidence I heard in his words.

"Are you sure you won't impale me with a claw?" I asked, voice raising in pitch as he descended toward me once more.

"No. So, don't move."

My limbs didn't want to move, anyways, so I didn't think that would be our problem here.

"Maybe you should just leave me here," I hedged as the tips of his talons gleamed above my head, extending out as he flexed them.

"Don't be stupid, you will most certainly die here if I do that." His sass took me off guard, yet it was exactly what I needed to relax as his clawed foot encompassed me. **"Can you hold onto one of them? I don't want to pierce you by closing them with you in the center."**

I leaned toward the talon in front of me, falling a bit as I wrapped my arms and feet around it to the best of my ability. *"Okay. You can close them more."*

He did as I instructed, and suddenly I was encased perfectly, with only small slits between his claws allowing light and air in. I felt as if I were in a cocoon, and the thought comforted me. I wouldn't fall from his grip unless he suddenly opened his claws. In my heart, I knew he would never do that.

Selfishly, I was happy that he'd decided on this method of transportation. As we launched into the sky and I felt the air grow colder as it flowed through the openings, I buried my face down against my chest. I couldn't imagine how I would have managed to hold on with the fierce wind and freezing temperature making my extremities stiff and all but unusable. I ran my hands up and down against my pants, trying to heat them up with the friction. When that didn't work, I settled on burying them behind my knees as I pulled my legs to my chest.

"Please don't open your claw. I'm not holding on anymore."

He screeched, making my wince at the sound. **"I'm now wondering if you actually wish to die. Is that the case? Please let me know, so that I can stop making attempts to save you."**

My eyes rolled behind my closed lids. *"No, I do not wish to die. I merely am trying to protect what little warmth my body is holding onto at present. Just warn me before we land and I will hold on again."*

"Anything else I can do to improve your flight, human?"

His sassy thoughts made me smirk. It seemed neither of us understood our draw to one another, yet we couldn't fight or deny it. What existed between us felt like a genuine friendship. If only friendship could keep me warm.

Time passed quickly and I felt the shift in the air pressure as we descended. I got into position before he even warned me, so when he announced that the ground was approaching, I gave him the go ahead. Slowly, his clawed foot opened and I glanced down. Torches of burning fire lined the front of the castle and confusion stirred in me as I let my feet dangle from his claw. When the distance was safe, I dropped down, letting out a huff as my bones rattled with the impact.

I attempted to walk and found my limbs moving with a bit more ease now. Doing my best to hurry toward the entryway of the castle to get away from Kaida's landing point, I managed to only stumble once.

Glee poured through me as I felt the warmth of the torches and wasted no time in lifting my hands toward one that was anchored to the icy archway.

"Do not go in there, human."

The sudden fear in Kaida's voice had me glancing back at him in confusion.

"Didn't we both agree that we needed to come here?"

I gasped as his eyes swirled and sparked like the clouds that were suddenly gathering above the castle, filled with streaks of sparking lightning. No part of it felt natural.

"Answers you have been searching for will be

found within but so will your death. Only you can decide if the price is worth the entry."

His voice seemed void of his personality, as if he was completely detached.

I swallowed the lump building within my throat as I glanced back at the massive doors of ice beckoning me forward. It felt as if I was being pulled toward them by a force bigger than myself, and suddenly I stood at the base of the doors, without remembering even lifting my feet. A loud groan filled the air as they began to swing inwards.

I couldn't escape whatever was waiting for me.

"I think I have to go in there, Kaida."

"I will follow you."

The strength behind his words slammed into me, and I turned back to find him ambling toward me, eyes back to their milky white voids I'd quickly grown to know. A deep sense of trust and love for this creature grew within me, like a ball of light burning brightly.

"No. I will not place your life at risk as well."

He let out a growl and puffed steam at me. **"I will not stay behind."**

A desire to keep him away from the ominous doorway filled me when I looked back into the void within the castle, darkness calling to me. This was for me to face alone, somehow I knew this without question.

An explosion of ice sounded behind me, and I whirled to find Kaida's way blocked, a wall of ice now separating me from him and trapping me within the arched entryway. He roared before I saw his body through the translucent ice, running straight for the wall. A boom came as he slammed into it, yet the ice didn't crack, even with such brute force hurtled against it.

"Trust me to do this."

Still, he threw his weight into the ice over and over, and suddenly, I felt his emotions without him needing to voice them. A possessive desire to protect me. The overwhelming need to stay by my side. His love for me.

It nearly brought me to my knees, and yet I remained unflinching in my decision to go on without him. That same love he felt for me poured through my own heart and soul in my quest to ensure he didn't die alongside me.

I wasn't sure who he was to me, but I knew that I would do everything in my power to protect him.

"Don't go!" he yelled into my mind, and so I began to build a wall there to keep him out, on instinct alone.

"Goodbye, Kaida," I whispered to him before sealing it completely.

He clawed at my mind but I forced myself to walk into the darkness ahead. Everything went black as the doors slammed shut behind me. The force of them closing echoed through the room. As I took a deep breath and continued forward, a voice whispered in the darkness around me.

"Welcome, Siyana. I've been waiting for you."

Siyana. As soon as I heard the name, I knew it referred to me. This knowledge of my name seemed to be the key to unlocking my mind, and my memories slammed into me with sudden force. It drove me to my knees as I groaned, faces and scenes rolling through me with alarming speed.

"Choose. Either you die or the dragon does," the unknown voice demanded, seeming to come from all directions around me.

Without hesitation, I answered.

"Me. Take me."

Chapter Twenty-Two

SIYANA

"COME ON WENCH, open that mouth and tell me how much you hate me now."

Theo's voice was the first thing I heard as the foreign world of ice and that sinister voice melted away, leaving me in a dark void. That odd dream left a feeling of fear gnawing in my belly, but I focused back on the sound of Theo's rumbling voice, anchoring me in the present.

It wasn't real. This was.

"Now?" I croaked, my throat constricting around the word. An overwhelming dryness filled my mouth and throat, as if I hadn't drank anything in weeks. I must have slept with my mouth open. I forced a small amount of spit down, swallowing thickly as I added, "Bold of you to assume I haven't hated you this entire time."

His deep, booming laugh had my eyes flying open in shock. After how I'd stormed out of that cavern, and the way we'd clashed about the bond, I'd thought he'd at least still be flustered and confused, like I'd been. But that didn't seem to be affecting the dragon in front of me, now.

Never before had I seen such a fierce yearning in his deep blue eyes as he gazed down at me. The intensity of his stare was almost overwhelming, drawing me into its depths like a moth to a flame. It seemed as if he were baring his very soul to me, willing me to understand the depth of his desire.

"Is your love language degradation, wench?" he asked, arching a single eyebrow as he waited for my response. He reached up, brushing away a strand of hair that was caught in my mouth to tuck it behind my ear.

My breath caught at the adoration I felt pouring from his every word and touch. He was still playful and teasing, but it felt rooted in something more now.

Confusion and butterflies took flight within my belly, warring with each other over how I was supposed to feel. This is what he always did to me, though. A few words and a glimpse into the real Theo and I always caved, despite any previous feelings of hurt and distrust.

Not again.

I scowled at him as I realized he was cradling me in his lap.

"No, this is my hate language, dragon boy."

A soft trill sounded on my left and my head rolled to the side, instantly feeling an overwhelming need to put eyes on Kaida after that harrowing dream. I knew it hadn't been real, but my nervous system demanded to see that my baby dragon was still exactly that, and that he was here and safe.

He was curled up and staring at me, tail flicking around in agitation as his gaze bounced between Theo and me.

"I don't think my dragon likes you, either," I surmised. I laughed at the thought, but my chest constricted, forcing a deep, painful cough from my lungs. Levity slammed into me with brute force, sobering me and bringing me back to the moment. "I feel like death," I murmured, my eyes drooping with the exhaustion I seemed to be fighting off by the minute.

"I'm glad you are awake, finally."

Sinda's voice filled my head, though the way she spoke now was much gentler than I remembered her being. My mind snagged on her last word after a few seconds, and I parroted, *"Finally?"*

I wasn't sure where she was, but as my eyes swept around the cave, I could only see the remaining unhatched eggs, Kaida, Theo, and myself. Even Katla, the little twin who hated me, wasn't present.

"Theo will explain. I'm hunting with Katla. We will be back soon."

The connection between us severed and I groaned, hating that I needed to depend on Theo for anything in this moment. "Why is it that Sinda seems to be able to come and go from my mind as she pleases? She broke through my defenses earlier today."

I turned my head back toward Theo as he hovered

above me, the action taking far more exertion from me than it should have. His lips thinned as his nostrils flared, just before he took in a deep breath.

"That wasn't earlier today. It was a week ago."

I blinked at him, confusion at his words swirling through my hazy brain. "No. It was just before I took that nap. I think I'd know if a week passed by, dragon boy."

"Then tell me why you're unable to move from my lap right now, wench? If you hated me as you claimed, you'd be pushing away from me, if you could."

His retort was full of his usual arrogance and had me bristling before attempting to move. All I managed was a measly rocking motion with my head in his lap, which resulted with him clearing his throat and something hardening beneath my skull.

If my eyes could have filled with fire, they would have at that moment. "Do you seriously have a hard cock right now, when I'm seemingly immobile in your lap?"

He snapped, "It's the dragon within me. Take it up with him."

My eyes narrowed in his direction, but I was distracted mere seconds later as I suddenly smelled the scent of bread. My stomach rumbled with aching hunger as he lifted a piece into my view. "Do you just blame him for everything? How convenient."

My question was ignored as he pressed the bread against my lips and demanded, "Eat. You need to recuperate your strength after the quickening. Sinda is hunting for meat for Kaida. You both were in a dream-state for seven days as your bond underwent an ancient trial."

My mouth opened from shock and he took that to his advantage, pressing the tips of his fingers and the bread between my lips and into my mouth. I growled and bit down, chomping on his fingers with as much strength as I could.

His words of a quickening and dreamstate were quickly forgotten with his unwelcome intrusion.

"Ow!" he yelped, snatching his fingers from my lips as I smirked in victory.

That'll show him to put his appendages in my mouth without being welcomed. Not that any part of him would *ever* be welcomed by me.

The thought had me internally withering at how often I seemed to be lying to myself as he growled at me. "You're insufferable. I'm just trying to make sure you're taken care of."

Something about those specific words broke open the freshly sealed wounds of rejection I'd felt multiple times with him.

"Who decided that was your job, Theo?" I asked, infusing my voice with thick sarcasm. "Because I'm pretty sure you made it clear that we aren't compatible and that our marriage will be over whether I want it to be or not."

Silence stretched as we engaged in a silent battle of wills, each of us glaring daggers at the other.

Eventually he caved, eyes rolling back in his head before fluttering shut. "I deserve that, and I'm sorry. I deeply regret how our last conversation went."

Well, well, well. Had the undine god broken free of Elysium and frozen over all of Edath? That seemed about as likely as Theo feeling regret.

"What was that?" I quipped. "For some reason my ears don't work when your eyes are closed. Look at me when you say that."

His eyes appeared again, flashing with sparks of blue as his dragon pupil narrowed and focused on me. "Why I like you is beyond my comprehension, wench."

The small admission had my mouth slamming shut and those damnable butterflies in my stomach multiplying in droves. *No.* I wouldn't let him in that easily.

He sighed heavily as he shook his head. "I won't blame my dragon for my words, despite the desire for the bond being forced by his needs. I alone decided to say exactly what I did, so that you would leave and be safe from me. From *us.* I thought it was the right thing at the moment, but when I returned to our alcove and couldn't find you..."

I wanted to ask him to continue. A yearning opened up in my chest that needed him to admit he felt what I did. Yet I remained silent, wanting him to be the one to bare his feelings and attempt to connect.

The ground shook and I knew a dragon drew close. From the way Kaida and Theo remained calm, I knew it had to be Sinda.

He glanced toward the entrance to the nest and sighed. I knew our moment was gone, just like that, and the armor he kept around his heart was clearly back in place. When he glanced back at me and lifted bread to my lips, there was no longer a soft nurturing energy to him. It felt stiff and awkward, and I hated my heart for the way it ached when all I wanted was for it to harden.

"As I said in the hot springs, stop messing with me. I'm not putting up with this any longer," I hissed, mustering as much energy as I could. His head jerked back as I continued, "You can't act like you truly care about me one moment and then simply return to the cold-hearted drackya who is merely keeping me alive for the purpose of our temporary marriage of convenience. I'm not some toy to occupy your time with. I'm a real person, with a beating heart and emotions."

As I did with my mind, I began to build a wall around my heart, exhausted and more than finished with his inability to be vulnerable and honest. As much as I resented him for his part in this back and forth, at some point I had to decide to be done as a player in this game.

That point was now.

"Be the real version of you, for both of our sakes."

Sinda and Katla dropped into the nest at the end of my whispered words and reconstruction of my mental wall, and I turned my attention to them. I felt Theo's legs move before gentle hands lowered my head to the ground in replacement of them.

I guess that was his choice, plain and clear. I was on my own.

This time it didn't hurt as much, because it was exactly what I expected of him. *Coward.*

He glanced back at me, and for a second my breath caught at how gorgeous the silver scales on his face looked reflecting with the light of the bonfire in the room. It was a shame that his personality didn't match that beauty.

"Sinda is politely asking you to open your mind to her, so that she may talk to us both at once, in regards to the quickening."

His words may as well have been imbued with his powers of ice, with the way they speared my heart. *The quickening.* The supposed reason I slept for a week and was now unimaginably weak. That was a welcomed change of topic and good use of what little energy I still possessed.

Instantly, I tore down my walls and spoke to her as I watched her place the spoils of her hunt at Kaida's feet, with me trying not to grimace as he tore through bone and flesh with ease. "Thank you for not breaking down my walls forcefully, though I'm still unsure of how you did that."

The thought was unnerving. I wanted to know that my mind was mine alone to share or not.

"Drackya cannot do that, if that's what you are concerned about," she mused as she crunched on her own prey, sending sprays of blood onto the scales around her mouth as well as the floor. My stomach churned at the gaping void of space where the animal's head once was. **"Only full-blooded dragons have the ability to tear down non-mated human's walls, and it still took a considerable amount of energy to get through your tightly constructed ones. I'd rather not have to do it again."**

Her admission only offered me an ounce of relief.

"Now, it is time to discuss what you and Kaida just went through, as there wasn't time to explain prior to the quickening. If you wouldn't have joined him quickly, there was a chance the bond would have been rejected."

"But I thought you didn't think I was worthy of the bond with him, so why would you ensure I had the chance to complete it?" The words were out of my mouth before I realized how accusatory they sounded.

Her chest expanded with a chuff and her laughter sounded through my mind. **"I like this fiery side of you. To answer your question, I did that because I accept that there are things in this world that I cannot decide or meddle in. Love and bonds are sacred, and every decision in relation to them needs to be in the complete control of those involved."**

I didn't miss the way her eyes slid to Theo, who stood above me, rolling his eyes at her before leaning back against the wall. I was so incredibly uncomfortable laying flat on the ground, incapable of sitting up and stretching out the tightness I felt in every inch of my body. It was on the tip of my tongue to ask him to help me to sit up and lean back against the wall, but I swallowed it.

I'd drawn a line, and I was going to stick to it, regardless of my personal comfort.

"So, I truly was asleep for a week, lost in some kind of trial?"

Her eyes shifted back to me for a second before returning to Theo and ignoring my question. **"You told me you would ensure she was provided for upon waking. Why are you not doing so now?"**

He scoffed loudly before crossing his arms against his chest. "I tried. She refused to accept my help."

"That's not what I refused, and you know it," I murmured, unable to bite back the words of resentment.

"Have you both considered relieving this tension through pleasures of the flesh? I think it would fix much of what is lacking between you."

I choked on my spit and began hacking profusely as it went down the wrong pipe. My vision blurred as tears sprang to my eyes and my chest tightened.

A warm hand touched my shoulder before gently moving to slip under my back and help me sit. A cold wetness touched my lips, and on instinct I opened them, greedily drinking down the water provided. I drank until my stomach hurt from bloating and my throat no longer felt like I'd inhaled the sands from Eruthya's deserts.

"We will not be engaging in physical intimacy," Theo answered, his voice far too close to my ear, sending an entirely unwelcome shiver down my spine. That was funny, considering he'd just had a hard cock from merely the touch of my head in his lap. "Now, can we please focus on the quickening and what they saw? You said the images you gleaned when Kaida sent them to you were unusual."

I was still stuck on Sinda plainly telling us to fuck out our problems, but quickly tucked it away. As my eyes opened and Theo took away the empty flask of water, I shoved down my pride and asked, "Can you please help prop me up against the wall?"

"And feed her some of your rations while we talk. I don't care what mental war you two have going on, but I will not let my offsprings' bonded die right after finding her. It is a pain that I do not wish upon anyone."

Her anguish and demanding tone had me reflecting upon the memory of Theo's mother being her bonded. She was right. Whatever Theo and I had going on couldn't be my focus anymore, I had a baby dragon to take care of and be around for.

I turned my head, making eye contact with Theo out of my peripheral vision and nodded my agreement. "I won't refuse, anymore. I need to regain my strength."

He let out a breath and quickly helped slide me up against the wall before settling in at my side with bread and dried meat in his lap. Kaida had finished his meal and got up to follow me, curling up on my free side but not before narrowing his gaze on Theo.

I felt the drackya bristle and ask quietly, "What did I

do to you? I'm your king and you will respect me, young one."

Kaida lifted his head again at his words and let out a hiss as his body rumbled. I felt his protectiveness floating through our bond as he gently settled his head in my lap, getting his bloody mouth all over my clothing. That was going to be tedious to wash off in the springs.

Theo grumbled to himself as he began to feed me. I focused on chewing and swallowing as quickly as I could, stopping myself from thinking of how intimate this felt.

In-between bites, as I felt the energy to, I recounted our time in the dreamscape from beginning to end and was met with silence afterwards.

"The quickening wipes the dragon's and human's mind of who they are, in an effort to ensure the bond is of pure intent and not for malicious or personal gain on either side. It leaves you at your most authentic and pure self. If either participant fails to choose to save the life of the other, without knowing why they would do so, it signals you are not worthy and the bond will dissipate."

Her words made sense, and I quickly swallowed my mouthful of bread before asking, "That sounds exactly like what happened–why would our experience be considered unusual?"

"Kaida is a seer."

My head snapped toward Theo, despite my utmost desire to not look into his eyes with his nearness. Some things were too important. "What?"

"Yes, Katla and Kaida are both seers. It has been countless centuries since the last set lived. They are always born in pairs, with one seeing the future and one seeing the present." Before I could ask which Kaida was, she answered. "Katla sees the present of any territory within Edath. On our hunting trips, I have taught her to use it to detect where our prey is. If news of her existence escaped this mountain, she would be hunted and bonds forced on her over and over, in an effort to control her power for gain. Kaida has more security, being bonded to you already."

So that meant Kaida saw the future. I thought back to his eyes swirling and sparking in the same manner as the sky during the quickening, as well as the way his words felt detached.

"From what I can deduce, I believe your quickening took place in the middle of Kaida having a premonition. There should have never been a third party there speaking to you, Siyana."

My blood ran cold at the memory.

Choose. Either you die, or the dragon does.

I would never let Kaida die, if I had a say.

"Sinda and I talked of the plan to go to Sanctum and find answers while you both slept," Theo offered as he lifted more dried beef to my mouth. I greedily chewed on it as I nodded for him to continue.

"If what you saw is the future, we have to take into consideration that it very well could be something we must face in search of the undine elemental god. Are you willing to fly there still?"

Before I could answer, my guard went on high alert as Katla left her mother's side and slowly moved toward us. Kaida's head popped up, and he issued a warning growl. His twin lowered her head and let out a whine as she continued closer, and my entire body went rigid as she stopped near my boots and looked at me.

"She's waiting for permission to approach," Theo whispered, startling me.

"Oh...oh!" I murmured, my heart beating frantically at the thought of her deciding I was once again a foe and biting my toes off. She waited so patiently and showed no signs of aggression, so I conceded, "You can approach."

Instantly, Kaida and her leapt toward each other, rolling around and playfully nipping at one another. I couldn't help but grin at the babies, loving to see Kaida enjoying himself as he should at this age. He quickly wore himself out, however, clearly not recovered from the quickening either as he flopped to his side and panted.

"Since the completion of the quickening, Katla now senses his energy within you, as we all can. You are now dragon kin, Siyana. Welcome."

Resolve formed in my heart with her words. I would ensure Kaida and myself were prepared for whatever came our way. I'd protect and cherish our bond, forever, but that meant admitting neither of us were ready to face any enemy.

I turned to look at Theo, admitting to myself that he was the best bet we had right now. "I want you to train us. Together and separately. I won't fly into Sanctum until I am confident we stand a chance, and I'm not too prideful to admit that we don't right now."

Sinda's approval rolled through my mind and I lifted my chin as I stared into Theo's eyes, waiting for a response.

"Then we will train every day and night once you've both recovered your strength, but don't expect me to go easy on you," he warned, a dangerous glint entering his eyes that I hadn't seen since he'd thrown me over his shoulder and paraded me out of my home.

I couldn't help the scoff that came from me as my brow pinched. "As if. I fully expect to be shown why you're feared. Because as of right now, I don't see it."

Chapter Twenty-Three

SIYANA

I'D LIVE to regret those words in the weeks that came and went.

As soon as I had an ounce of strength, Theo had me walking and then running laps within the tunnel system, with Kaida learning to fly through them alongside me. Thankfully, with my bond to Kaida, I wasn't in danger of being a small snack for an unsuspecting dragon. Our path had taken us by large caverns of multiple dragons sleeping peacefully, and none had stirred with my presence.

That was just our morning warm-up, with the afternoons consisting of hand-to-hand combat. At first, Theo had been surprised by my skill and ability to hold my own...when he wasn't using his magic. However, as soon as he introduced the magic to our fights, I was no longer a match. It didn't matter how many times I attempted to memorize his moves and tells like I would Brenson. Theo was completely blank, giving nothing away.

Recently, he'd turned to taunting me, as if goading me into an agitated state would make me fight any better. All it did was fan the flame of resentment for him that burned in my heart, the inability to equal him in combat only adding fuel to the raging fire. It served as a reminder of how inept I was in this world, and it felt like salt in the wounds of him not thinking me good enough to be his mate–even if I didn't *want* to be.

Our talks diminished to only speaking to one another when absolutely necessary, and only in regards to Kaida's needs and training now that we'd moved back to our own alcove. Sinda's mate had stayed away per her request while the quickening had occurred, but he had grown increasingly impatient, and it was safest for us all to leave.

The nights brought a level of tension I'd love to be rid of, when we were forced to lay together on our small bed of shrubbery. Thankfully, Kaida distracted me from the forced proximity with his incessant snoring. Still, sometimes my body reacted of its own volition from being so close to Theo. Occasionally, our limbs would brush when one of us moved, and without fail, we'd instantly still, like we were breaking a rule and trying to not get caught by the other.

The small touches seemed to be occurring more often in recent nights, and it was proving harder and harder to not seek relief from my growing needs. It wasn't like I had any moments of privacy to please myself. Despite not wanting to seek emotional depth with him any longer, I still had eyes that appreciated the lean, muscular build he put on display as he stripped down to his trousers every night.

This afternoon, when Kaida's stretch of training with Theo came to a close, the little dragon promptly collapsed, exhausted from the demand his wings were taking as they tried to build his endurance for the trip. In a matter of just weeks, he'd somehow doubled in size, and I was already missing the sweet little baby he'd been when we first met and bonded.

He rolled onto his side and his wing flapped over with the move, smacking him in the face. I winced, wondering if it hurt, but his snores quickly echoed around us, and I relaxed.

Theo stalked toward me as I finished my stretching routine, voice slick with sarcasm as he gestured toward Kaida with a tilt of his head, "Intellect isn't a flower that grows in every garden, I see."

"Don't call him stupid," I quickly defended, jumping to my feet as fire burned in my belly. "He is still a baby and is trying his best. You see how exhausted he is."

I took extreme offense to Theo's words. I was beyond proud of my dragon and the tenacity he showed at such a young age. He should be off frolicking with his sister and other siblings that had since hatched, and I'd be a liar if I didn't say that I still felt immense guilt for taking him away from his family. Despite the countless times Theo and Sinda had both reassured me that dragons didn't share the same familial attachments as humans did, I still couldn't help but wonder if he'd be happier surrounded by his own kind.

He gave it all up for me, and I wouldn't let anyone talk poorly of him.

Theo's hand lifted to pinch the bridge of his nose. "You assume the worst of my words every time, Siyana. I simply meant that it was amusing to see his wings still act of their own accord. It is typical of younglings."

I bristled at his use of my name. We'd given up the wench and dragon boy nicknames after the conversation following my awakening from the quickening, as the tension and anger built up to new heights. It still felt odd when he called me that, despite the weeks of him choosing my full name over the nickname. It didn't sit right within my chest to have such formality.

"Whatever," I responded, bouncing on the balls of my feet and rolling my neck around. "Let's get to training. We're wasting precious time with each day we stay here."

I desperately needed to work off some of this pent-up energy or I was going to combust.

At this point, I wasn't even sure I hated him anymore. Perhaps I hated myself for the pull I felt toward him, the temptation of his body as he wound through training sessions, muscles tightening and untightening, sweat glistening.... After everything, I thought the feelings would fade, and yet they only seemed to grow alongside my annoyance. And still yet, it seemed so easy for him. He was formal and detached, showing no signs of frustration other than with my inability to make what he deemed acceptable progress in our training sessions. Worst of all, the only thing my mind seemed to focus on was how he wasn't as affected by me as I was by him.

Pining after him left me resenting myself, if I was being honest. I wanted to turn it off as badly as I wanted to break this curse and secure the safety of the people in my kingdom. I thought of the women's lives that had been lost, and the thought of more being taken as I remained stagnant in my training forced me to work harder every day.

As I waited for Theo to compose himself to start our fight, his eyes fixated on the wall behind me, seemingly distracted by something. I glanced behind me, half expecting a dragon to somehow have snuck up on me, but when I saw nothing but an empty tunnel, I turned back with a raised eyebrow. "Hello? Are we going to spar or what?"

"Hold please," he whispered, lifting a hand, "Lucius is talking to me about a new issue arising."

My curiosity won over my budding anger at him giving me the hand, and I waited patiently for him to fill me in. There had been a few attempts to kill Lucius over the weeks, but neither Theo or him seemed particularly bothered by it, saying the culprits were easily killed in response. How they weren't bothered by multiple attempts at his life, I didn't know, nor could I fathom the grit it required to simply continue on in the face of such adversity.

I watched with rapt fascination as Theo's face ran through a wild array of emotions, from shock, to intrigue, and finally to confusion. Now *that* was new. He never reacted to Lucius like that. Each emotion was easily portrayed by the way his lips moved, from agape, to pursed, and then pressed into a thin line. Or maybe I just had an obsession with looking at his lips and needed to get a grip.

I missed the days before I knew the softer and possessive sides of Theo. The bliss of ignorance was far preferable to the knowledge that made me yearn to see the softer parts of him at all times. It was so much easier to fear being his wife when I thought him a cold-hearted brute. Before I knew he would protect me and cradle me to his chest possessively when I called out for him. The tender way he held my hand and fixed my wounds. How he'd opened up and shown me the wounds his father had left behind and the immense weight he felt from taking on his birthright as king. The way he suffered the burden silently, giving me only the briefest glimpses into his struggles.

"It appears your friends have made the trek to my castle to demand your return," he breathed out, focusing back on my face. "They said they aren't leaving, no matter the danger to them that Lucius has warned them of."

That was high on the list of things I never expected to come from his mouth. "Which friends?"

"Tillie, Mira, and...Brenson," he answered, the last name showing the first bit of fire within Theo that I'd seen in weeks. Perhaps he wasn't as unaffected as I thought.

I cleared my throat at the tension building with the mere mention of my friend. "Will Lucius be able to protect them until we're back? I worry about Tillie and Mira being there, just as we feared for my safety as an unmated human."

Theo's eyes narrowed and he averted his gaze, opening his mouth and closing it.

"What?" I demanded, sensing he wasn't telling me everything.

His jaw clenched and the veins on his forearms bulged as his hands clenched. "I will tell you this, but you have to promise to not freak out."

My heart all but jumped into my throat. "You can't start with that! It immediately makes people freak out, Theo!"

His eyes rolled before he sighed heavily. "Don't be so dramatic. Your precious Brenson is fine. It just seems that Lucius has taken an interest in Tillie, in a similar manner as my dragon feels to you. Now, can we continue with our training? We need to leave within the next few days. It cannot wait any longer."

Without waiting for my response, he rid himself of his tunic, causing me to narrow my eyes. If he thought he was going to distract me with his body, or stop me from thinking of Brenson and my friends in general...Well, he wasn't entirely wrong, but two could play that game if it got me the answers I wanted. Surely I could catch him off guard and prod him until he cracked. It was clear he didn't give a shit to give me answers as we stood now.

I stripped off my vest and tunic, leaving me in only my black brassiere and trousers. Instantly, he stiffened, his eyes falling to my breasts as my skin pebbled with the brisk chill of the cave, despite our fire. He seemed to snap out of a trance and demanded, "What is the meaning of this?"

"You think you're the only one who can play that game?" I questioned, stepping closer to him, enjoying the way he took a step back. "Or are you too riled up with jealousy that Brenson is here to rescue me from you to even remember what my question was, about Lucius protecting them?"

His nostrils flared, his eyes sparking with glittering blue magic before he took slow, calculated steps forward to close the distance between us. My body seemed to come alive a "You don't know how dangerous the game you're playing right now is, wench."

Yet I did. I knew exactly where teasing and taunting him went, if from nothing else than at the very least from my display of pleasuring myself in the hot springs. Was I trying to get the same rise out of him now? Already, I was pleased at the renewed use of my nickname. My brain wasn't working on logic, deciding to shut off entirely and give in to the emotions spurring me on instead.

My hand lifted to trail a finger down his chest as I stared up at him from beneath my lashes. "Are you thinking of how Brenson will ravish me after so much time apart? The way his mouth will devour mine." I trailed my hand lower, drawing to a slow stop just above his trousers. "How his hands will travel down my body just like this."

He trembled beneath my touch, but I wasn't sure if it was from barely restrained anger, or desire. Perhaps both, which was exactly how I'd been existing recently.

Suddenly the cave spun as my feet were knocked from underneath me. I attempted to throw my hands out to break my fall, but thick arms wrapped around me just before my head could hit the floor. A large hand cupped the back of my head tenderly. Theo's body pressed atop mine as his head dropped close to my ear. "You may think you can win by distracting me, but that only works if you aren't as equally distracted and have a clear mind."

I bucked my hips, attempting to move him from me, but I knew how this went. It was futile, given his size and weight. Instead, I switched my efforts to banging my fist into where his kidneys would be if his anatomy was similar to ours in this form. He grunted and snarled at me. "Stop that. I'm not moving until we figure this the fuck out. Right now, wench. This ridiculousness has dragged on for far too long."

He lowered my head to the ground right before he

lifted his upper body to snatch my wrists in his grip. His weight shifted into his hips, driving down into me, and I squirmed at the feel of his hardness pressing against me. At the very least, it seemed we were on the same page about not actually being disgusted by the other.

"Figure what out, Theo?" I snapped, letting all of the emotions out that I'd been suppressing for weeks. Fury rose within my chest as I continued, "That I'm a complete idiot and can't get over this draw to you, no matter how many times you make it clear you don't want me? That you'll leave me as soon as this curse is broken without a second thought, and I'll be left thinking about you because I can't get you out of my stupid head!"

At some point in my rant, my anger had joined forces with the anxiety I felt about never seeing him again. It wasn't rational. None of my feelings for him were. The worst part was that my last admission was tinged with my true emotion: grief.

I was already grieving being shipped back off to my home, with no chance to speak on what I wanted. All I wanted was to have a fucking chance to choose my own future.

My hands were jerked above my head suddenly, pinning them there in one of his large hands as he bent back over me. Our chests brushed against each other as he asked, "Do you want to stay at my side, at the end of this?"

The question threw me completely off-guard, and suddenly I felt completely naked beneath him. As if he was forcing my soul to the surface, bearing it to him merely for his own viewing pleasure. The question burned as hotly as my anger, as my attraction.

"I...I," I stammered, averting my gaze to the side, unable to hold the intensity of his stare with how close he was to my lips. My body squirmed as an overwhelming need to escape him overcame me. I didn't want to tell him the truth. I didn't want to give him a chance to reject me once more.

His free hand came up to grip my jaw, harshly enough to tilt my head back, forcing me to look into his searching eyes. "No. I'm giving you the chance now, to tell me what *you* want. I should have before, but I thought I was doing the right thing. The odds of a drackya finding their mate were already lower than you think, even before the curse. So what do you think the odds are of you being mine, when I demanded your hand in marriage before even meeting you?"

The thought of him finding someone else had my lips thinning and my breaths quickening in my chest. My lips fell open, but I found that I couldn't summon the words he wanted.

"Tell me, wench. What are the odds?"

"None!" I yelled, tired of this question. "The odds are against it."

His grip on my jaw loosened enough for his thumb to rise up and brush along my lower lip. My lips parted instantly as my core tightened, desire flooding my system. "Now I want you to tell me if, despite knowing that, you want to give into this, knowing the possible outcomes? I can't get a taste of you and let you go if it isn't you. I'm too fucking infatuated with you, wench."

My breath hitched with the admission as his thumb dipped into my mouth. "The amount of times I've pictured these sinful lips wrapped around my cock." I closed my mouth, running my tongue along the pad of his thumb and he groaned, flexing his hips down in the process. "The way you haunt my every waking and sleeping moment."

I released his thumb and he dragged it out, running the palm of his hand down my cheek as his fingers sank into the hair on the side of my head. Our foreheads touched as he lowered his face toward mine. My heart was beating so wildly, there was no way he couldn't feel my reaction to his words. To the heat of his body. To his admission, equally as damning as my own truth.

"Then why have you denied me at every turn?" I asked, hating the vulnerability in my soft tone. I swallowed, trying to vanquish the unwanted emotion, before continuing, "You've made these past few weeks seem so easy, with the distance we've built between us."

A rumble flowed from his chest into mine, making my nipples pebble through the thin brassiere. "Easy? That is the last word I would use to describe shoving down my desire for you. It was easy to focus on training and hoping that you and Kaida progressed enough to ensure I didn't lose either of you when we leave this mountain. It was easy to incite your anger, in a desperate

SHARDS OF DESIRE

attempt to remind myself that you didn't want me, when I was so close to giving in. It was easier to think of you not wanting me anymore than to think of expressing my fucking need for you and you rejecting me."

My mouth suddenly went dry as he pulled his head back and brushed his thumb along my temple.

"Because that's what I deserve, Siyana. I deserve for you to reject me after what I've put you through. You deserve someone better than me, but I'm coming to realize I'm not as self-righteous as I thought." His already deep voice dropped to an almost growl as he bit out, "I don't care if there's a better match for you out there. I'll freeze them within a block of ice and drop them into the ocean without a second thought if it means you remain mine."

This was what I'd been wanting, but was it too late? Could I trust his words, or would he take them back tomorrow?

As our eyes locked, I couldn't help but notice the raw, unbridled yearning in his gaze. It was as if all of his desires were laid bare before me, and I could feel every emotion coursing through him. The intensity of our eye contact was palpable, drawing us closer together with an irresistible pull. In that moment, it was as if nothing else existed except for the fire burning between us as our lips brushed against each other for the first time.

Could I give into my needs while still protecting my heart?

"Fuck it," I breathed out.

Chapter Twenty-Four
THEO

It was like a glimpse into the afterlife of Elysium as she surged up to meld our lips together. Never before had I felt like I was floating in the clouds while in my human form, until now. It was like being home, tasting her on my lips.

Her intoxicating scent enveloped me, igniting every nerve in my body as her teeth sank into my bottom lip, pulling it into her mouth with a fierce hunger. I surrendered completely to the raw passion of the moment, my hand abandoning her dark tresses and instead gripping tightly onto her neck, driven by an animalistic desire that rode me mercilessly.

My fingers closed around her throat as I pulled back and asked, voice slick with desire, "Who do you belong to?"

I'd never been as infatuated and aware of the way she

had me eating from the palm of her hand, ready for any crumbs she offered me.

In no surprise at all, her eyes narrowed, challenging me before that pretty little mouth even opened. "I belong to myself, dragon boy."

The dragon within me roared, slamming against the constraints wrapped around him, and I was only barely keeping him at bay. He urged me to show her just how much of a liar she was—that she'd belonged to us the second our eyes clashed as she walked into her father's council room.

We'd tried to fight it, yet we had still ended up here. It was time to accept that I couldn't rid myself of the haunting way she occupied my thoughts. Every iota of my restraint and will-power I possessed had gone into the last few weeks, and it seemed that well had finally dried up. I was left now with a hunger only she could satisfy.

It was time to right my wrongs. If she wanted me, who was I to deny her any longer? I'd show her exactly how dragons treat their mates, if that's what she wanted.

Our ragged breaths mingled and I released her wrists, crushing our lips together. My tongue plunged into her mouth, twisting and dancing with hers as my hands roamed down her trembling body. Fingers traced along her smooth shoulders before seizing the weight of her breasts, kneading them roughly as she arched into my touch and let out a throaty moan. This was only the beginning of my plans for her, as I savored every sound she made and learned exactly how to make her mine.

I rolled her nipples between my fingers and pulled my lips from hers, trailing kisses down to her jaw until I settled at the soft flesh of her neck. She turned, giving me further access and my beast reveled at the submission, whether she realized what she was doing in the moment or not. A rumble grew from deep within me as I sucked on the tender flesh she offered up.

"Theo, I need more," she panted before her lips closed around the bottom of my ear, nipping at me. "Unless you think you can't handle it."

She was playing with fire, insinuating such a thing.

A squeal sounded from her as I moved my hands to her waist and lifted her legs to wrap around my hips as I stood, quickly. I backed her against the cave wall, and just as I was leaning in to taste her again, a loud, disruptive snore echoed, making me falter.

Kaida. I'd forgotten he had collapsed into a slumber not far from us.

It sounded like he was choking on his own breath. Truly, I'd never heard such a thing.

We stared at each other for a few moments, panting with need before she cracked a smile. "Kids, am I right? Always killing the mood."

Frustration and longing pulsed through my veins as I bit down on my lip, nearly drawing blood. "Don't you dare mention kids unless you want me to make them with you right here and now."

I could see her pupils dilate at my words as her tongue darted out to wet her lips. The air between us was heavy with anticipation as my throbbing cock pressed against her covered heat, begging for entrance. It was a pivotal moment—would we let Kaida's interruption push us back into our old patterns, or would this be the time when everything changed?

As if reading each other's minds, our hands reached for one another, refusing to go back to how things were before. And I knew deep in my core that I couldn't ever go back, not after experiencing the way her lips felt on mine. How her moans echoed in my ears. The way she writhed under my touch, desperate for more.

She was mine, body and soul, and I would make damn sure she admitted it before the night was over.

As our lips clashed in a flurry of pent-up need, I palmed her ass and lifted her from the wall. I knew the path to the springs like the back of my hand, not needing to see to get there. We were quickly plunged into darkness as I walked us toward the spot where I wanted to get on my knees and repent.

I opened my mental connection to any dragons within our vicinity, allowing them a quick warning as I came in contact with a few. *"If you value keeping your vision, you will leave the springs within the next two minutes."*

Apparently, even my voice belied my lust, for not one dragon grumbled in resentment of my demands. Thoughts of understanding flowed back before I closed them off. I was thankful no one fought back, because at this rate, I would have made good on my threat to remove their eyes if they lingered and saw what I was about to do to their queen.

No man, woman, or beast would ever lay eyes on what was mine.

Her lips moved to my ear as we descended into the heat of the springs, her breath hitching as she murmured, "Are you sure you can handle being in here with me, dragon boy?"

My cock strained in my trousers at her question. I wanted to shove it into her mouth every time she gave me an ounce of that sass, but it was also one of her qualities that I deeply admired. She'd never once backed down from me, despite her open hatred and fear of me when we first met.

Somehow, she had the most courage and stubbornness out of anyone I'd ever met, man and beast alike. She'd make a fine queen, of all of Andrathya. I'd worship at her feet in public, but in private, I would say my prayers between her legs.

"Close your mouth before I give in to my desires to fill it," I answered, loving the way she pulled back, showing a beautiful flush to her cheeks.

Maybe my little wench wanted to serve her king after all. We'd get there in time—this moment was about her and correcting my behavior from the last time we'd been here together.

Her legs loosened from around my hips until her feet gently touched the ground. She wasted no time in reaching for the strings of my trousers, undoing them and delving her hand down to palm my erection. I strained in her hand, marveling at how differently it felt to be touched by another, instead of myself.

"Fuck, Siyana," I groaned at as my toes curled and my eyes fluttered.

"Don't call me that," she snapped, tightening her grip on the base of my cock before beginning to stroke me. "Sia will do, if you don't wish to refer to me as wench or queen. Both are titles that I gladly claim."

She might have been joking, but she had no idea just how in line with my thoughts her words were. My eyes opened as I grabbed her wrist and lifted her hand out of my trousers, barely holding on to my thoughts of ensuring the entirety of this moment focused on her when her bottom lip stuck out in a pout.

"Do you not want me to touch you?" she asked, dropping her hands to her side. "If I'm not—"

I quickly cut her off as I bent down to undo her trousers, ensnaring her lips in the process. "So you want me to call you my queen?" I mumbled against her mouth as the clothing fell to the ground, pooling around her boots.

Her lips parted as I lowered myself to my knees and took her boots in my hands, pulling them from her feet. From this height, I could scent her arousal as I turned my eyes to look up at her, finding my lips even with her lower abdomen. She stepped out of her trousers as I pressed my mouth to her skin, licking and nipping a path down to her thighs. My hands roamed from her ass to her hips, the tips of my fingers digging in possessively.

Glancing up at her, I whispered, "Let me show you just how willing I am to serve my queen."

She nodded as my fingers found the sides of her underwear, the silent question clear. I dragged the material down her legs, inch by inch until they hit the floor. The scent of her left my dragon desperate to taste her arousal, to sample the proof of just how much she wanted us, no matter what her mouth might say at times.

To my surprise, her brassiere was tossed down to the side, distracting me briefly from the mound in front of my face that I was barely holding back from burying my mouth in. She lowered herself to the ground, leaning back until she was resting on her elbows and smirking at me.

She was temptation on a silver platter. Her body was somehow even more tantalizing than I'd pictured in my dreams. I wanted to spend days here, running my mouth and hands over every inch of her curves. It was interesting how I'd changed her out of her cold, wet clothing upon her first night in my castle, in an effort to keep her alive, but I'd never given myself the chance to truly glance at her. If I were ever in that position again with her, there was nothing that would keep me from ravishing her.

Her legs spread, revealing that pretty pussy I'd watched her dip her fingers into, pleasing herself all those weeks ago. Our eyes locked and my jaw clenched as I forced my words out.

"This is your last chance to walk away. I'm not saying it would be successful and that I wouldn't chase you," her eyes widened at that, and the animal within me wondered if she wanted to be hunted like prey. That could be arranged. My heart rate spiked and I barely stifled a groan at the image in my mind. "But I know that once my mouth touches your pussy, you will be trapped until I deem we are done. I won't be able to stop. So tell me, is this what you want?"

I expected a moment of hesitation and fear to rise up within her as it had the last time we were here, but she simply shook her head at me and stated in a confident, even tone, "I'm not walking away this time, no matter what happens."

It was all I needed to hear before I got on my hands and knees before lifting her legs and settling them over my shoulders as I lowered myself to the ground completely. This was the altar in which I'd sacrifice myself, though not for one of the elemental gods as was the ancient way of dragons.

The elementals had done nothing to deserve my faith, but Sia? She'd done everything.

My nose nestled into the sparse hair of her mound as my tongue flicked out to run along her for the first time. Her hips bucked as I did it again several times, noting that she seemed the most sensitive at the top. I may not have been with a woman before, but I was a predator built to sense every movement of my prey, and I'd use it to unlock exactly what made her come undone.

Already, I'd memorized the speed and location her fingers had displayed, but I wanted to discover this first— on my own. To know I didn't need assistance.

My arms curled around her legs, my hands finding her hips and holding her down as I pressed my face in further. My lips closed around the sensitive bud that seemed to be what made her tick, and I sucked, long and hard, before flicking my tongue across it. Instantly, she rewarded me with a moan as her hips strained to move. I doubled down, repeating the motion over and over until her legs quivered atop my shoulders.

A growl rumbled from my chest and up my throat, and she let out a gasp that had me looking up at her. Our eyes clashed as her mouth parted, panting out, "You're far too good at this."

There was an air of jealousy in her words. One that I knew far too well, in relation to thoughts of her with Brenson.

I grinned against her wet pussy before responding, "I've only ever touched your flesh, Sia. Do continue to be territorial, though. I quite like this possessive side of you."

Her head fell back and she let out a breathy sigh as I returned my tongue to her. As I focused on delivering her the highs of unrelenting pleasure with my mouth, I dragged a hand down and toward her center, running the tips of my fingers along her arousal to make them slick.

I sank a finger inside of her and began to move it in

and out as she'd done with her own two fingers. We'd build up to two, considering mine were far thicker than her own. She'd need to adjust to everything about me, if I didn't want to harm her. I found a rhythm of flicking my tongue on her swollen bud and building up her pleasure with my finger that had her hips rocking as much as they could in my ironclad grip.

Something within me knew she was searching for more with the motion, but I wasn't ready to give it to her. Her pleasure was on my terms.

My own arousal was reaching new heights as she moaned my name, the breathy sound echoing through the cavern. "Theo, please."

Her words had me growling out, "Please, what? Tell me."

I moved my hand on her hip across her abdomen, using the full weight of my arm to hold her down as I slipped another finger in, stretching her and curling my fingers up. The motion made her gasp and beg again, "Please. More."

"I need you to do something for me first," I said, speaking into her mind so as to not take me away from my feast.

"What?" she panted out in return, not bothering to speak back to my mind, or perhaps not even realizing that speaking into her mind was what I was doing right now. "Anything. Just tell me."

"Look at me," I demanded, increasing my pace with

my fingers to drive her closer to the precipice of pleasure that she was moments away from toppling over. When her eyes dropped down to look at me between her legs, I said, "Tell me you're mine. Tell me, and I'll give you everything you need."

Her eyes narrowed at my request, but I instantly clamped my lips back around her and sucked hard as my fingers stilled, besides curling up and down to reach the tender spot within, making her lids flutter and a soft moan escape her parted lips.

"I want you looking into my eyes and admitting that you're mine. We both already know it's true."

Her moans turned into cries as I resumed my pace with my fingers, slowly building up in speed as I reached up with the hand across her breast to pinch her nipple. "Shit," she breathed out as I rolled her nipple in the same manner she had seemed to like earlier, "I'm so close."

Her words had me nearly finding my own release without her even touching me.

A possessive growl sounded once more from my dragon, pushing me to cover us in the scent of her arousal.

"Tell me, Sia," I begged, knowing I wouldn't be able to stop myself from giving in to her needs, even if she didn't answer me. I was too far gone in my obsession to see her shatter for me. *"Admit that no one else makes you feel this way. Tell me you're mine."*

I watched with rapt fascination as her lips parted and her eyes widened. The walls of her pussy clenched around my fingers and I growled, sensing her release coming.

"I'm yours."

Her words sent me into a frenzy as I worked her pussy with my mouth and fingers, continuing even as her head dropped back and she screamed her release.

I wasn't done with her yet—far from it.

"You're so pretty when you say you're mine."

Her hands found my head, pushing me back as I slowed my pace but didn't back off. "Theo! I'm so sensitive now."

A renewed hunger awoke within me, wanting to see just how many times I could get her to fall apart with my body. I pulled back and smirked at the relief she showed, her shoulders curling forward and a heavy sigh falling from her.

"I'm not done with you yet," I admitted before grabbing her hips and pulling her over me as I laid on my back. Her hips shifted to allow her legs to settle on either side of my head as I pulled her down onto my mouth.

The new position had her legs truly trembling, and she squirmed as my tongue licked her again. My hands fell to grip her ass, hard, urging her to move back and forth on my mouth.

"Theo! I...I need a second—oh!" she cried out, and I felt her arousal covering my lips and the way her hips began to rock at their own pace without my urging. "My legs, they—"

"You've lain with a human man before, but

never a king of dragons. You're about to learn that dragons finish their meals, so, I don't care if you're trembling and begging me to stop."

Chapter Twenty-Five

SIYANA

MY HIPS GROUND back and forth across his mouth as my head tilted back, the tips of my hair brushing across my ass as I lost myself to the sensation. Never before had anyone made me feel so wholly devoured and revered.

Theo had an uncanny ability to make me feel like his prey and the most precious thing he'd ever held all at the same time.

When he told me he wouldn't be able to stop once I agreed to this moment, I hadn't imagined him refusing to let me off of him until I'd had a minimum of three orgasms. Never in my life had I experienced back-to-back releases, let alone three.

How I was the first person he'd touched sexually was beyond me at the display of skill. I suppose what one didn't have in experience could be made up for with enthusiasm, and that was something he had in spades.

"I can't—" I panted, overwhelmed with the sparks of

pain and pleasure that came with the lashing of his tongue as it danced around my clit. It was too much.

"I'm. Not. Done. You can and you will."

His possessive growl into my mind had me building up once more despite my pleas to him that I couldn't. How did he know what my body could handle better than I did?

It was truly like our bodies had belonged to lovers in a past life, with the ease in which we settled into intimacy once we both gave in.

Fuck, I was so obsessed with this dragon. He'd worn me down both emotionally and physically in our weeks together, challenging me to reevaluate my small-minded thoughts and opinions about the world outside of my castle.

I couldn't imagine going back to that life now. I wasn't the same woman who hid away her thoughts and desires. No matter what I did, I'd never fit back into the box I'd confined myself to for so long.

The confidence I felt in who I was and what I stood for had chills running along my arms as he growled into my mind. **"So fucking beautiful, and all mine."**

This was what I wanted when I'd declined countless suitors through the years. I wanted someone who would challenge me to be the best version of myself, even if it was a messy and painful route to get there. I didn't want to live a stagnant life, wasting away in the corner as a man took the lead.

"In case you need to hear it, too, I'm yours, Sia."

My core tightened, my release rushing through me with his words. Tears built in my eyes at the powerful emotions that came with it. It felt like a fucking spiritual experience having his mouth on my pussy and his voice in my mind at the same time.

A satisfied rumble flowed through him as he finally released his hold on my ass that kept me rooted to the spot. Bliss rolled through my mind as a tingling numbness set into my limbs. I had enough sense left to scoot down so he could sit up. As soon as he had the space, his arms wrapped around me, cocooning me against him as I settled in his lap. My head fell into the crook of his neck as I soaked in the moment, desperately clinging to the hope that we wouldn't go backwards after this.

Fingers trailed along my back in a random pattern as I burrowed in closer to him. The shift of my hips had his cock pressing up against my core, igniting my desire once more, despite feeling entirely spent mere seconds before.

Knowing I was the only one who would touch him in return had an equally possessive need surging up in me. He'd told me he was mine, but I wanted to show him exactly what that meant.

Bringing my hand down between us, I reached for the top of his trousers, wanting to pull him out and sink down onto him. Before I could make contact, he pulled back and stopped me.

"I don't want to rush this," he whispered, staring down into my eyes. I could obviously feel his desire to do exactly what I wanted, but I had to respect his words. Perhaps it wouldn't be a bad thing to slow this down before we did something we could never take back.

"Can I at least feel you?" I asked, moving off of him and settling at his side before he could respond. "You got to touch me. Fair is fair."

While I appreciated his ability to slow things down when I wanted to jump into the deep end, I couldn't help but wonder why I hadn't felt him reach out with the bond at all yet. I'd prepared myself for the warmth and lightness that came with it.

His half-lidded eyes traced the features of my face before landing on my lips. "What did you have in mind?"

I lifted my hand to run over his cock, that strained impressively against his trousers, loving the way he inhaled sharply with such a small touch. "I want to connect with you in the same way."

He nodded, and I wasted no time in pulling his trousers down before he could change his mind. For the second time, I was seeing his cock, and it was possible that I'd forgotten just how thick it was. I swallowed hard, thinking of what I'd planned in my head.

Could I even comfortably fit my mouth around him without my jaw aching within minutes? Or my teeth scraping against him?

"Afraid, wench?"

His teasing words had me scowling and grabbing his cock. It was ridiculous, how we could easily rile each other with the same tactics. One would think we could see through the words in the moment, but without fail, we each took the bait every time.

I worked my hand over his impressive length, unable to touch my fingers together around him. Maybe I *was* scared of it. Gratitude rolled through me at him urging me to slow down when I'd rushed to try to move to sex. There was no way I was ready for it.

Crawling over his leg after urging him to spread them, I settled between them, leaning down but leaving my ass in the air. His hands quickly came to gather my hair from my face, digging in possessively at the roots as he held it back.

"I'm not afraid of any part of you," I finally answered before opening my mouth and guiding the tip in. I wrapped my lips around him tightly, sucking and pulling back to tease him.

He groaned, but it was unlike any sound I'd heard from him before. Perhaps it was more a mix of a growl and a throaty groan. His fingers tightened in my hair as he admitted, "I'm afraid of you, wench. I'm afraid of the spell you have on me, despite not having any magic within you. I'm afraid I'll lose myself in you and not want to handle everything else waiting for us outside of this mountain."

His words spurred me on, reminding me that I was the first person he would experience this with. Losing himself in my touch is exactly what he'd given me earlier, and I'd be damned if I gave up before I returned that same gift. Being able to turn yourself over to the moment, surrendering the mental load that plagued you, in favor of the way your partner was making you feel...It was a mortal magic.

My tongue lavished his tip, licking up the beads of cum that pooled with my touch. I took him in deeper, forcing myself to relax my jaw in order to accommodate his size. I ran my tongue along the underside of his cock as I slowly worked my mouth up and down.

"Gods, this is unreal."

His hoarse words were music to my ears, and I knew from the way his balls clenched as I reached my free hand down to grab them that he wouldn't last long. I wanted to toy with him and drag it out, as he had done for me, but if he enjoyed pleasing me as much as it felt like he did, he'd already been teasing himself for a long time now.

He deserved this release. I'd save my tactics for another day.

His hands moved around in my hair until one held it all at the nape of my neck. I couldn't help but wonder what he was doing with his free hand. A smack echoed through the room before a slight sting settled on my ass.

Had he just spanked me?

The sudden touch had me jerking and choking on his cock, which earned a hum of approval from him.

"Am I enough to satisfy you, wench? Do I fill you to the brim?"

I blinked back tears as I pulled back slightly, somehow moaning around him with his words. The mouth on him was sinful and dangerous. I wasn't sure I'd survive it.

"Answer me."

I resumed my sucking and licking, working up and down his cock, learning the bulging veins on the underside that promised me loads of pleasure when I felt bold enough to try to take him inside of my pussy.

Another smack echoed, this time harder than the last. His hand smoothed over the tingling skin as he hummed.

"Are you ignoring me on purpose, wanting to be spanked? Naughty wenches don't get what they—"

I took deep breaths through my nose as I worked him down into my throat, making him falter in his words. As much as I loved where this was going, I didn't want this to be about me again.

"You're not the one in control right now, Theo. Give in to me."

I gagged a little again but was thankful as thicker spit entered my mouth, coating his cock and lubing the edges of my stretched lips. Using my hand at the base of his cock, I worked him up and down until he was grunting.

"I can't wait to feel you inside of my pussy, claiming me completely when you finish."

His hips jerked with my words before a feral snarl sounded in my head, and it felt like his beast talking as he rumbled, **"Don't say that. I won't be able to hold back."**

I increased the pace of my hand over his length as I pulled back to focus my mouth's attention on his tip.

Swirling my tongue around it, I tossed back, *"That's the point. I want you to finish in my mouth so I can swallow you into me."*

I didn't know where that came from, considering I'd never wanted such a thing before. My words weren't a lie, though. I wanted every bit of him. It was all *mine*. After holding back from each other for weeks, I didn't have a filter or the ability to refrain from letting every single thought flow freely now.

"Shit, Sia," he breathed out, using his grip on my hair to force me down further onto his cock, bobbing my head in a rhythm that had him quickly spilling into my mouth. I swallowed him down greedily, continuing to bob my head up and down until he was all but dragging me off of him.

His breathing was ragged as we stared at each other, and I smirked. "Sensitive, huh?"

He barked out a deep laugh before pulling my head toward him, sealing our lips together. I was shocked that he didn't care that I had the taste of him still on my tongue. Somehow, it turned me on even more as he kissed me so deeply, I wondered if there would ever be a piece of my body he didn't touch.

I all but melted under his touch until he pulled me down next to him, breaking off our kiss as he let out a deep breath. "That was incredible."

I curled into his side, feeling the most satisfied I had ever been in my life. His arm wrapped around me, anchoring me to him tightly and making me smirk against his chest.

"So, what now?" I asked, scared of the answer, but well aware that we couldn't shy away from it any longer.

There was no going back from what we did, and I just hoped that there wouldn't be any regret on his part. After all, he'd said he was saving his body for his mate. What if...what if that still wasn't me?

"Mmm," he rumbled, splaying his hand against my lower back and resting his head atop mine. "I'd like more of all of that."

I cackled, smacking my hand on his chest lightly. "That's not what I meant and you know it."

His lips brushed against the top of my head and I felt his jovial mood dissipate, taking my smile with it. "I guess that is for us to figure out, isn't it? I can't tell you where we go from here. It's a feat that my dragon was satisfied enough with marking each other with our scents to put off demanding the bond be established."

Well, at least that answered my earlier thought.

"I don't know how long I'll be able to resist initiating it again," he admitted with a heavy sigh that made my head move up and down with the breath in his lungs. "What I do know is that we need to head to Sanctum. I know you feel like you haven't made progress in our training, but you have. Unfortunately, there will always be a gaping disparity in our prowess, due to my magic."

It was my turn to sigh, deflating with his astute observation. "I don't know how I'll be able to protect you or Kaida if something goes wrong."

I rolled to my back, forcing him to loosen his grip so I could stare up at the sparkling ceiling alongside him. How things had changed since the first time I'd seen it.

Silence wrapped around us as we each fell into our own thoughts. For the first time in weeks, I wasn't filled with anxiety and pent-up anger. Sinda had been right about pleasures of the flesh, but I'd go to my grave before admitting that to her.

"Whatever happens, know that I will lay my life down before letting anything happen to you or Kaida. There's nothing I wouldn't give to ensure it."

His admission, though sweet as it was, had the smallest iota of dread taking root in my gut.

"Let's just hope it doesn't come to that."

Chapter Twenty-Six

SIYANA

"No. Absolutely not."

"Theo, there is no other option," I reasoned, dropping his saddle to the ground, knowing he wouldn't shift until this was settled.

His eyes locked onto Kaida, who was looking around in awe, seeing as this was his first time out of the mountain. It brought me immense joy to see his eyes widen and his tail flick around as his head craned in every direction, taking in the expansive blue sky that provided an idyllic backdrop to the snowy mountain range. I imagined this is how parents felt when their child first experienced the world with them.

It was a beautiful day for us to head toward Sanctum. Despite truly being in the thick of winter now, there wasn't a cloud in the sky for the time being, and we really needed to take advantage of that before any came. Rain or snow wasn't high on the list of things I wanted to experience on this journey. Though, I knew it would be a relatively quick one if Theo would just accept my plan.

Despite knowing I was right, he wasn't budging because of his ridiculous dragon-sized ego.

"We can take breaks," he reasoned, arching an eyebrow at me. "This is unheard of, wench."

Kaida walked toward the edge of the alcove and my heart all but leapt into my throat, scared he'd launch into the sky, not understanding we weren't in a cave system anymore.

Theo was quick to stand in front of him. "No! You are not allowed to fly out there yet."

My hands flew into the air. "See! There is no other choice but to let him ride on you with me. He's going to get lost," I reasoned, my voice growing panicked, "or he's going to hurt himself pushing that hard to keep pace with you!"

Nerves clawed at my stomach at the thought of either option. He was just a baby. We couldn't ask that of him. While he'd made immense progress in his training, I wouldn't risk pushing him too soon. I'd never forgive myself if he was lost in this big world he knew nothing about, or if he injured his wings during these formative growth phases.

Thankfully, even though his endurance wasn't quite up to par, he excelled at tapping into his ice magic when training with Theo, earning some hard-to-come-by praise. I'd been assured that the only real threat to him at this point would be an older dragon. However, the unspoken truth still lingered–Theo was only including the threats we knew of in our world. Heading into Sanctum opened us up to a plethora of unknowns, the unfamiliar place full of possible risks to all three of us.

Leaving Kaida behind wasn't an option either–he threw a fit when I brought it up last night. It would be even more dangerous to try to leave him behind just for him to possibly try to escape and follow on his own.

Kaida hunched down, a low growl coming from his belly as he narrowed his white eyes on Theo. My hand lifted to hide the smile I couldn't contain. My dragon knew something had shifted between us, and he wasn't a fan.

Last night, when we'd returned, Kaida had run his nose all over me, huffing and hissing. When we sat to share dinner, Theo had entwined our fingers together, lifting my hand to kiss the back of it, but Kaida was having none of it. He'd woken up from a deep sleep, as if sensing the contact, and made it his business to come sit between us, making it impossible for us to hold hands any longer.

I wasn't sure if he felt jealous of my relationship with Theo, in the sense that they were both dragons at heart. By nature, they were territorial creatures when they claimed an item or person. It seemed I'd quickly become a prized possession to them both. It could have also been spurred on by my offer for him to stay behind while Theo and I went to Sanctum.

"Don't take that tone with me, Kaida," Theo argued, holding his finger up in a scolding manner that made me giggle.

I couldn't remember a time in my life when I'd giggled before meeting Theo. It was absurd to think about. I felt like a child with a crush, yet we were already married. Perhaps that was for the best, though, because for some reason, I suspected Theo wouldn't know what to do with a courting period if it smacked him in the face.

Kaida nipped at the air in front of Theo's hand, testing his boundaries. To the latter's credit, he didn't flinch, standing his ground with clenched fists.

I couldn't wait for Kaida and me to be able to mind-speak, so we could secretly push Theo's buttons together. Glee filled me at the thought of the antics we'd get into. While I felt we had a good read on each other's emotions and needs after a month together, I was eager for him to reach the age where he could reach out and speak to me. I'd quickly learned that as a hatchling, the only person a dragon could communicate with was their mother, but even then, it was with images and not words. Soon, though, he would be able to have short conversations with me. As he grew, so would his energy and strength to focus on the bond for longer ones.

"If you want me to carry you on this journey, you will listen to your queen and behave. Am I understood? I will not be turning back if you fall off and get lost."

My mouth opened to argue, but Theo eased into my mind. **"Wench, I don't actually mean that. Of course we would find him, but he needs to understand the rules are in place for a reason, to keep him safe."**

Kaida's head craned around as he widened those big eyes at me. He knew exactly what to do to get me to fold. I pursed my lips, wanting to cave to whatever my little guy wanted, but I knew Theo was right. Much to my chagrin.

I crossed my arms against my chest. "He is right, Kaida. You need to be a good boy and stay right next to me once we find a spot for you to be strapped in."

His head bobbed up and down before he let out a trill and sat back on his hind legs, waiting patiently now. I crossed over to him and rubbed his chin as the wind rushed into the alcove, whipping my hair around. A rumble of contentment sounded as he dropped his chin further into my hand, as if I could hold the weight of it up. I let out a grunt at the sudden shift.

"We need to get going while the current is still on our side," Theo warned as I chuckled and pressed a kiss to Kaida's cheek. "The flight will be relatively quick, as long as Kaida cooperates."

He was right. Enough time had passed this morning already, with his quick trip back to his castle to deliver my letter to Lucius for my friends that assured them I was fine and to please return home. While I'd wanted nothing more than to see them myself, I feared I wouldn't leave them if I did. Despite falling into a sense of routine with

Theo and Kaida, and being accepted as dragon kin, my heart still yearned for my loved ones from my life before.

Was there a world in which I could have both?

My hand fell to the hilt of the new sword strapped to my side, one that Theo had brought back for me. A comforting sense of peace filled me at the familiar sensation. It had been too long since I'd held a blade, and it meant more to me than I could put into words that he'd truly listened when I spoke of my love of it during our training sessions. I might not have the best hand-to-hand combat skills, but with this, I knew I could offer some form of protection for us.

Kaida began to hop around, his few minutes of behaving quickly over with. I couldn't blame him. This had to be incredibly exciting, to finally see life outside of the caves, and I was eager to watch him take in the world, but my lips pursed over the current dilemma ruminating in my head.

I hadn't quite figured out exactly how we were going to anchor him onto Theo, but we'd have to figure it out once he shifted. If Kaida felt the air catch his wings, he would likely take off.

My eyes fell to the supply sack at Theo's feet, and I arched a brow. "Do you still have a ridiculous amount of rope on you, by chance?"

We'd each had our own and I'd never needed to look at his, but a sneaking suspicion told me he might.

He grinned as he bent over to lift it open. "Why? Are you wanting me to tie you up and do nasty—"

"Theo!" I snapped, cutting him off with wide eyes glancing between him and Kaida. "Not in front of the baby!"

He stretched back up as my cheeks flushed with heat, thinking of his words. The rope dangled from his hand and my mind drifted to the ways we could utilize it in a manner I would actually like. At least in comparison to our previous experience.

"Kids really ruin everything," he sighed, walking over to us and extending the rope for me to take. As my hand wrapped around it, he tugged me in toward his chest, wrapping his arm around my lower back. "I haven't even gotten a kiss today, wench. Don't tell me you regret what happened yesterday."

There was an open vulnerability in his tone that shocked me, despite his overall joking demeanor.

My head shook in response. "No, I don't regret it at all, I just..." I stumbled, drawing my bottom lip between my teeth as I sought the words to explain the roiling mess of emotions I was still sifting through myself.

How did I feel? If I was being honest with myself, all day a nervous energy had buzzed through me anytime the thought of initiating physical contact with him came to mind. At the end of our conversation last night, we agreed to merely take things as they come, but after spending a month fighting our feelings, it felt strange to just...let that go?

His forehead dropped to rest against mine as he

murmured, "I was only joking. There's no pressure to give me physical intimacy, Sia."

My hands rose to rub against his arms as I took a deep breath. I was so in my head about all of this and here he was, being sweet and merely wanting affection. It was exactly what I should have wanted from him, considering I'd been so scared to wake up today and see if he would be back to the familiar hot and cold dynamic I'd grown accustomed to over the weeks spent with him in our alcove.

I'd laid awake for a majority of the night, my mind running through scenarios of all the reasons that I shouldn't continue forward with Theo. The main one that haunted my mind was the thought of him having a mate somewhere out there that wasn't me. I didn't want to truly open up to him, body and heart, just to have him ripped from me if he found that person.

Warmth covered my cheek as his hand rose to cup it, and my eyes fluttered shut. I'd never been in love in my life, and the draw I had to this stubborn dragon made me think that we could get there one day.

"I'm scared," I admitted on a heavy exhale, deciding to keep my eyes shut, finding it easier to get the words out this way. "I'm scared to truly give this a chance and find out in the end that you'll be ripped away from me by your mate, or that you'll realize you don't actually want this."

"Open your eyes."

The soft demand had me caving, and I found myself

wanting to hide away as he pulled back to stare deeply into my eyes. It was odd, being so open with my vulnerabilities, when just yesterday morning we couldn't even have a normal conversation. While we were taking things slow physically, it somehow felt like the emotional journey was on an expedited course in my heart.

My heart flipped in my chest as he brushed his thumb across my cheek. "I can't pretend to know what we're supposed to do now. You're my first everything, Sia. I'm learning as we go." He leaned in to press his lips to my forehead, making my toes curl in my boots. "I'll probably fuck up more than once, knowing me."

I couldn't help but laugh, enjoying the quick way he lifted the feelings that weighed on my shoulders as heavily as gravity. I took another shaky breath and brought my hand up to rest on top of his, leaning into it as he glanced back down at me.

His lips curved into a soft smile at my touch and I melted. He was invested in this and finally opening up to the possibility of us after rejecting it multiple times. I couldn't run from him because of the fear that set my nervous system on fire.

I owed him the same chance.

I owed *us* the chance.

"Yeah, you definitely will," I agreed, smiling back at him. "I, on the other hand, will be extraordinarily perfect."

His lips thinned as he glowered at me. A vibration spread from his chest into mine and I smirked.

"What, dragon boy?"

"You make me want to do dirty, unspeakable things to your mouth nearly every time you open it. It's incredibly trying to hold myself back."

I pressed up onto my tip toes, throwing my arms around his neck, and his hand settled back around my waist. Teasing his lips with my own, I whispered against them, "Then we better break this curse so we can get back home and put that to the test."

Home?

His question was full of tentative hope, and my chest exploded with warmth. I hadn't realized I'd even made the connection that I'd accepted the dragon's territory as my new home until the words had come from my mouth.

Home.

You are so fucking mine.

His lips crashed against mine and I greedily opened up for him, sweeping my tongue against his as my eyes closed again. The ball of warmth in my chest expanded until my entire body felt positively on fire. It was criminal, the way he lit me up with such ease.

Just as his hand dropped onto my ass, a blast of warm air sent my hair flying forward. I jumped back, whirling to see Kaida staring at me, and despite him lacking an iris, I swear there was an accusation in his eyes.

My dragon was jealous of my other dragon.

How had this become my life?

I leaned back as Theo's hand gripped my waist,

drawing me back into him. His lips came down to rest against the shell of my ear and I shivered as his breath tickled me.

"We need to set some boundaries with our child. He's really becoming a cock-block."

Chapter Twenty-Seven

THEO

"Great job, buddy!" Sia called out to the smaller dragon, whom I'd somehow been convinced to allow myself to be tied to with a rope.

I swore this was her version of long-term payback for tying her to me on that horse. She could tell me she was over it all she wanted, but I knew my girl could hold silent grudges. I'd be hearing about how I almost killed her the first day we met until we actually did die.

Not only had Kaida ridden on my back for a majority of the trip, but I also had to slow down every time Sia asked me to, to allow him to stretch his wings and fly. I was merely a resting zone and guide for the little shit.

That was a stretch of the truth. I suppose I didn't *have* to do anything, but ever since I'd stopped fighting this draw to my wench yesterday, I found myself filled with this consuming need to ensure she was satisfied and fulfilled—my pride be damned. I didn't want to give her a single reason to walk away from this now that I'd had a taste of her.

I craned my head around to watch him out of one eye, finding him gliding and doing small barrel rolls like I'd taught him in the caves. The end of the rope being tied around his ankle allowed him far too much freedom in my opinion, but after trying to compromise with my wife, we'd ended up doing exactly what she wanted anyways.

Is this what marriage truly looked like?

Pride and annoyance warred for the main slot in my brain as her energy remained focused on Kaida. To say I had been struggling with jealousy since finding her in the quickening with the small dragon would be an understatement.

Light spilled through a break in the clouds, illuminating the pinkness that bloomed on her cheeks anytime she grew cold. Her lips turned up at the corners as she smiled and clapped for the small blue dragon showing off for her. A brightness had appeared within her eyes when she'd bonded to him, to which I was grateful. At the same time, I was insecure of how a bond between us would make her feel if we were lucky enough to establish one.

Would he come first, or would I?

My mother had made it abundantly clear that Sinda would come first before my father my entire life. As a child, I'd never understood how that was possible. We were taught from a young age that finding our mate was of the highest honor and to be cherished. Perhaps it wasn't the same for the human involved in the bond, only the drackya.

As if sensing my nervous thoughts, Sia's head turned toward me. While the smile she gave Kaida was full of warmth, it was nothing compared to the way she looked at me now. Eyes wide, her braid whipping in the wind behind her, and utter joy lifting her cheeks as the edges of her eyes crinkled with her smile. The silver hilt of her sword gleamed at her hip, and if we weren't in the sky, I would shift back, forever tempted to let her ride me in another manner.

She truly looked like a queen.

She looked like mine.

"Hey, handsome."

I fucking preened beneath her, my wings stretching out further as a shiver ran the length of my body, causing my scales to scratch together. I hated how soft she made me, yet I also didn't want to go back to who I was before she'd broken through.

"You find my dragon appealing?"

I internally groaned at the eagerness in my tone. We'd never discussed her thoughts of my dragon, and I'd just assumed she tolerated it when I needed to fly us somewhere. While I knew full-well that the curse was created to ensure humans were repulsed by us, that insecure part of me still yearned for her acceptance.

It already felt like a miracle that she'd shifted from the disgust upon looking at me in the council room to accepting my cursed human body. Could she grow to accept my beast in its entirety?

She shifted in the saddle as her smile tapered off, the action sending my hope plunging into the pits of my stomach, swallowed whole.

Perhaps I needed to focus on the wins I'd already achieved with her. They were enough.

I glanced back at the sky in front of us for a moment to check for any threats. The sun was beginning to fade behind quickly gathering gray storm clouds as we approached the southern tip of Andrathya that bordered Sanctum, setting me on edge.

"Appealing may not be the right word," she hedged and I deflated, having my fears confirmed before she continued. **"I find your dragon breathtaking. Your scales glitter beneath the sun, as if clear gemstones have been broken up and fused within them. The way you fly through the sky, as if you're truly one with it as the clouds wrap around you like a friend. The ice that glistens on the tips of your spikes, deadly and beautiful all at once."**

"Oh."

Her tinkling laughter filled my mind. **"Oh?"** she parroted back.

I wasn't prepared for such a description of myself, and for the first time I could recall, I felt bashful. *"Thank you."*

Her hands rubbed across the scales near the saddle, making me rumble at the feel of her not only touching me, but accepting me as I was. **"You're welcome, dragon boy."**

Fuck, I swear I'd find a way to claim her in this life and any other our souls found themselves in. It didn't matter that we still were unsure of the bonding that would undoubtedly happen. In this moment, she was mine, and I was hers, and everything else that existed outside of that could perish.

Streaks of lightning filled the darkening clouds over the mist-filled central territory of Edath. The rapid intensifying of the storm had me on high alert and second-guessing if I'd made a mistake in allowing the two of them to come. It was as if the sacred space sensed our intent to invade it, warning us to turn back.

To my knowledge, no dragon from Andrathya had ever entered the land. I'd asked those who dwelled within the mountain before we left, and even the most ancient of dragons couldn't recall an instance of one of their kind, of our kind, venturing to Sanctum. I hoped that even if no one living had, that perhaps one of the elders before them had passed down information. All of their answers had been similar, steeped in fear of the energy that radiated from Sanctum.

I truly believed it was the portal to our elemental gods, or the new home of the witches after being hunted to extinction by dragons. There was no other logical reason for the tales of magic that existed within all of the myths and rumors of the territory.

"Call Kaida down, please. He must stay down

*as we approach Sanctum and the bordering king-
dom's lands. It is not up for discussion."*

She didn't argue, instantly filling me with relief as I felt Kaida settle in behind the saddle. I touched his mind, finding it open to me for once.

"If we run into danger, you need to take your rider and protect her. Leave me behind. Do not go back to the humans of our lands, though, no matter what she says. They are not to be trusted yet."

He didn't respond, but that was to be expected at his age. I just had to hope he received my instructions.

Our trip had been uneventful thus far, having chosen to skirt the mountains on the western side, opposite my kingdom, to avoid the drackya. Upon crossing through the human's lands, we'd simply used the low-hanging white clouds to blend in and soar through without issue. I had taken note of the ballistas that had been mounted to the castle walls, though. They hadn't been present when I'd come to claim my wife, so why were they adding to their defenses now?

The thought was disturbing, and I'd tucked it away to discuss with Sia after we completed the current mission. There was no need to add to her mental load now, when we could do nothing about it at present. Already, her mind was too full of worry with her inade-quacies as a human and her limitations, despite more than surpassing my expectations of her skills. It was my hope that in bringing the sword back for her that her heart would settle some.

My eyes quickly swept over the expansive jungle of Eruthya approaching in the distance on our left. Though the forest was thick, I knew their zephyr dragons could be hiding with ease amongst it, or camouflaging themselves with their scales. I detected no movement at the border, only noting small specks in the distance flying around the hearth tree. Rain clouds scattered across their domain, pouring into the lush domain.

"I've never been able to see the other lands like this," Sia admitted, her excitement and wonder clear. **"That is the largest tree I've ever seen."**

It was easy to forget how sheltered she was as a human in Andrathya. As a whole, the kingdoms did keep to themselves, but it was curious that our humans didn't bother to educate themselves on what happened outside of their walls.

An obvious reason that they needed this treaty with us to last, if war ever came to our borders. They'd be mere fodder for others to pick off, existing within their small, ignorant bubble.

"That is where the ley line runs to—their hearth tree. It's where the zephyr dragons and humans live, together," I explained before tossing my head to the other side. *"Can you see the highest mountain peak on our right, in Isomythia? The humans and lithi dragons live inside it, similarly to the cavern system you saw in our mountains. They supposedly have used their abilities to shape entire cities within*

theirs, built around their ley line within the mountain.”

Before she could respond, an alarm sounded in my head, my beast sensing imminent danger. My head turned in all directions, trying to detect where I felt it coming from.

“Theo, what’s wrong?” she asked, her voice filling with unease. **“Kaida and you both began to act on edge at the same time.”**

I was relieved to hear that Kaida’s instincts were coming in swiftly. They would need his danger sense if anything happened to me.

The storm in front of us swirled in the sky and strong gusts of wind began to batter my wings. I held strong, cutting lower in the sky as the mist began to flow around us.

“Hang on tightly, both of you!” I yelled at their minds. *“I don’t know what we’re flying into, but it doesn’t feel right. Do not get separated.”*

Within minutes, we were completely enveloped. Despite my excellent vision, the mist was too thick for even me to see through. I refused to descend any lower, fearful I’d fly us directly into trees, but after what felt like we’d flown for miles with nothing coming into view, I wasn’t sure if anything else even existed in this land.

My wings began to feel heavy as the winds suddenly disappeared, leaving me to hold us in the air at a standstill.

“We can’t stay up here, Theo. We can’t defend

R.L. CAULDER

ourselves in the sky when we can't see anything. Let's go lower and find the ground."

While I knew there was truth to her words, a gut instinct told me that there was no safety to be found on the ground. Some preternatural knowledge told me there were even further risks waiting for us there. Ones that I wouldn't be able to defend us from in my current form as easily as I could in the sky.

Could I risk changing into my human form and settle for the magic I could wield to protect us?

It was like the sky itself decided for me, weighing down on my wings and body, making me feel as if I was being crushed to the ground. Tendons strained within me and I knew I'd risk serious injury to my wings if I didn't give in. I tried to maintain an even balance as we hurtled down, but I knew I was likely rocking Sia and Kaida around as I pitched from side to side.

Please let the ground find us, soon.

As soon as I said the words in my mind, my feet slammed into the dirt-packed ground, sending waves of pain through my legs at the jolting shock. Thankfully, the weight that had pressed us down lifted the second my claws touched down.

"I think it best if I shift back now. How quickly can you and Kaida get off and settled?"

Silence greeted me, and I craned my head around, trying to get eyes on them. **"Sia?"**

Fear rocketed through me as I tried to turn my head and body in every way possible to get a glimpse of them. I forced myself to stop, focusing on the weight I should feel on my back from Kaida.

I'd been so focused on the force that sent me down to the ground that I hadn't even noticed I didn't feel him on my back once the pressure lifted.

"Sia!"

"Kaida!"

No, no, no. I couldn't have lost them.

A roar ripped from my chest and out of my jaws as despair bowled over me.

How had this happened?

A sinister voice came from seemingly all around me from within the mist. "Tell me, dragon king, what would you give up in order to find what it is that you seem to have lost?"

Chapter Twenty-Eight

SIYANA

"KAIDA!"

"Theo!"

My heart raced as silence echoed back at me.

It was like descending into the quickening all over again. One moment I was safely strapped into the saddle, and the next I was on the ground and seemingly alone. I, at least, held onto my memories of who I was in this warped reality.

It felt like hours had passed since I was separated from Theo and Kaida, yet determination filled my steps, carrying me onward. I wouldn't give up on finding them. We'd all known that we were descending into the unknown when choosing to come here, but I was positive that none of us thought the chaos would start this quickly.

With a hand on the hilt of my sword, I trudged on, continuing to call out their names in a desperate attempt to find them. But all I heard was the howling wind that blew the thick mist around my body, pressing against me like unwelcomed incorporeal hands. My heavy breaths puffed through my nose and over my lips, dissipating the heavy mist only for it to move back in seconds later.

It was eerie, the way there were no sounds or signs of life anywhere. All that met my eyes was mist swirling so thickly around me that I could barely see my hand when I raised in front of me, bracing myself for a jolt if I were to run into something I could see coming. Even glancing down, I could barely see the ground beneath my feet, dead vegetation appearing and disappearing again with each step I took.

A familiar voice cut through the air so suddenly I let out a startled gasp and jumped back, eyes darting around as my heart beat wildly.

"Welcome, Siyana. I've been waiting for you."

A chill crawled down my spine, pulling an involuntary shudder from me. No. It couldn't be. *Could it?*

Dread filled my stomach like a heavy iron weight, dragging my stomach down until it felt like it touched my feet. Flipping it violently, until I felt like I might vomit. We'd talked of the quickening we'd experienced somehow occurring within a premonition from Kaida, and Theo had even linked it to the possibility of it being in the lands of Sanctum. The fear that the possibility of what happened in the quickening becoming reality had been palpable, driving me to the point of denial.

I spun around, my body coiling with tension as I

braced for the worst. Instinctively, my hand tightened on my hilt, ready to wield the sword. "Who are you, and what do you want?"

My body tensed in anticipation as I strained to hear the sound of steps, waiting for the disembodied voice to tell me to choose who died, either myself or my dragon. I knew how this would go, yet this time I wasn't going to offer myself up. I refused to accept that either myself or Kaida must die. Perhaps it was foolish of me to hold on to that belief, but I couldn't allow myself to fall into a pattern of fatalistic thoughts. Still, I waited for the voice, dread wrapping around me like a vice.

Yet it didn't come.

"It matters not what I want, yet I do know what *you* want, mortal. To find your missing companions. To seek answers I don't believe you are ready to hear." He spoke in a voice that echoed with the faintest noise–something that whispered of the rushing rivers running throughout Andrathya, carrying fish from the ocean and through our lands.

Suddenly, the mist began to swirl a few feet in front of me, slowly spiraling into the shape of a person, not entirely corporeal, but seemingly made up of water and ice. Slowly, facial features and appendages became more clear. His eyes were like frozen sapphires, glistening with unspoken power, and his body seemed to shift and swirl like a blizzard in motion.

The undine elemental god. It had to be. There was no other explanation for what I was seeing.

My throat tightened as I tried to speak, but my words came out as a mere stammer. "Did you...did you take them?"

I could feel the weight of his gaze upon me, and I couldn't help the tremble that ran through me in fear. But still, I forced myself to stand tall before the enigmatic deity.

"I have been watching you," he admitted, disregarding my question and startling me simultaneously. "You have defied the odds set by the curse of a powerful witch—the very same curse that shrouds the lands of Andrathya. You've drawn closer to the dragons with each step you've taken. I must admit, you have impressed me, human."

Despite my overwhelming fear, I couldn't help but feel a glimmer of hope at his words. But then the reality of my situation hit me once again. If he didn't have Kaida and Theo, he needed to let me be, so I could find who did.

"Where are they?" I demanded, my voice shaking with both anxiety and determination.

The elemental god tilted his head, strands of mist curling around him like serpents as he regarded me. "You are just as strong-willed in person as I was hoping. It will serve you and your companions well. Perhaps it will even save their lives."

There it was. He knew where they were and that danger would befall them.

"Please, don't hurt them," I pleaded, barely above a

whisper.

I wasn't above begging a god for mercy, but I also wasn't above trying to kill one, either.

"The path ahead is treacherous," he warned as his body began to dissipate, swirling around me in a burst of flurries. I spun on my heel, following his energy before it returned to his previous form again. "But if your heart is pure and your intentions true, you may yet find what you seek."

The gravity of his words settled heavily on my shoulders as I prepared to face whatever challenges lay ahead. I had to, for Kaida and Theo. I wouldn't allow myself to be a useless human, waiting for one of them to find and save me.

"Follow the path if you have the courage."

A soft light began to glow throughout the mist that obscured my boots. Curiosity overtook fear as I knelt down to inspect it. As soon as I touched the pulsating energy, a surge of power coursed through me. But just as quickly, a burning pain spread through my fingers and I jerked my hand back as a mocking laugh filled the air.

"Silly girl," the undine god taunted, the voice suddenly feeling like it was at my back. I jumped to my feet as they continued, whispering directly into my ear, "You think you can tap into the ley line directly? You're not a witch or a dragon—you weren't meant to wield that kind of power."

"How do you know I'm not a witch?" I questioned, genuinely curious if any still existed, seeing as Theo never mentioned catching the one who laid this curse to begin with. "Can you tell me, are they all dead?"

"You cannot trick the trickster, mortal," they answered, now sounding faint. "I know you are seeking answers about your curse with that question. I have threaded double-meanings throughout my words for millenia, do try to remember that. Though I appreciate the audacity of your attempt, however, so I will say that there are no undine witches left."

An answer that only led to even more questions.

So, there could still be others, from the other elementals. I tried to recall if Theo had ever mentioned which elemental line the woman his father slept with was from, but I drew a blank. If she was dead, the only true hope we had left was the god before me.

"That was a free answer, the next one will cost you, so choose wisely, when you wish to ask another," they warned, the sound of their voice now a mere trickle in the mist around me. "Follow the ley line if you wish to find your companions."

The clear instructions had me spurring into action, running as fast as I could along the blue, pulsating line of magic. As I stumbled over a root and nearly fell, I was shocked by the first sign of life here besides myself. I steadied myself and continued on with renewed hope, following the ley line until I stumbled into a clearing completely void of mist.

It was so strange, finally seeing something other than a wispy white void around me, that I almost didn't believe it as I drew to a sudden stop in the clearing. I quickly scanned the area for the undine god or anyone else, but found myself alone with four standing stones, arranged neatly in a square. Between them all was an opalescent-toned swirling void.

I walked slowly alongside the blue ley line that connected to the nearest stone before placing my hand on the rough surface. It hummed with energy beneath my fingers–perhaps the stone was a conduit for the immense power that had burned me prior. Each of the other stones had their own ley line running from it, and it wasn't hard to piece together the colors and directions spreading outward from this center point.

To the left was a vibrant green ley line heading toward the eastern kingdom of Eruthya. To my right was a violet streaked ley line running toward the western kingdom of Isomythia. My gaze lifted to the southern ley line opposite ours, which burned as brightly as I imagined the molten lava on the land of Salarya did.

Sanctum was truly the center of all of the magic in Edath. The connection to the gods and the powers granted from them. It took my breath away to see such raw power at its core. I couldn't imagine many got the opportunity to see this, and as I took hesitant steps toward the portal, I would bet that even fewer took the risk of traveling through it.

Whether it was because they weren't idiotic enough to travel to Sanctum like we had, or because they weren't enticing enough for a god to take interest in, as the undine had us, remained to be seen.

Indecision gnawed at my chest, my brain warring with my heart in what felt like an unwinnable battle. This had to be where I needed to go to find Theo and Kaida. The ley line had led me here, and according to the undine god, it would take me to them. But did I trust that information? He had openly admitted to being a trickster, to using doublespeak, and finding amusement in my own attempts to subvert him in my search for information.

It took all of a few seconds of looking around, knowing I'd simply get lost if I tried to search elsewhere, before I took a few more steps toward the opalescent portal. The tips of my boots were mere inches away from making contact, and I had to take deep, steadying breaths to stop myself from backing away. The fear of this unknown began to take root, knotting in my stomach and causing a slight tremor in my hands.

I had to risk it for them.

With a surge of adrenaline, I stepped into the center of the swirling magic and closed my eyes.

Please don't kill me.

For a moment, nothing happened. But then I felt a tingling sensation all over my body, and before I could comprehend what was happening, the stones were gone and bright white light consumed me. Weightlessness left me spinning in the void and I shut my eyes, feeling nausea rise up, the threat of me spilling what meager breakfast I'd forced down this morning very real indeed.

When I suddenly felt solid ground beneath my feet once more and opened my eyes, I found myself at the base of a towering mountain range that I recognized. I turned on my heel, knowing that if my thoughts were correct, Theo's castle would be behind me. But we couldn't be back home, could we?

The castle before me wasn't Theo's, yet I did recognize it. The icy walls glittered with crystals that reflected the sunlight like prisms. Rows of torches lined the path toward the large doors, and there, perched upon one of the walls was my dragon looking down at me, from the same castle we'd found in the quickening.

Our eyes connected and he let out a loud trill. I opened myself to our bond and felt his concern and relief pouring into my mind. I sent those same emotions back to him tenfold, thankful, at least, to have one of them on my side once more.

Kaida.

I couldn't help but smile as he swooped down to land beside me, knocking up a spray of fresh snow with his tail. I rushed to his side, throwing my body against his chest as I did my best to hug my arms around him. His head dropped to my back, a rumble sounding from him and vibrating against my heaving chest. I gulped breaths greedily, relief pouring into me from the contact with my dragon.

"Hey, buddy," I whispered as a tidal wave of

emotions suddenly clogged my throat. "I was so worried. It turns out your premonition was correct."

He nuzzled against me affectionately as I took a deep breath, trying to keep the tears of relief from cascading down my face.

But then another thought crossed my mind—where was Theo?

"He's safe for now," came a familiar voice from behind us. My heart skipped a beat as I turned to see the undine god once more, but this time in a human form as he approached.

Tall and imposing, he exuded an air of power and an ethereal quality that was both captivating and terrifying. His icy blue eyes seemed to pierce through my very soul, while his flowing light-blue hair cascaded down his back like a frozen waterfall. Every movement he made sent shimmering ripples through the air, as if he was surrounded by an invisible aura of frost.

Kaida growled from behind me and I held out an arm, scared of what the god would do if he attacked. The iron weight of dread threatened to pull me to the ground, but I stood straight, steeling my reserve as I faced the undine god before me.

"Now, Sia, I hate to be the bearer of bad news," he said, holding his hands out as twin daggers of ice appeared in them. "Either you die or the dragon does."

We had known it would come to this, but my heart twisted painfully in my chest anyway.

I wasted no time in drawing my sword, ready to fight until my heart stopped beating to protect Kaida.

"I don't mean the dragon behind you," the god clarified, smirking at my confusion as the tip of my sword began to fall toward the ground. "I mean the one who has already offered to sacrifice himself for you."

My breathing turned shallow, coming in small, panicked gasps as the realization hit me.

Theo.

The dragon spoken about in the premonition had been him.

Chapter Twenty-Nine

SIYANA

"STAY BACK, KAIDA," I demanded, my tone far more harsh than I'd ever been with him.

It was necessary—I couldn't allow myself to be distracted by his involvement. He was mine to protect, and that was exactly what I was going to do.

His trill and stomps behind me told me he would do as I said, though he wasn't happy about it. I didn't need the dragon to be happy–I needed him to be safe.

My heart raced as I launched forward, my sword gleaming in the dim light. With all my training and skill, I aimed the blade straight for the god's neck, hoping to end his life quickly. But as I drew closer, I couldn't help but wonder if a beheading would even work on a being this powerful.

Yet I couldn't hesitate now—my movements were swift and precise, honed from years of dedication. In mere seconds, I stood before him with my blade inches from his skin. But he was just as quick, effortlessly evading my attack with a grace that defied his immense stature. His ice daggers clashed against my sword as he parried. No matter how many blows I landed against the icy weapons, the divets I managed to make in them were healed almost instantly by his magic.

Not for the first time, I couldn't help but wonder how anyone could stand a chance against a magical deity. Hadn't Theo proven to me time and again that I could hold my own, until magic was involved? But I couldn't give up—there had to be a weakness I could exploit somewhere. Everyone had one, right?

A mocking laugh escaped him as I paused my assault, gasping for breath in the frigid air. Each breath was a brutal torture to my lung, and as loose strand of hair fell into my face, I blew it away as I carefully studied my adversary. There had to be a way to disarm him, but it dawned on me that he could simply conjure up more weapons with his magic. It was apparent then that I had to stop him from summoning them in the first place. But how?

He didn't use any gestures or incantations to cast his spells—it was as if he commanded the elements with merely his thoughts. So then, how could I prevent his thoughts? Was it even possible?

"This has been unexpectedly entertaining," the god admitted, letting his ice weapons melt away and drip onto the ground. "It has been a long while since I've felt the urge to meddle in the affairs of those in my topside domain. You have impressed me by not faltering, even after being pulled into my mirrored realm, where my powers are at their strongest."

For a moment, the revelation interrupted my thoughts of disarming him. A thousand new questions sparked in my mind, and I swallowed thickly around the urge to ask all of them at once.

"I couldn't help but notice that your castle is in the same location as the drackya's," I observed, noting the glint in his eyes. "Do all elementals reside in this mirrored realm?"

"Mmm," he murmured, tilting his head as he regarded me. A slow smile spread across his face, and my stomach twisted uncomfortably at the sinister twist of it. "I did warn you that more answers would cost you, mortal."

Shit.

My body froze, encased in the grasp of frigid magic that twisted around me like a deadly serpent. My sword, once an extension of my arm, now lay useless at my side, held in place by the same icy tendrils that bound me so effectively.

The god stood before me, his eyes blazing with triumph as he surveyed his helpless prey. I could feel the cold creeping into my bones, threatening to turn me into a frozen statue from the inside out. Panic began to claw its way up my throat as I realized the gravity of my situation. I hadn't come this far to become a forgotten relic of the time a mere mortal had challenged the undine god.

"Such bravery, but you are no match for me," he taunted, his words sending shivers down my spine. I grit my teeth, defiance burning in my chest as I refused to back down. "You've put up much more of a fight than any other mortal before you, so for that, you have my begrudging respect."

I didn't want his respect—I wanted his defeat.

A surge of defiance rose within me and I gritted my teeth, refusing to back down. "If I die here, Theo will avenge me, tearing you limb from limb," I spat, already imagining the god's death in return.

I may have seen the warm side of Theo that he kept locked away deep within his heart, but I also knew the ruthless and feral nature that lurked within him—and even that was just a fraction of what he was truly capable of.

In the midst of our standoff, a small roar echoed from behind me—not that of a full-grown dragon, but one that was representative of Kaida's first attempts at using his true voice.

"Forgive me, Sia," a sweet voice spoke into my head. **"I cannot sit and watch."**

"No! Kaida!" I yelled just as the god's eyes snapped to the space behind me, switching focus. To my horror, I was bound tightly in my prison of ice, unable to turn toward my dragon and urge him with my eyes as well as my words. "Fly away!"

Shards of ice began to rain down as a shadow flew above me, cresting over my head and toward the god. A wall of impenetrable ice lifted with ease, a shield that encased the god from my dragon's futile attempt to protect me.

"Kaida, please," I begged as my eyes stung with tears, causing my vision to blur. *"Please leave me."*

Just as my dragon descended, talons out and aimed at the block surrounding the undine elemental, the ice shattered. Kaida's wings quickly expanded, in a likely attempt to shield me from the onslaught just before my eyes slammed shut, preparing myself for impact.

The ground shook and my eyes flew back open. Doing a quick mental sweep, I was relieved to feel no injuries to myself. When my eyes dropped lower, a scream ripped from my throat at the sight before me. Kaida was pinned to the ground with a large taloned foot on his throat and chest. A pure white dragon with sapphire eyes stood in place of the human form we'd seen from the god. He was, without a doubt, the most fearsome and intimidating beast I'd ever laid eyes on. Each of his glittering scales was tipped with shards of ice, covering him like a second layer of armor. His tail swept behind him, the ball of fearsome spikes at the end belying the fact that he would easily skewer a person with one easy swing of it.

In that moment, as I watched Kaida struggle and cry out in pain, I knew true terror for the first time. The tip of one of his gleaming black claws pulled back from its dangerously close position at the smaller dragon's heart.

"I do not wish to harm you, little one." The god

seemed to speak without moving his mouth, though he was not infiltrating my mind. It was as if the wind itself was his messenger. His large, scaled face descended toward Kaida's thrashing body, letting loose a billowing cloud of steam from his nostrils that engulfed the smaller dragon. "Stop squirming or I might harm you, accidentally, of course."

I tugged at the ice trapping me, thrashing around wildly as I yelled, "You're going to crush him!"

Those sapphire eyes lifted, trained on me as his taloned foot lifted ever-so-slightly. "I would never harm such a perfect creation, one born from my own power."

The sheer offense in his tone as he admitted to creating the very dragon he was nearly crushing had my mouth clamping tightly shut.

Call me dense or naive, but never before had I wondered how the dragons had come into existence. For as long as our texts could recall, the dragons had simply lived alongside humans. I'd known of drackya and witches being of the elementals' creation, but they hadn't started to appear in our texts until the more recent centuries. Dragons had simply always been there, part of our prehistory that had never been questioned.

I didn't intervene as he freely offered more information, instead letting him rant as I checked on Kaida.

"The dragons were the very first of our creations to occupy the human's realm, offering a foothold into their world, as we cannot stay there ourselves. The dragons have served their purpose beautifully, cementing our tie to the human realm. It is *our* magic that runs through your world as ley lies. It is the very same magic we used to sustain the first dragons, creating ecosystems in which our creations could thrive. Over the span of their first millennia in your lands, the dragons and their connection to our magic through the ley lines changed the human realm, irrevocably."

"Are you okay?"

"Yes, I...I think so," he answered, his voice trembling even mentally. **"I'm sorry I wasn't strong enough. Theo will be mad. I was supposed to protect you if he wasn't here."**

I couldn't stop the few stray tears from leaking from my eyes to hear the warbling admission from my dragon. *"Theo will be so proud of you. You flew in to protect me, against someone much more powerful than both of us, despite me telling you not to."*

Fuck, where *was* Theo? We needed him.

Still the elemental droned on as Kaida continued to wiggle beneath his claws. "Life grew boring, as the humans and dragons continued to live separately. There was nothing for us to observe from our realm through their eyes, thus the drackya and witches were created and sent to the topside. We watched new civilizations rise and flourish until the drackya and witches became natural enemies, fighting for the energy from where the ley lines occupied in the central areas of each kingdom. With the dragons naturally taking the side of drackya and forming alliances, the witches were hunted to near extinction."

"So, the elementals created these beings because you were dissatisfied with your lives in your own realm," I mused, keeping up the conversation to try to buy time to figure out some type of plan. There had to be *something* I could do. Perishing without first putting up a fight simply was not an option. "If company and entertainment was what you wanted, you should have just kept your creations here."

The ground vibrated as he stepped back, lifting his foot from Kaida's wriggling form. My dragon shot into the air, flapping his wings one, twice, before pulling them tightly against his sides and skidding to a stop next to me. Through it all, Kaida never stopped growling at the massive beast.

"What entertainment can truly be found in observing creatures that you can easily control, easily bend to your will at your own whim?" he rebutted before collapsing back into his human form in the span of seconds. The sudden change in his appearance and size was jarring, my brain taking a second too long to catch up. His tone was flippant and full of arrogance as he continued, "We needed the unknown variable provided by the humans to truly keep us entertained. Though many of your kind are the same—selfish, greedy, and cruel–there are a few, like you, who manage to surprise us."

The ice holding me captive melted away as he drew closer to us. It didn't seem like he actually wanted to kill either of us, at least not yet. But why? What was the point in keeping us here, gloating about the creation of dragons, drackya, and witches?

It was like being splashed in the face with ice-cold water, the way the obvious truth hit me.

The curse was a way of providing him that entertainment he craved. If the undine god were to help us break that curse, ending his current tantalizing form of entertainment, he would want something in return. But what did I have to offer him that he would find more amusing than the unnecessary anger and grief felt by those most affected by the curse? That remained unclear.

"You told me to choose between Theo and myself," I said, bringing us back to the very beginning of this fight. "I choose to offer myself."

I kept my voice as even and confident as I could manage, but inside I was shaking, fear searing through my veins. I was gambling here, taking a huge leap of faith based on the little information I had gleaned from our conversation thus far. If humans were the key to his entertainment, would he simply kill me here? I was beginning to think not.

The cold lingered in my bones as I watched him, arms wrapping around my shaking body as he drew to a stop in his tracks. A bone-deep shiver passed over me as his eyes took in my body, from the hair atop my head to the tips of my toes and all the way back again.

"Well," he started, that same slow, sinister smile from before returning to his face, "since you have both offered yourselves, it seems I must find a way to encourage one of you to...forfeit."

He'd taken the bait.

"I don't like this," Kaida murmured while shuffling closer to me and extending a wing protectively over me.

I took a few small steps forward, refusing to cower behind him. I couldn't allow him to pull the god's focus from me. Not when I had him hooked. "Then what would you have me do?"

"Trust me, Kaida. We will all leave here together."

I wasn't sure if that was a promise I would actually be able to keep, but saying the words felt like the first step in manifesting my desired outcome. If I said it enough, I would eventually start to believe it too.

The god's hands came together in a loud clap, sending shockwaves over us, the world around us morphing. Suddenly, the mountain and castle were gone, and instead, I found myself at the bottom of a large, stone arena, staring up and up and up, the stands stretching as far as the eye could see. Incorporeal figures made of various forms of water and ice filled the seemingly endless stands as I turned around slowly. The echoing booms of their loud cheers and shouts overwhelmed me as I struggled to understand what was going to happen now.

Kaida growled at my side before suddenly disappearing. Panic once more filled my being, leaving me with a racing heart and quickened breaths.

"Sia!"

My heart fluttered at the sound of Theo's voice. It was so faint, the noises of the fake crowd drowning him out, but I scanned and scanned until I spotted him standing next to the god at the very top of the arena. They stood near a platform that jutted out beyond the stands, like an observation area that sat directly above a large gate in the arena. His hands and feet were bound with a pulsating energy that reminded me of the ley line itself, glowing a vibrant shade of blue, beating in a rhythm that made it seem alive. I watched as the restraint grew to cover his mouth, forcing itself between his lips and wrapping around to the back of his head.

Wisps of his white hair flew around his head as he thrashed in the constraints.

He seemed unharmed from what I could tell, and relief took root within my chest, growing into a wild, uncontrollable thing when I spotted Kaida next to him. A cage of the same magic trapped him as well.

"Please don't do anything to risk yourselves," I begged them both, staring up at them imploringly. I was met with silence in return, the path between our minds feeling severed in some way.

The god strode forward, and a long, billowing cape made of what looked to be blue silk glided behind him, long enough that it reached the floor. For an awful moment, I found myself wishing his legs would get caught in the material, twisting and twisting until he fell and met his end on the stone floor of the arena. He raised a hand, and suddenly all of the spectators quieted, leaving an eerie calm in the noise's wake.

"The rules of today's challenge are simple," he began, but the creaking sound of heaving metal met my ears, pulling my eyes to the iron gate on the arena floor. "If you can defeat the beast, I will give you what you seek and release you."

What beast was I expected to fight?

"Should the drackya king decide to intervene to protect you once the battle begins, the magic binding him will dissipate, allowing him to come to your rescue."

Theo stilled at those words, head craning in the god's direction. Hope fluttered to life in my chest before meeting a premature end. My blood ran cold at the god's next ones.

"The cost of his intervention will be his dragon. Should the drackya come to your aid, he will forfeit the magic from within him, leaving him a human."

Chapter Thirty

SIYANA

My breath caught in my throat, and my hand tightened around the hilt of my sword until my knuckles hurt.

Forfeit his dragon.

Tightness clawed at my throat as the rules played in my head over and over. The undine god being unable to resist a new form of entertainment was what I had taken a bet on. I hadn't doubted he would pull some sort of trickery, but the stakes of my bet were nothing at all like I could have imagined. The cost was too high, and I was afraid Theo would willingly pay it.

I refused to look at Theo or Kaida, dropping my eyes to the arena floor instead. I couldn't think of them. They were safe for as long as I had my life and the fight left within my heart. I was thankful now that we couldn't speak to each other mentally, needing the silence of my mind to carry me through this trial.

I had to do this for them. *For us.*

Chains rattled as the gate groaned open, the sound of it locking into place echoing through the air. It was as ominous as it was unsettling, sending chills of fear down my spine. I felt the hairs on my arms stand on end as I stared into the dark depths beyond the gate that led from the arena floor.

Acid filled my stomach as the ground began to shake, a tremor running through it to my boots.

Whatever was coming was much larger than myself. I slid a foot back as I fell into a battle-ready stance, shifting my hips to allow my knees to bend and hover slightly forward. Pulling the hilt of my sword between both of my palms, I took a deep breath, trying with all my might to dispel my nerves.

They had no room in this battle. I couldn't put myself at a disadvantage before the fight even began.

"I am nothing if not fair," the elemental called out as from the depths of the shadowed hall now, a blood-red dragon's head emerged, orange eyes burning like their magic had eternal flames in their depths.

My pulse spiked. Was this an ember dragon?

"I created a dragon for you to fight, though I didn't imbue any extra magic into him. He is a standard ember dragon, with the simple ability to breathe fire. That is his one weapon, as your sword is yours."

I couldn't help the snort of incredulity that came from me. This was fair to him? Fascinating.

Perhaps I would have taken that as a compliment, if there wasn't so much at stake.

I kept my gaze trained on the dragon that had stepped fully into the arena. Bouncing lightly on the balls of my feet, I was prepared to launch myself in any direction to avoid an attack. His large head swung around, slitted eyes taking stock of our surroundings as steam poured from his snout.

Using his distraction to my advantage, I took the opportunity to quickly try to gauge the size of the dragon in comparison to others I had encountered in my time away from my father's home. From this distance, I felt that I could safely assume he was around the same size as Sinda, whose size I was familiar with both close up and from far away. This was always the first thing I did when facing a new opponent.

Assess and compare strengths and weaknesses.

Speed would be on my side, but the sheer size of him would cancel that out. If he lifted a foot, intending to crush me, the diameter for where he needed to strike was massive. I would have to not only choose the correct direction to avoid him before he brought it down but also hope that I could get to the edge of his hit zone.

The same went for his tail. Thankfully the ridges and spikes that started small at the bottom of his tail, progressively becoming larger as they moved up toward his back, wouldn't be an issue, unless he could twist his tail around to impale me. As it was, I could attempt to duck, jump, or throw myself to the side if it swept toward me. That move, at least, would be heavily projected and give me time to react, but considering I was about the same size as the skinniest part of his tail, I was once again at a disadvantage to the beast.

"Best of luck, mortal."

The god's words broke me out of my inspection of my opponent just as the dragon seemed to focus on me, swinging its neck around and pointing its snout in my direction.

I quickly surveyed the arena, finding the walls around us were far too tall to even consider trying to climb. The only exit appeared to be the hall from which the dragon appeared, which still stood directly behind him. Perhaps I could use the more narrow hall to my advantage to fight from, instead of the large arena that left me vulnerable and open to attack from all sides.

Time was up for my inspection as the dragon opened its jaw and unleashed a torrent of fire as it lumbered toward me. I quickly darted to the side, pumping my arms and legs harder than I'd ever pushed them before as my heart leapt into my throat. This was the true beginning of my trial.

I felt the heat of the dragon's fire breath licking at my back, but I refused to glance back, focusing instead of interspersing my path with sharp and unexpected turns to throw the dragon as far off my trail as I could manage. Eventually the heat dissipated and I took the opportunity to glance over my shoulder, breathing heavily as I saw a glow building from his belly. He came to a stop, giving me a chance to put the pieces of information I'd gathered, together.

So there was a finite amount of fire that he could blast me with before he needed to produce more, it seemed. The faint glow from his underbelly was the perfect cue for me to watch for, and with that in mind, I took the risk of turning back and heading toward him. If I wanted a chance at survival, I had to see how quickly he could begin to attack with fire again–my survival depended on my understanding of the extent of his abilities. If I stayed far enough away, he might perceive me as not being much of a threat and hold onto the fire until he felt it was needed again.

A growl vibrated as his lips peeled back, spit dripping from his razor-sharp teeth and dropping to the ground, causing the stone to sizzle and heat waves to appear in the air above it. So his spit contained some level of heat as well.

Just as I began to build confidence in my ability to catalogue the ember, he lowered himself slightly, haunches bunching before he launched himself into the sky. As his jaws opened once more, his wings flapped, lifting him higher. The god must have encased us in a magical barrier, though, because after a moment, the dragon was forced back down, as if he had bounced against an invisible wall of force.

He quickly righted himself, hovering just below the space where he'd smacked into the barrier before cascades of flames tore through the air, coming directly for me.

"Shit!" I squeaked, equally impressed and terrified of the distance the flames could travel.

I sprinted toward the open hall, knowing there was no other place to find cover. The dragon could stay in the air indefinitely, wearing me out until I made a mistake or was left with no stamina to escape the flames. The only way I stood a chance was if he came back down to the ground and fought on my level.

His earlier attack had left scorched, hot lines that glowed across the stone floor, but with the path I needed to take to get to the hallway, I was left no choice but to run directly over them. The bottoms of my boots hissed with the contact and I gritted my teeth as the heat quickly passed through to my feet as I reached the other side. Now I knew I couldn't afford to let him cover the entire arena floor with fire either, the heat of his breath attack working against me on multiple levels.

I was quickly running out of options for finding a path that would allow me to get close enough to the dragon to even wield my own weapon against him.

Still, I refused to concede. Every enemy had an opening. I just needed to buy myself enough time to find his.

Darkness passed over me as I retreated into the hall, the heat of flames blasting the opening at my back. My chest heaved as I gasped for air, whirling back around as the heat faded once more. It seemed he'd run out again.

My thoughts raced as I desperately tried to piece together what little information I'd gathered, knowing I had limited time until either the stone floor would be too hot for me to survive running on or until my own stamina failed me. It required every bit of energy I had to keep up the pace required to avoid his flames, and I wasn't foolish enough to think I could keep it up for long. Nor was I foolhardy enough to believe that the dragon wouldn't begin to formulate his own plans of attack, easily seeing how limited my own prowess was at a long-distance.

I needed him up-close and he needed me far away, or pinned to one spot, to use his fire accurately.

My eyes blinked rapidly as my brain snagged on that thought. The only way he'd risk coming close enough for me to use my weapon was if I was pinned to one spot, unable to flee, giving him an opening to funnel his flames into.

This hall was the perfect trap for both him and me. All that mattered was who executed their plan best.

My palms began to sweat as my heart skipped a beat, and I took a moment to wipe them on my trousers, passing my sword between my hands as I did so. I shuffled back and forth on my feet, nerves twisting my stomach into a mess of churning bile as I waited.

The rhythmic beat of the dragon's wings sounded, growing closer as his shadow cast over the opening.

That's it. Come down to my level.

I wouldn't get a chance to surprise the dragon again. If I didn't get this right, I was dead, plain and simple.

The only option was to either die alone or be victorious. I could not allow Theo to give up the very essence of his being to protect me. Never before had I felt such immense pressure weighing on my shoulders for the sake of someone else.

Someone who matched my own fire and would never let me settle.

Someone who made me ache deep to my core when I was in his presence.

Someone who forced me into uncomfortable growth.

Theo.

Not only was I fighting for him to keep his dragon, I was fighting for the life I desperately wanted the chance to explore with him once we got the answers to break this damnable curse.

To see if we'd still choose each other when we no longer had to for the sake of a treaty.

My chest expanded as I took a deep breath, seeing the talons of the ember descending in front of the opening. A strange sense of peace passed over me as my truth poured through my mind.

I would choose Theo, over and over again.

He may drive me absolutely insane at times and have his own personal work to do, but I wanted to be there when he finally realized he could let others in and heal from the scars of his past.

I didn't want to picture anyone else at my side, infuriating me until my hair turned gray and my skin wrinkled, belying the beauty of the time that we'd spent together.

The ground shook beneath my boots as the ember settled down onto the arena floor, far enough away that there was still a gap between the opening and him. That same space allowed his snout the room to lower until it was level with me. He thought he had me right where he needed me to char me down to bones.

Yet a smirk of determination pulled my lips up at the edges. It bounced on the balls of my feet, mustering the arrogance needed to bluster myself into actually implementing this truly insane plan.

It was now or never.

Tingles spread through my body as I planted my foot back, kicking off toward the beast.

I rushed in with my blade following behind me, watching in anticipation as the fire built in his belly. It felt like déjà vu rolling through my body as I stared directly into the jaws of death as they opened before me. This time I didn't run away. I couldn't evade him, needing him to think he had me trapped and unable to escape the hellfire of his breath weapon.

The orange glow of fire built from within his throat, and I knew I had to time this perfectly. I only had one shot to shift directions and take him by surprise, using his limited line of vision against him.

Once his jaws widened, stretching until they were fully open and prepared to spill fire down this tunnel, he wouldn't be able to turn his head in order to see me. Turning would force the fire in a different direction, and what would be the point of trapping me just to waste his most devastating weapon? He may have enhanced long-distance vision, but what he didn't have was excellent depth perception, due to his eyes facing out on the sides and not forward. I would exploit that very weakness of dragons here and now, but to do so would require a level of bravery I've never before had to conjure.

As his growl trembled through the ground and I watched the first flecks of a spark on his tongue, I bit down, my own jaw clenching as every nerve ending in my body screamed for me to flee.

Wait.

I pumped my legs faster as molten fire spewed into his mouth with the same force of a geyser spitting boiling water into the sky. Impending heat began to blister my cheeks just as I passed through the narrow opening between the arena floor and the opening in the wall. My eyes closed briefly as the fire consumed my vision, blinding me as I planted my right foot into the ground.

Now.

I threw my body over my shoulder at the last second with all the power I could muster, pulling the hilt of my sword and my elbow up to jaw level. I swung my sword around with me as I barrel rolled through the air and to his side.

I saw Brenson's look of surprise flash through my mind when I'd initially come up with this move during our final morning of training. At the time, I'd used his poor depth perception due to his late night of drinking against him. Unlike that morning when I'd pulled short of cutting deeply into Brenson's neck, I let out a scream as I drove all my energy through my arms, placing my other hand on the hilt as the tip of my blade flew toward the dragon's eye. My aim was true, sinking deep within the orange serpentine eye all the way up to the hilt.

The dragon's roar of pain reverberated through my body, shaking me in the seconds before he jerked his head away from the source of his anguish. I lost my grip on my weapon, the force of the dragon trying to escape his pain flinging me bodily away from him. Rolling over and over, all of my focus was on my stomach twisting with nausea...until my body hit the arena wall, forcing me to a hard stop as the breath was knocked forcefully from my lungs. Briefly I wondered if it hadn't been enough as I picked my head up to watch my opponent.

Was the sword not long enough? The force of the thrust not great enough? The desperate determination I'd forced through my trembling limbs not feral enough?

Seconds later, the beast stilled and his slitted pupil blew out, round and lifeless as his head flopped to the side, the force of it shaking the ground beneath my feet. The hilt of my sword was barely visible with how deeply embedded it was.

I'd done it.

I'd slayed the beast on my own.

My nervous system was wrecked from adrenaline and fear, making me uncertain of whether I wanted to shake from the shock of it all or scream my relief. The decision was made for me as a figure climbed up from the other side of the dragon's snout.

He shook his head, the waves of his white hair now

long enough to cover his dragon eye. Soot was smeared across his cheeks and neck as he walked toward me, fury blazing in his eyes and swiftness in his gait.

"Theo..." I breathed out, shaking my head in disbelief of what I was seeing. My body trembled at the implications of seeing him here with me on the arena floor, my knees going weak before giving out beneath me. I crashed to the ground, falling hard on my shins as I blinked away the tears stinging my eyes. "No. No. No."

He'd jumped down.

Chapter Thirty-One
THEO

TEARS BURST from her eyes as I fell to my knees and gently gathered her in my arms, tugging her against me as her body shook with the force of her sobs.

"Hey, wench," I murmured, my body finally regulating as I held her and felt the steady thrum of her heart beating against my chest.

She was alive.

I swore things moved in slow motion as I pictured the fire licking at her body, burning away the woman who stole my heart. Something had snapped within me, my dragon and I falling into agreement that she was to be protected—no matter the cost.

"You stupid fucking dragon!" she screamed as she buried her cheek against my chest, lifting her hand to hit against my shoulder. "I had killed him, and now it doesn't even matter!"

Of course she was pissed at me, meanwhile all I felt was relief. That was my wench, assuming the worst of me and my intentions.

My hands grabbed her face tenderly, tilting it up until she was forced to stare at me. "Please don't cry for me. I'm not worthy of a resource as precious as your tears."

Was she this bereft because I'd lost the same part of myself she hated only two months before? It simply could not be.

"Why would you give your dragon up for me?" she questioned, absolutely hysterical as she began to hyper-ventilate, ignoring my pleas that she calm herself.

It seemed she was truly distraught, but wouldn't me being a human be more in line with her interest and life?

Whatever the case, my chest constricted at the anguish pouring from her. I wrapped my arms around her tightly, holding her close and burying my nose in her hair, breathing her in as she fell apart.

Her question rolled through my mind, and while I could think of a hundred answers, only one mattered. "Because I can't imagine a life in which you don't exist, wench. Somewhere along the way, you became as deeply ingrained within my soul as my dragon."

"I..." she struggled to say between the ragged breaths blowing against my neck. "I had it. I killed it. Why did you sacrifice your dragon right at the end?"

My nostrils flared as I nodded against her hair. It was unfortunate that the beast was dead as my feet touched the ground, but I'd done what I needed to in the moment, and I wouldn't apologize for it. "All I saw was the dragon beneath our platform, pinning you in the hallway and about to engulf you in flames. I didn't think, wench. I just jumped down, ready to take him out or die with you."

She pulled her head back, and I lifted mine to stare down at her dirt-smudged face, tear tracks running over her and cheeks and ending at her chin. Her bottom lip quivered as she sucked in a breath, seeming to attempt to calm herself. This was the dirtiest and most broken version of her I'd ever seen, yet I'd never before found her quite so breathtaking.

Here she was, heart shattered into jagged pieces, the pain on display for the world to see as she sobbed. And all of this...for me.

I lowered my head, touching our foreheads together as I breathed in her scent, the stench of sulfur masking the citrusy, woodsy scent I had grown to love. "All I know is that I couldn't stand there and simply watch as the other half of my god's damned heart risked her life for me, simply to allow me to keep my dragon."

"But..." she rebutted, her voice cracking as she did. "Your dragon is who you are, Theo."

Our breaths mixed together in the space between us. I desperately wanted to taste her lips, but I needed her to understand first. "Me without my dragon is anguish, but I'll still be alive. Me without you, wench..." I trailed off, unable to get the words out as emotion clogged my throat for the first time since my mother passed. "It's unimaginable. It would be like being alive while my heart was dead in my chest, no longer beating."

"I can't bear knowing I'm the reason you gave half of your soul up," she admitted as fresh tears pooled in her eyes. "It's too heavy to carry in my heart."

I lifted my lips to press against her forehead as she hiccuped. "And I couldn't bear the thought of you giving your life up for me to keep it."

Before Sia could reply, my head snapped to the left, the hairs on the back of my neck standing on end and alerting me to the presence of the undine god. He stood at our sides, staring down at us with his hands clasped behind his back. The grin he wore tore a growl from my chest, my dragon threatening to surge out of me for the last time, just so I could rip the skin from his bones.

All of this was because of him. He'd made my wench inconsolable.

"Well, it appears we are at an impasse," he chirped, like life just couldn't possibly get any better for him. "Just as her blade pierced his brain, killing him, your feet touched the ground of the arena after breaking your binds to interfere."

Sia jerked from my hold at his words, pushing to her feet to glare at him as I stood to my full height next to her. I entwined our fingers together, squeezing lightly as she vibrated with rage. Fury rocked me to my core, but I was more afraid of what she would try to do to him than what he could ever possibly do to us, in that moment.

"I did what you asked," she spat, bitter and full of rage. "I killed the ember on my own without interference. You can't take his dragon."

While I did understand her rationale, this god had already proved to not care about reason, preferring to take joy from our misery. This right here? This was the perfect opportunity for a heaping spoonful of it.

He tsked in return, holding a hand up to stop her from continuing. "He willingly gave his dragon up the second he made his decision to intervene and the magical restraints dissolved."

Just what I expected.

My teeth ground together as he added, "But, in the spirit of also acknowledging that you did *technically* complete the task given to you, mortal, I will offer you a new trial."

Swallowing the growl rising in my chest, I stared the undine god down. I didn't like this one bit. Whatever he was going to offer had to have an even heftier price tag attached than what was asked in the first trial, especially if he was giving up the opportunity to take my magic and dragon.

"No," I quickly disagreed, stepping forward and letting go of Sia's hand. "Take my dragon and let us be done with this."

"Theo!" she yelled, her voice hoarse from crying. She stepped back to my side, clasping my hand between both of hers. I turned to gaze down at her as she implored with wide eyes, "At least hear him out, please."

Her fingers squeezed my hand tightly, and my heart thudded wildly within my chest. Everything in me screamed not to give this god another minute of my time, but I couldn't deny her. Not when she made it clear that my choice to give my dragon up for her would haunt her.

"Fine," I relented, looking back at the elemental whose eyes were bouncing back and forth between us, a gleeful smile tugging at his lips that more than proved that he couldn't get enough of our discourse. "Spit it out, but we're not agreeing to it before hearing it."

He hummed as his lips split into a full-fledged grin. "It's simple this time."

We stood our ground as he approached, walking around us in a slow circle before coming to a stop at our front once more. I only barely resisted the urge to lash out at him.

"Initiate the mate bond," he demanded, earning a gasp from Sia.

My eyes instantly narrowed, and it was on the tip of my tongue to tell him to go fuck himself, but he kept speaking, stilling my tongue for the time being.

"If you are mates, I will ensure the curse is broken," he offered, splaying his hands out before his smile fell. "And if you aren't, well, that won't be my problem to deal with."

The callousness of his words had my body tensing up to the point of shaking, but Sia snapped me out of it as she stepped forward and tilted her chin up, staring up at the elemental with seemingly no fear.

I'd never stop being in awe of the way she never cowered or wilted in the face of danger.

"We accept."

My mouth popped open as the elemental looked us over. "My, my, little mortal, how the plot thickens."

"Sia!" I whisper-yelled, yanking her back to me harsher than I'd intended. "We need to decide this together!"

Before we could talk, the elemental intervened, taking back over the conversation. "She's already agreed, King. I will keep the seer with me, where he will be safe, for the time being."

Sia's eyes blazed with determination as her head whipped toward him, her braid flying out behind her as she did. "I want him returned to us, now."

"Oh, mortal," the elemental practically purred at her as he brought his hands up to his center, "I don't think you want him to see what is about to happen."

This time I knew what to expect as he clapped. After descending into the portal, I was held in an ice-covered copy of my own castle for what felt like hours before he'd transported us to the arena with the same gesture of his hands.

Reality shimmered around us, blurring as if we were walking through a wall of water. I gripped Sia's hand tightly, not trusting that we wouldn't get separated again. Moments later, though, we found ourselves within a stone chamber that glowed with the light of the countless candles peppered throughout.

I quickly glanced around, searching for an escape, but there was none, only a large bed covered in rose petals, a steaming bathing area, and a small hutch with drinks and flowers next to us that occupied the space. The flickering light of the candles being the only source of light casted dancing shadows on the walls. Wherever he'd transported us, there were no doors to come and go, only four seamless walls and a roof over our heads.

A heavy sigh crossed my lips, my head falling forward and hanging heavily. We were trapped here, and at the whim and mercy of a god that wanted nothing more than to see us fail. And now, part of my soul wasn't the most important thing on the line.

Small hands trembled as they grabbed at my own, the warmth of her skin instantly soothing my rattled nerves. Instinctively I turned my hands over, holding her in return.

"We always knew we would end up here one day," she whispered, her soft voice drawing my head back up to look at her. "It was a miracle that your dragon hadn't attempted to force the bond again, as is, but we both knew that it was coming for us sooner rather than later."

I slammed my eyes shut as I bit down on my bottom lip. I hated that she was right. I hated that there was nothing I could think of to get us out of this situation now. Even if we had to go through with this, *this* wasn't how I pictured it being—forced and under the voyeuristic watch of a god.

She deserved better than this moment.

"Look at me, Theo," she demanded softly, her voice gaining confidence as her hands stopped shaking in my own. "You know I'm right."

It didn't matter if she was right. We shouldn't have been here.

I relented quickly, opening my eyes as I shouted, "I would have given up my dragon to avoid this! To avoid the chance of losing you!"

She shook her head and answered in a gentle voice that completely contradicted my own. "You might have thought it a viable option, but I didn't—your dragon is a part of you. Perhaps it makes me greedy, but if I'm going to have you by my side, Theo, I want all of you." A beautiful pink stain bloomed on the apples of her cheeks as her eyes dipped down to my chest. "I just want *you*, and this is how we find out if I can have that."

Her words had my heart cracking open and my cock hardening in turn. Fuck, I needed her. I needed to consume her and feel her all at once. There would never be a moment where I had enough of her.

My dragon stirred at her words and I placated him, just barely, telling him that his time would be upon us soon enough. I just needed a bit longer, to ensure that I could make this as special as I could, under the circumstances, before she offered her soul to him.

"You already have me," I admitted, voice hoarse as I

struggled to hold myself back. "How could I possibly deny that you are not only everything I want, but exactly what I need as well?"

I reached out to the table full of freshly clipped roses near us, grabbing one and gently sending magic through my fingers into it, encasing it in a delicate layer of ice. Turning back, I ran my free hand up her hip as I pressed my chest to her back, bringing the rose around as my other arm wrapped around her body.

"I should have known that you could handle that dragon without me," I breathed out, pressing a soft kiss to her neck as she took the flower from my hand. I loved the way she immediately stretched her head to the side, giving me better access to her soft, sweet skin. "You may look as delicate as this flower, like you could shatter with one wrong move, but you also have thorns that make you a weapon. Your knowledge of the blade. Your years of dedication to honing your body's endurance and stamina. The wicked mind of yours that never accepts defeat, against all odds."

Her breath caught as her ass pressed back against my hardened cock, making my hands grip her hips hard.

"But the truth is, it didn't matter how long you battled that dragon. Because the second he burnt even a single strand of hair on your head, I would have been down there. I told you long ago that you were under my protection as my wife, but now you are just simply *mine* —including every strand of your hair."

Her hips ground back against me, wiggling despite

my best efforts to hold her still as I fought to not unravel where I stood. My restraint was barely there, and my cock twitched heavily with my desire. I unraveled as the sounds of her breathing turned shallow and ragged, indicating her needs heightening alongside my own.

"I need you, Theo," she admittedly breathlessly. "All of you."

And all of me she would get.

Chapter Thirty-Two

SIYANA

"I HAVE my own deal for you, wench," he growled out, spinning me in his arms and making my core clench as I felt his need for me pressing against my belly. "Since you seem to be a fan of those today."

His light ribbing made me smirk. *Asshole.*

I watched his eyes flash over to the wisps of steam rising from the tub in the back corner, and silently he grabbed my icy flower, placing it down gently on the table before walking us over. I didn't miss the way his lips peeled back ever-so-slightly as the steam wafted over us. Without a doubt, he wasn't enjoying the warmth, but I was beginning to realize that he didn't make a lot of decisions around what *he* wanted.

No, my king lived to give me what I wanted.

I turned to lay my hands on his chest, pushing up to tease his lips with my own, loving the growl that vibrated his chest against my own and had my nipples hardening.

"What's your deal?" I asked before nipping at his bottom lip and looking up at him from beneath my lashes. "Better make it a good one if you want me to agree to it, dragon boy."

We both knew I was bluffing. I'd agree to anything he wanted.

Never had my heart been so full that it felt like it would burst within my chest. Ever since watching him appear next to the dragon, I felt full to the brim. He'd been willing to give up such an integral part of himself, for me, claiming I was the other half of his heart.

I'd offer myself on a silver-fucking-platter for that.

His hands traveled over my body as I leaned in, capturing his lips fully. I teased him with my tongue as he began to peel my clothing off, each piece dropping to the floor with a soft swish. As I helped strip him in return, I was uncomfortably aware of the heat in my body–I felt as if I was on fire with the anticipation of what was to come. While nerves were still present within me at the thought of the bond, I was beginning to believe that there was no one else out there for either of us.

We had to be mates.

My eyes fluttered as he pulled back, forcing me to take a breath as our foreheads touched.

"The deal is that you let me show you what you mean to me right now, without a bond forcing us to choose each other. Let me take care of you, please," he begged. "I've learned something since meeting you that has helped me make peace with what happened between my parents, even before the curse happened."

My pulse sky-rocketed at the mention of them, knowing it was such a heavy topic for him—and the source of a lot of his burdens and trauma.

He brought my hands up, threading our fingers together and squeezing them tightly.

"I learned that a bond means nothing if you aren't committed to the other half of your soul," he whispered, bringing our joined hands to his lips before pressing a kiss to our knuckles. "I learned that the bond doesn't do the work for you. You have to continue to choose that person every day that you're lucky enough to have them."

Butterflies erupted in my stomach as he pressed a tender kiss to my lips before whispering against them. "I'm choosing you, wench. Every day. I don't care what the bond says at the end of this. I want you, forever."

"Damnit," I whispered as my eyes burned with the heat of tears. With a sniffle, they fell, rolling over my cheeks to my jaw. "I don't think I've ever cried so much in one day before."

His answering chuckle rolled through me as he relinquished my hands and brought them up to cup my jaw. I stared into the eyes of a dragon and a man, wondering how I'd ever found him repulsive.

"I think I'm falling for you, dragon boy," I admitted breathlessly as I brushed away the tears before they could hit his hands.

A smirk pulled the corner of his lips up before he answered, "I think I fell for you the second I had to tie you to me on that horse, wench. I just took awhile to come around to accepting it."

My brow rose as our joint laughter filled the air, causing my tears to abate. I took a deep, shuddering breath, releasing it between pursed lips before I smiled and laughed. "You don't say."

Seconds passed and as silence descended, he tugged me toward the tub, helping me in, though he remained standing next to it. A moan fell from my lips at the instant relief the hot water gave my aching muscles, making me all but melt as I sank completely into the warmth. I hadn't realized how exhausted I was after everything we'd been through. How many hours had it even been since we'd left the safety of our alcove? I hadn't the slightest clue.

"Don't offer the water what belongs to me," Theo growled as his hand moved to my braid, slowly untangling the strands with deft fingers. "I thought you'd know by now that I won't share any part of you—including the sounds that come from your mouth."

Fuck me.

How he had me going from tears to desire roaring through my body in minutes was a magic all its own.

Soon enough, my long waves were released from their constraint and floating around me in the water as I struggled to find the words to respond. My toes curled as his hand sank into the hair at the base of my neck, tugging it back gently and forcing me to gaze up into his piercing blue eyes. "Tell me you understand what it means when you say you're mine."

His free hand dipped into the water with a lathered sponge, running it over the tips of my nipples. My body shivered of its own accord at the light, teasing feel of it.

"I understand," I replied, my eyes rolled back as he changed the trajectory of the sponge, pushing it between my breasts and down my abdomen.

"I don't think you do," he said as I focused back on him, my lips parting in anticipation as his mouth drew closer. "But we have forever for me to show you what it means."

While I truly loved the sentiment that he was choosing me, no matter what the bond told us at the end of this, I held back the doubt rolling around in my mind that he'd be able to make good on that. Could he have the will to deny what his dragon wanted—his true mate —if it wasn't me?

No, now wasn't the time to think about that. But the doubt still tickled in the back of my mind.

When he let go of my hair, I was panting and desperate for more, but he seemed to focus in, finding the task of cleaning me a top priority. By the time he'd scrubbed every inch of my skin, I felt as if I would erupt if he didn't replace that sponge with his hands soon.

"Dip your head back into the water," he instructed as my hands gripped the edge of the tub.

He had no idea how close I was to launching myself

out of this tub and telling him I wasn't waiting any longer. But this moment was about both of us, and I would be a fool to ignore the gentle reverence he was giving me as he cleaned my body.

By the time my hair was cleaned to his standards, my chest heaved as I pictured what I hoped was coming next. There was a slickness between my legs that even the water couldn't wash away. He leaned over the tub, pressing his lips to my temple as I felt fingers grazing the inside of my thigh.

"You did so good, waiting as I prepped my next meal," he praised, pressing two fingers down on my clit and rubbing in a torturously slow circle. My hips bucked in the water. "I find myself suddenly ravenous after such a long day."

"Gods," I breathed as my eyelids fluttered shut and my head fell to rest against the edge of the tub.

His pressure increased as he answered, "They aren't here, but I am."

Suddenly his hands slid to grab my waist, hoisting me out of the water as if I was as light as a feather before setting me on my feet. A towel was wrapped around me, slowly wiping off errant droplets as his hands traveled over my skin, his heat radiating at my back.

The towel dropped from around me, leaving nothing between our bodies as his cock bore down against my ass. Lips pressed against my neck as his fingers trailed over my arms, pebbling the skin in their wake as they traveled to my breasts.

I couldn't take this at his pace anymore, needing to feel him inside of me. The weeks of frustration and desire had only been curbed by our time in the springs—not sated. After what we'd gone through today, I would settle for nothing less than taking him deep within me, claiming him as mine.

Turning abruptly, I found him wiping off the soot from his face with the damp towel. Thankfully he wasn't covered in it like I had been, because I was not going to wait for him to take his own bath. My hands pushed at his chest, demanding, "Get on the bed, Theo. It's my turn to get what I want."

His eyes widened imperceptibly before dragging his bottom lip between his teeth and smirking. "Yes, my queen."

I took in his wide back and toned ass as he turned, muscles flexing with each long stride he took to the bed. Once he turned and settled on the edge, leaning back on his hands, I took slow, measured steps toward him. His cock was long and thick, waiting for me as it strained toward the ceiling, begging for my touch.

"What is it that you want exactly?" he questioned, raising an eyebrow as he brought one hand around to stroke the base of his cock.

I stopped between his legs, knocking his hand out of the way. "To take what's *mine*. You aren't the only one with a possessive need." I fisted his cock firmly, stroking up and down his length. "I want you to feel my body gripping your cock, claiming you as you spill inside of me."

"Shit, wench," he breathed out on a ragged breath. "Keep talking like that and you're going to feel me spill into your hand."

We couldn't have that.

His pants and groans spurred me on, and I reveled in knowing that I was the only one to bring him pleasure. Pushing on his chest with my free hand, I demanded, "Lay back. I don't want to wait any longer."

While I knew just how much he loved to make me orgasm with his fingers and mouth, tonight wasn't about leisurely learning, it was about claiming, and we'd both fought this for too long.

I released his cock long enough to crawl onto the bed and straddle his hips.

His head lifted up, eyes trained on the distance between my pussy and his cock as I lined him up. "Sia, are you sure you're ready to take me?" he asked with a husky tone as his hands settled on my hips, squeezing. "I wasn't expecting to take you so quick—"

Maybe I'd regret not having the hours of foreplay I knew he'd be more than happy to give me, but I was aching to be filled—now.

Cutting off his sentence, I lowered my hips down, pressing his tip into me before releasing my hold on him. While I knew how big he was from holding him in my hand, nothing prepared me for the feeling of him stretching me in this way.

"I'm fucking sure," I answered as I forced myself lower, taking him inch by inch. Already, my body felt so tightly wound up from the anticipation that even the feel of just a few inches inside of me had me tensing up.

A groan fell from him as his head collapsed back onto the bed, eyes still trained on the union of our bodies. "You're so damned wet for me, wench."

A bite of pain laced through me as his tip buried itself in me and I worked to take in his shaft. My teeth ground together as my jaw tightened. I'd thought I could take him without preamble, but I instantly regretted it. It didn't matter how slick I was with my own arousal.

I whimpered as his hand found one of my nipples, rolling and pinching just as his other brushed against my clit. Euphoria danced through me and a new rush of wetness coated me, letting me sink down another inch.

My teeth drug my bottom lip between them, biting down as I danced on the cusp of pleasure and pain.

"I don't know if I can," I whimpered, knowing there was still so much more.

"Do you want to know why I know you can take me all the way into your pussy, Sia?"

I wasn't sure when I shut my eyes, but his question shocked them back open as I looked down at him. The heat that smoldered in his gaze made me gasp. He may be part human, but that gaze was fully animalistic—like he wanted to devour me.

"You can take my cock because you were fucking made for me," he encouraged as his hips flexed up ever so slightly, making my eyes flutter. "I'm going to fit inside of you, but it's going to push you to your limits, the same way we push each other outside of this bed."

I rocked myself up and down his length slowly, trying to figure out how I'd manage it. I wanted to so damn badly.

"I know my wife doesn't back down from a challenge," he murmured, brushing his thumb back and forth against my clit at a speed that had me clenching around him.

His words left me craving more of his praise, and I began moving up and down a little faster, finding myself sinking onto him further as waves of my arousal continued to coat his cock.

"There you go," he praised, making me moan and crave even more of it. "Look at you taking me deep inside. So fucking perfect."

Waves of pleasure shot through me as I worked myself on him, feeling him hit a spot deep within me that had stars exploding behind my eyelids. "Oh," I moaned as my head tilted back, "you feel so good, Theo."

"Moan my name again and I won't be able to let you take this at your pace anymore," he warned, challenging that brat within me to do it again. I knew I was past the worst of the pain, that I could take whatever he could mete out.

"Theo," I moaned as we locked eyes.

True to his word, he rocked up into me, in one swift thrust, burying himself deep. My mouth dropped open at the feeling of him, and for a moment, we didn't move or speak. The sounds of our pants filled the air as his hands snaked around to grip my ass firmly in his palms.

I found myself instantly craving more, spurring me to rise up before dropping myself back down onto him. A harsh cry slipped over my lips as his fingers dug in my flesh, encouraging me to do it again as he lifted me up.

"Shit," he hissed as I rocked down onto him again, my walls clenching at the end. "Stop clenching around me like you want to squeeze the cum out of me."

The picture his words painted in my mind had me grinning as I began to fuck him in earnest, panting out, "That's exactly what I want."

Now that the pain had subsided entirely, I let loose, loving the sound of our bodies slapping against each other as I rode him—hard. Never before had I felt so thoroughly filled and claimed. One of his hands left my ass, returning to lather attention on my clit, brushing against the swollen bud hard.

Sparks exploded within my core as his growl filled the room, and his hands were suddenly gripping my hips tightly. He took over, using his grip on me to slam me down, over and over as his hips bucked up.

Somehow he reached even deeper within me, and my head tilted back as my cries of pleasure echoed through the chamber. "Yes! I'm so close, Theo."

My words sounded like a plea, and they were. He delivered, slamming into me, hitting deeper inside of me in this position, and his hands gripped my hips even tighter. Increasing his pace, he left me no time to breathe as my climax built up to its precipice.

He grunted, his pace suddenly slowing, making my head fall back down to glare at him. But when I saw his eyes sparkling with the magic that warned of his dragon's presence, I knew that we were at an impasse.

The bond was beginning to surge from within his dragon.

"I can't hold it back any longer," he admitted hoarsely, still hitting deep within me, making it hard to think about anything other than the pleasure rolling through me.

"So don't," I answered, lowering my chest to his and sealing our lips together. *"Claim me."*

I pulled back to stare into his eyes as I continued to rock up and down on his cock. Deep fear reflected back at me, and my chest squeezed at how much he cared for me.

"Trust in us. I do."

My words seemed to wipe away his hesitation as he lunged for my lips and tangled our tongues together.

"This is forever. No matter what, wench. Remember that."

His words accompanied the weightless, floating sensation that seemed to coax my heart out of my body, just like I'd felt before in the springs. Tingling warmth coated me as I gave in, letting my essence branch out to meet his own that called to me. I felt like I was floating in the clouds, close enough to touch the moon that I knew was beaming down outside.

My climax welled within me, the moment, the sensation altogether too much but somehow still not enough. Bearing down, I cried out, ignoring the way our bodies began to glow from the inside out, our veins suddenly sparking with the same blue, magical ley line energy in this realm.

I shattered, calling out his name as he did mine. His hips stilled and I felt him release within me.

A tidal wave of energy released as something shifted within my chest. The bed shattered beneath us as the rest of the furniture within the room went flying into the walls, breaking on impact. I slammed my eyes shut as his arms wrapped around me tightly, rolling me to lay beneath him. I shouldn't have been surprised at his attempt to shield me from danger. He'd proven time and again that he'd always protect me.

We were plunged into near darkness as the candles extinguished all at once, right before the walls themselves cracked, allowing in shimmering rays of moonlight.

As silence settled, I opened my eyes and gasped.

"Your eyes," I breathed out, hands shaking as I lifted them to a face I didn't recognize. "Your scales."

The magic pulsating beneath our skin began to fade as he turned his lips to kiss the palm of my hand.

"They're gone," I said, running my hands along his smooth skin, missing the scales that I'd once used to mark him as my enemy. "The curse is broken."

His lips crashed into mine. **"And you're my mate."**

Chapter Thirty-Three

SIYANA

MY BODY and mind were engulfed in a whirlwind of emotions as Theo's lips devoured mine, leaving me gasping for air.

My husband.

My mate.

At that moment, I felt like I was finally whole for the first time, with his arms wrapped tightly around me. Our smiles were blinding, radiating pure joy and triumph as he pulled back to look at me. We had overcome all obstacles to be together, our souls now merged as one.

But amidst the euphoria, I noticed a tangible link between us that pulsed with raw power, the remnants of the magic that had bound us together, I assumed. It was a magnetic force that solidified what we had always known: we were destined for each other.

"How is this possible?" I asked, my heart racing with disbelief that everything we'd wanted had come to pass.

"The curse shouldn't have broken so quickly. The undine god hasn't even appeared yet to know that we completed the bond."

I had to wonder if he was watching us now as a shimmering door of ice appeared on a wall nearest us, the soft rays from the moon illuminating it. The god's voice carried on the howling wind seeping in from outside. *"Come claim your seer and be gone from my realm."*

Kaida.

My heart leapt at the opportunity, and I all but shoved Theo off of me. I rushed to my feet to get dressed, feeling a little bad at my immediate rush to leave our little bubble to ensure Kaida was okay. "I love you, but I—"

I stopped mid sentence, realizing what had just come from my mouth. Was it too soon to say that, after everything that happened?

Shit. What if it was?

We stood there, staring at each other in the near dark, me with wide eyes and Theo with absolutely no expression on his face, but his cock hardened again as the seconds passed.

It seemed he wasn't against the words, but he didn't rush to return them, making my anxiety grow doubly in my chest. My hands came together, my fingers twisting around each other as I fought the urge to look at the ground.

"I mean, I love you as a person," I back-tracked, heat rising to my cheeks and the tips of my ears, the flames of embarrassment too big to hide. "I—"

He took one long stride toward me, grabbing my face roughly and cutting me off. "Don't you dare take it back. Say it again."

A lump swelled in my throat at his demand, but I swallowed it down, reaching for the bond between us to quell my nerves. What did I have to hide? We were already married and now had a mate bond between us. These were just words.

So why was I so nervous?

"Fine," he said quickly, cutting off my nervous internal battle. "I'll say it. I love you, Siyana Takkar. You are the air I breathe, the ice that fills my veins, and the reason I wake up each day, looking forward to what it might now bring to me. Before you, I existed in the shadows of my own life, wishing that I could find a way out, but too afraid to take the steps."

An array of emotional and heartfelt thoughts swirled through my mind, but my mouth let out the first sassy thing that came to it. "Takkar, huh? I don't recall agreeing to change my name."

My words were in complete jest, but truly I had never even thought of such a simple tradition, considering we'd skipped the formal wedding ceremony.

He raised a brow as his hands fell to my waist. "I don't recall asking you if you agreed to our marriage either, but here we are. You should know by now that I will claim you in every way I can. If they aren't a beast that can smell my scent on you at all times, I will ensure they at least know you're mine through name."

A chuckle rose within me. That was my possessive mate.

"I love you, Theo Takkar," I admitted, my voice clear and confident this time as I brought my arms up to rest around his neck. My fingers threaded in the soft, white waves of his hair at the base of his neck. "Thank you for seeing the good and bad—"

"Bratty," he corrected, smirking.

I ran my tongue along my top teeth before clicking my tongue at his cheekiness. I deserved that.

"Yes, thank you for loving my stubborn and bratty sides, as much as I likely drive you crazy with them," I relented before lifting to press a quick kiss to his lips, melting into him briefly before dropping back onto my heels. "You challenge me and make me a better person, and I hope you never stop. I hope we continue to push our boundaries of comfort, growing from the discomfort it brings. I hope we are strong enough to fix the damage between our peoples now, uniting the two halves that were always meant to be a whole."

"We will, darling," he promised, "We will do it all."

While I'd forever love being his wench, the new, softer nickname had a nice ring to it, making my heart flutter. I hated pushing past the feeling, pushing past what was a momentous occasion, but the undine god still had Kaida, and our life wasn't complete without him.

Quickly, we threw our dirty clothes back on, making me long for clean clothes and our bed. Soon enough, I promised myself. For now, I'd just remain grateful that this trial was over and that we were all going to leave here together–as long as the elemental stopped toying with us. The curse was broken and we had no use for him, but I couldn't help but wonder what he'd demand next for the sake of entertainment. We'd passed his trials, and I wanted to go home.

Would he truly just let us leave that easily?

After tugging my fur vest on, I pulled my damp hair over my shoulder, wishing for the first time that Theo had the fire of an ember, so I could dry my hair.

"I heard that. Don't you dare wish for a different dragon or we will never leave this room as I remind you why I have everything you'll ever need," he warned before tossing my boots at my feet.

"But I didn't say it!" I defended as I watched him pull on his clothes, sulking a bit that we couldn't continue to get lost in each other's bodies. "I didn't even think it to you mentally!"

He tied the strings of his black trousers before tucking in the bottom of his white tunic. "You didn't have to. Perks of the bond being complete. You can still learn to block me out, though."

My mouth popped open. "So you heard my entire internal panic about saying I love you?"

"Yes, now let's go see our little menace," he said, grabbing my hand as I stood back up, pulling me toward the door.

He didn't give me a chance to dwell in my embarrassment, which I was thankful for. As digesting this new aspect of our bond took every iota of my brain power.

The wooden door creaked open toward us on its own accord, inviting us into a seemingly empty hall of ice, but I recognized familiar portraits hanging on the walls. They were larger versions of the ones between mine and Theo's chambers in our castle.

"This is my throne room," he explained, sensing my confusion as I glanced over at him. "It's eerie, the way he seems to exist within our world, but through a thin veil that lays just over the surface."

I had to agree with his sentiment. Was there anything the gods couldn't see from their realm? It didn't sit right with me, how much the undine elemental seemed to know about us, but I couldn't dwell on it for too long. I couldn't do anything to change it or block them out, to my knowledge, and there wasn't a chance that the god would offer up how to do so.

Long ago I'd lived within the mortal bubble of my castle, with little knowledge of the drackya and dragons, let alone the elementals. Still, even then I was but a pawn to beings such as the elementals, and I hated to accept it. As long as he didn't harm us, I'd try to forget that a watchful eye could be hovering above us at any moment.

At the end of the glimmering hall of ice we found the undine god sitting on a throne of ice, with Kaida sitting far too close to his side for my comfort. My dragon seemed lost in a vision as he swayed slightly, not taking note of our approach at all.

"What is going on here?" I asked, nerves taking flight in my stomach and spreading outward to soar through my body.

At the sound of my voice, Kaida seemed to snap out of his trance. He trilled and practically fell over his feet trying to run to us. While very graceful in the air, he still hadn't figured out that dragons weren't built to run on land.

Theo held out his hand, commanding the smaller dragon, "Do not crush her!"

I opened my arms wide as Kaida skidded to a halt, his claws digging into the icy floor to do so. "Hi, buddy!" I exclaimed, rubbing my hands on the thick skin between his eyes like he liked. He pushed harder against my hands, making me laugh.

"I missed you, Sia," he gushed into my mind, melting my heart.

How had I somehow been blessed with two perfect dragons after growing up fearful of them? In my life before, I had never been able to comprehend a world in which humans and dragons could coexist. Life had a funny way of challenging me.

Relief had my body relaxing, seeing that Kaida was perfectly fine and hearing the happiness in his voice.

"I missed you too. Has he been treating you okay?"

"We had interesting talks of the future," the undine god stated, eyes locked on Kaida as he steepled his fingers beneath his chin. "You are lucky to be bonded to such a strong dragon, mortal. If he weren't bonded, I'd think of keeping him here with me."

His words set off my internal alarms, but I forced myself to stay calm. If he wanted to force Kaida to stay here, why go through this?

"I am lucky," I agreed, my words clipped with forced politeness.

I turned as Kaida left my side, keeping the god in my view as I watched the smaller dragon approach Theo. I hadn't even realized that he had stepped to the side to give us our moment.

My breath caught in my throat as Kaida sniffed him, jerking his head back quickly. Theo lifted a hand, letting it linger in the air between them in an offering. Just when I thought my heart couldn't be any more full, Kaida lowered his head, pressing against Theo's hand and letting out the softest trill of acceptance.

My boys.

They separated moments later, coming to stand on either side of me. With Theo grabbing my hand and Kaida pressed into my side gently, we faced the undine elemental, together.

He pushed from the throne to stand at the edge of the steps, peering down at us. We stood strong, not cowering beneath his harsh stare. For the first time, a piece of me pitied the god as I looked up at him trying to lord over us. It seemed like a life lived in lonely eternity here. When I told Theo he was trapped in a prison of ice, alone, this is exactly what I pictured.

R.L. CAULDER

No friends or family to turn to. Occupying his time with the short lifespans of mortals and his creations, our years likely fleeting seconds to an immortal deity. Did he even have dreams or aspirations anymore, or did he just simply...exist?

It went to show, you could have all the power in the world and still be miserable.

"How did you break the curse?" I asked, knowing he wouldn't entertain us much longer after he'd already demanded we collect Kaida and leave.

I couldn't leave before knowing the answer. Or else it would haunt me forever.

He sighed heavily as his eyes roamed across the three of us. "I suppose I've stretched this out as long as I can, and you've risen to each trial I've presented to you. I will give you the answer as a reward."

The anticipation built within me, my body tightening up as his lips parted to continue.

"You broke the curse by simply fulfilling the requirement of the witch: A human must bond with a cursed drackya of their own free will, establishing that true love can exist without the lies and deceit of their predecessors."

It felt like being kicked in the gut as I processed his words. This couldn't be the truth, yet his words lined up with the exact timing that the curse broke. Theo's own shock radiated through my mind, echoing my own feelings.

"So, all we had to do this entire time was complete

our bond?" I asked, needing clarification that it was, in fact, that simple all along.

Theo growled at my side, and I elbowed him gently. *"This isn't the time to piss off a god, sweetie."*

He glanced at me out of the corner of his eye. **"I don't give a shit if we piss him off, *honey*. I'm over his antics. We didn't even need him to begin with."**

"So everything you put us through was just a game to you?" I asked, my voice filling with venom. All of the anguish and fear we'd felt and overcome. It was all for his twisted pleasure. "Instead of telling us that to begin with, you forced us through your trials?"

"You can judge me all you want, mortal, but until you know the feeling of eternity, your opinion means nothing to me," he defended, eyes narrowing at the clear judgment in my tone. "Though you may not see it, my actions weren't entirely selfish. I navigated you into scenarios in which your true devotion was put to the test, paving the way for you to get exactly what you needed in the end."

Theo cut in as my mouth opened, effectively silencing the tirade I was ready and willing to go on. "Was Sia ever in true danger from the ember dragon?"

The undine god chuckled darkly at that before turning and walking back up to the throne, seeming to grow bored of us already. "No. It was a figment of my imagination, as is everything in this territory that you can see. It may have seemed real at the time, but I can't create embers, only undines."

It was such a simple truth that I kicked myself mentally for not realizing that in the moment. I'd been so focused on the safety of Kaida and keeping Theo whole that nothing else crossed my mind.

"That sword was never long enough to pierce through to a real dragon's brain. It simply stopped because we had achieved my intended results at that point."

I bit down on my lip hard enough to draw blood, the warm metallic liquid dripping into my mouth and spreading across my tongue. I'd given that battle everything I had. Although Theo had jumped down in the end, I'd carried such a sense of pride in thinking I'd slain the beast.

To find out it wasn't true was a staggering blow to my ego.

"Now if you don't mind, I'm being summoned by another elemental, who claims to have found a witch for us all to watch."

He was so nonchalant, proving once again that we were all just playthings for the gods. For the first time, I wished myself a witch, so that I could curse him to feel all of the heartache, the entire gambit of emotions, he'd needlessly put us through, just to find out in the end that we were pawns simply being used for entertainment.

Theo tensed at my side. "Is the one who set the curse on the drackya of Andrathya still a threat to us? You owe us that answer, at the very least."

A swirling portal appeared in front of the elemental

as he glanced over his shoulder at us once more. "No, she was the last undine witch to die." He stepped to the side, gesturing toward the portal. "Now, I'd suggest you leave before I decide I don't like either of your tones and decide to keep you here as I've done with the previous visitors I've received."

His words were like a jolt of lightning to my chest, but it was a heavy reminder that we'd never heard of anyone returning from Sanctum. As much as a fiery hatred for this elemental burned within me, we were all still allowed to leave, and for that I owed him my gratitude.

"Let us depart," Kaida urged, nudging me forward with his large head.

He didn't have to tell me twice as the heavy glare of the god had me tugging Theo up the steps. As we passed by him, our eyes met, and I found myself hoping that I'd never have to stare into them again. It felt like a miracle to be walking out of here with our lives. Because something in my gut told me that if we ever saw the undine god again, that wouldn't be the case.

I gave into the swirling sensation of weightlessness in the portal, holding on tightly to Theo's hand as I closed my eyes and waited to feel the ground beneath my feet once more. A bright white light flashed before I heard the crackling of a fireplace. My eyes opened, taking in the now-familiar chamber before Theo tugged me to him and lifted me up. I wasted no time in wrapping my legs around his waist and burying my face in his neck, though

I found myself missing the small scales that used to be there.

"We did it," I whispered against his skin. "We're home."

A huff of air blanketed us, and Theo turned us as I glanced over at Kaida sitting politely to the side, like he was waiting his turn. We looked back at each other and dissolved into laughter as Theo slowly lowered me to the ground before pressing a kiss to my forehead.

"Such a cock-block, still."

I walked over to Kaida, giving him scratches and a kiss between his eyes until a throat cleared behind me. Kaida's snout nudged me to turn, though my brow scrunched together in confusion as I did.

With the light streaming in from the balcony, basking us all in the early morning glow cresting on the horizon, Theo dropped to one knee.

"I know this is a little late and more than backwards, seeing as we're bonded already," Theo hedged nervously as his cheeks flushed. His hand raised up, a dazzling sapphire ring pinched between his fingers. "But I wanted to know if you will marry me, willingly this time?"

I closed the distance between us and dropped to my knees, grabbing his face and pulling his lips to mine.

"I couldn't think of anything I want more."

Epilogue

SIYANA

SEVEN YEARS LATER...

"You know the laws," I growled out with the tip of my blade pressed to his throat, not pulling back as he swallowed hard, making the sharp edge of my blade draw a thin line of crimson to the surface.

Fury burned in my veins, so icy-hot I wondered briefly if it was the magic of the bond sparking.

"I know, but have mercy, my queen," he pleaded weakly, staring up at me with barely concealed hatred in his dull, gray eyes.

Did he really think he was that good of an actor? The second I took my sword away, he'd attack. His back was against the wall for breaking our law and stealing a human from our southern territory. It had been years since we'd had to hunt down a drackya and dole out justice.

I bared my teeth at him as my jaw clenched. "Do you think you're above the other drackya that met their own fate for the lives they destroyed? That you deserve to be released?"

The need to skewer him here and now was strong, but I resisted the bloody urge, forcing myself to take deep breaths.

"Are you okay, darling?"

The concern in Theo's voice served as the perfect grounding point for my frazzled emotions. ***"I'm fine. It's just bringing up old wounds."***

"No," the criminal answered, dropping the thin facade and allowing his full disgust for me to bleed onto his face as it twisted into a sneer. "I just thought you a stupid bitch."

Kaida and Theo let out low, warning growls from behind the drackya, their large forms menacing and providing me backup. I held my free hand up, halting them from ripping his head off for insulting me. That was one thing about my boys—they didn't allow anyone to disrespect me.

A chilling laugh fell from my lips as I moved the tip of my sword up his throat to rest under his chin, forcing it up more as I stared down at him. "I didn't become the queen of all of Andrathya—humans, drackya, and dragons alike—by being a stupid bitch."

My father had conceded the throne quickly to Theo and me shortly after our return from Sanctum. We'd traveled there after we discovered his plans to attack the drackya, thinking he could catch us, unsuspectingly. Brenson had been integral to feeding us the information from the inside, after rising in rank to attend council meetings.

I rolled the hilt of my sword in my hand as I grinned at the memory.

Well, perhaps conceded wasn't the correct term. I'd *taken* my birthright from him, with my dragons forcing him off of the throne, cowering and shaking in fear like the pathetic man he was. It was insane, to think of the dutiful princess I'd been the last time I'd seen him, being taken by our then enemy for the hopes of doing right by our people.

When I'd sat in the throne he'd warmed up for me, watching him oscillate between pleading for me to understand and apologizing for the wrongs he had done to me, I'd only had two words for him: *Thank you*.

Because of his disregard for my life and the marriage he'd forced me into, I was exactly where I needed to be, living a life of love that I would have never been able to find if I'd stayed. After making peace with realizing I could both hate him and be thankful for his actions concurrently, I'd told him to take my mother and leave. I didn't care where they went, as long as it wasn't in Andrathya.

The human woman trembled at my side, bringing me back to the present, hugging the scraps of her bloody dress to her body that his talons had cut into when he'd snatched her. She was brave to stay here after we'd rescued her, with two fearsome dragons still on either side of the drackya who had taken and harmed her. It was still odd to see Kaida full-grown, bigger than Theo now. He'd always be our baby, though I'm sure the woman next to me wouldn't view him as such.

I expected her to flee, but as I observed her, there was a defiant blaze in her gaze as she looked at the sniveling man beneath my sword. It would serve her well as she forged a path ahead after being attacked.

"Our tribunal agreed to exile those in the past who did this," I informed her, watching her closely to see her reaction. "It serves as an extended death sentence, forcing them into the other kingdoms' lands, where their dragons will see an undine and attack. It is now law throughout Andrathya. He knew the consequences for what he did to you."

She nodded once at me, still keeping her eyes trained on the drackya. "So that is what will happen to him?"

"The first thing I will do is kill you before I leave," he spat at her. "If you would have just been quiet and accepted the bond, I wouldn't be in this position."

There were the words I needed to hear to forgo allowing him a meager existence in exile.

I pulled my sword back, smirking at the confusion clouding his eyes. Sweeping my blade down, I took his head from his shoulders before wiping the blood off on the grass to the best of my ability before sheathing it.

The woman let out a startled gasp, taking steps backward as the head rolled toward her feet, his long dark hair collecting twigs and leaves as it did. Her wide brown eyes swung to me, searching for answers it seemed as her mouth opened but no words came.

"I find it interesting he thought me stupid," I mused, as my dragons circled to stand at my back, "considering if he'd polished up on his knowledge, he'd know that the subsection to that law is that exile is only given to the drackya that accept the verdict without further harm being incited."

I felt no regret over the path Theo and I had agreed to, to seek justice for my people's lives lost before the curse was broken. Forming a tribunal had been easy, already having trusted allies that we knew would take the positions seriously, helping us see all sides and coming to joint decisions. Together, Theo, Alstrid, Sinda, Brenson, Lucius, Tillie, and I had decided exile to be fair.

Mira had declined our invitation, far too invested in her position as commander, the first woman to hold the title. After her meteoric rise through the ranks, we'd finally achieved our joint dream of training other women to join our army. The hopes were to never need our now-strong forces, but I had the utmost faith that we'd now be prepared, as our humans and dragons found their bonds as riders resurfacing.

To Theo's utmost dissatisfaction, Brenson had proved worthy of a rider bond, leading the charge in helping others become fearsome pairs that now watched over our borders.

As king and queen, Theo and I traveled between the southern and northern castles, spending half of the year in each, but thankfully in our absence, those on our tribunal helped keep a watchful eye, upholding the new laws we'd all created.

"I shouldn't find it so incredibly alluring to see you behead someone, considering I am not innocent myself."

While my husband felt immense guilt over letting the women he'd released into the wild, thinking they'd return to us, that guilt had only grown over the years. He truly understood the depth of being alone in this world, every time a report came from our patrols, that they'd found an exiled drackya, dead at Andrathya's southern border.

I lifted a hand to the shimmering silver scales of his snout as he swung it down to rest on the ground at my feet. *"We've been over this, Theo. You held no malice in your heart when you let the women go, thinking you were offering them mercy. We all make mistakes—it's learning from them so they aren't repeated that matters."*

"So, what now?" the woman asked, lifting a shaking hand to tuck a strand of her pale blonde hair behind her ear. "Can I go home?"

I tilted my head at her question as my eyes swept over her injuries. The blood that soaked into the edges of the ripped sections of her clothing made them seem worse than I'd originally thought, but I still wanted her to be cared for before we had an escort take her home.

"Will you consider staying and letting us tend to your wounds and provide you with a safe place to rest before making the journey home?" I asked, tentatively hoping she'd trust us after we'd protected her. "We have an inn for humans in town that will have everything you need. You'll be safe there until you feel well enough to travel back. We will, of course, assign a guard to your carriage at that time."

Though we'd come far in a short time in unifying our people after the curse broke, it was slow-going enough that any non-bonded humans rarely or purposefully journeyed to us here. I wouldn't be surprised if she resisted, not trusting the other drackya here.

Her lip quivered at my offer before her hand lifted to brush against her eyes misting with sudden tears. "Yes, I think I'd like that."

"Oh," I answered lamely, shocked at her willingness to trust us, and the drackya in town, after what had just occurred. I was quick to correct my tone, not wanting her to misunderstand me. "I mean, that's great!"

A soft smile pulled at her lips as I walked toward her, gesturing toward the path that would have us in town within minutes, as we were at the edge of the forest already. "If I may ask, what made you agree to stay?" I asked hesitantly as we began to walk side by side. "I can only imagine your distrust of our people here after what just happened."

She was silent until we drew to a stop atop the hill that overlooked the bustling city. "I figured that in the end, there are always going to be good and bad souls, no matter the appearance of the body they're trapped within —humans and dragons alike."

"There is hope for the future of Andrathya, after all," Kaida said, praise filling his words as he ambled to my side, the ground trembling lightly. **"We must keep moving forward."**

He'd grown so wise, so quickly. I leaned against his leg as I answered, *"You're right. We can't give up now."*

"Wait—" I called out as the woman began toward town on her own, realizing I didn't even know her name. "What's your–"

"Sylvie," she provided, cutting me off as she looked over her shoulder at me. "I'm sure I can find the inn on my own. You've done enough. Thank you, all three of you."

As she turned back and began her walk, my eyes began to burn with tears as we watched from afar. The second she crossed onto the cobblestone paths, people rushed to her side to offer assistance, quickly walking her down the road to the inn.

This was what we'd fought so hard for.

"Can I shift back, now?" Theo asked, drawing my

head to find him behind us. **"You know I hate being seen in dragon form next to Kaida when we're in town."**

"No. If I'm not allowed to be naked in front of others, then neither are you. We left in such a hurry that we forgot a change of clothes. We can go home now, though. She is in good hands."

He grumbled in my mind before I climbed up Kaida's tail to my seat. **"You never ride me anymore, wench."**

My head whipped to him just as he hunched down, preparing to launch into the sky. *"Last night begs to differ."*

"I think my memory needs a refresh when we get home."

As we quickly soared through the sky toward our castle, I reminded him, *"No time for that. We're already running late. We need to fly to the southern castle. Brenson's wedding is this evening, or did you forget?"*

His response was dry as we landed on our balcony. **"Forget is a word for it."**

"He is literally getting married to Mira tonight," I scoffed. *"When will you ever accept him as a friend in my life?"*

"Ask me in another year," he retorted after shifting back, making me shake my head.

Men.

Kaida snorted out a puff of icy air as I dismounted, as if I was going to forget to give him a goodbye kiss. I never did.

I pressed my lips to his snout. **"Behave yourself. Treat her with respect and she will come around eventually."**

Despite being invited to the wedding, Kaida had opted to stay behind, suddenly finding himself fascinated with a sweet water dragon that had been born the winter after him. It continued to boggle my brain how quickly dragons developed physically and mentally. If he were a human, he'd be considered a large toddler, but within his species, he was the equivalent to an adolescent.

Selfishly, I wasn't ready to share his time, but he deserved to find love. One day, when Theo and I were no longer here, despite our extended lives, Kaida would need the love and support of a mate to fill the rest of his days with happiness. Though he was likely still many, many years away from choosing a mate to settle with for life, I couldn't believe it was even on the horizon.

A heavy knock echoed through our room as Kaida took off. I turned toward the sound, finding Theo already pulling on pants before padding over to the door. He yanked it open, and in true Tillie fashion, she wasted no time bustling through the room.

As her eyes fell on me, she let out a frustrated huff of air. "How did I know you wouldn't be ready? You never change!"

She shooed Theo from our room with her hands.

"Get! I need to work a miracle to get her ready in time. Go find Lucius and help him with your nephew."

I smiled at the mention of little Gawain. He was ten months old and full of the most precious skin rolls. He'd begun to drive his mom and dad crazy recently, as he began to tune-in to his affinity for water. If I thought about it for too long, it still freaked me out to know that human mates could carry drackya offspring. Though they remained in their human form for at least the first five years of life, it was still odd to think one day they'd be able to shift into a dragon and that they'd been carried by a human at their conception.

"She could go exactly as she is now and she'd still be the most beautiful woman in existence," Theo rebutted before the door shut behind him.

Tillie's lips pursed as she dragged me over to our bathing area. "It's sickening, how in love you both still are all these years later."

I flicked her with the water on my fingers after feeling the temperature of the bath she must have prepared earlier. "Don't act like Lucius isn't constantly falling over himself just to make you smile every day."

A gentle smile lifted her lips before she sighed. "You're right. It's just been hard to find time for us since Gawain was born."

I quickly shed my clothes and stepped into the tepid bath, knowing we definitely didn't have time to fetch new, warmer water. "Let us watch him for a night, so you can have time together to reconnect. You know we'd be happy to."

While Theo and I weren't ready to have our own children, we loved showering our nephew with love before returning him back to his parents. Being an aunt and uncle fit our desires perfectly for now.

Soon enough Tillie had worked her magic, getting me dressed and ready for an event as queen. The long bell sleeves of my dress shimmered like ice beneath the sun as I moved them in the light, admiring the new material. Fixing a hairpin that she'd stuck in tightly enough to give me a headache, I let out a huff. While the style did need to last as we flew down, I'd rather have a mess of hair than be in pain. That was the main difference between Tillie and me, but I hadn't bothered arguing with her on it, choosing to wait until she'd left to find Lucius and Gawain to leave.

Our door clicked open and I spun around, finding Theo with a supply pack ready to go. "I'm not forgetting this again. I refuse to be stuck as a dragon, forced away from your side for even a moment tonight. You're far too beautiful to be left unattended."

He tossed it onto the floor as heat crept into my cheeks with his hungry gaze sweeping over me.

"My queen," he murmured, pulling me into his arms before pressing a kiss to my forehead. "It will be hard to keep my hands off of you and remember our titles tonight while in public."

"Tonight I don't want to be the king and queen," I

breathed out, tangling my fingers into his soft waves as I pulled his lips down to mine. "I just want us to be a dragon boy and his wench."

Continue to explore the lands of Edath in the next book, journeying to the fiery dragons of Salarya.

Embers of Wrath: https://mybook.to/EmbersofWrath

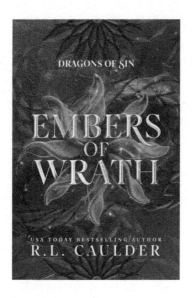

Made in United States
Orlando, FL
07 January 2025

57005698R00225